T0149763

Vacant Places

THE NOVELS OF STANLEY MIDDLETON

A Short Answer
Harris's Requiem
A Serious Woman
The Just Exchange
Two's Company
Him They Compelled
Terms of Reference
The Golden Evening
Wages of Virtue
Apple of the Eye
Brazen Prison
Cold Gradations
A Man Made of Smoke
Holiday
Distractions
Still Waters
Ends and Means
Two Brothers
In a Strange Land
The Other Side
Blind Understanding
Entry into Jerusalem
The Daysman
Valley of Decision
An After-Dinner's Sleep
After a Fashion
Recovery

VACANT PLACES

STANLEY MIDDLETON

NEW AMSTERDAM
New York

First published in the United States of America in 1990 by
NEW AMSTERDAM BOOKS
171 Madison Avenue
New York, NY 10016

Published by arrangement with
Century Hutchinson Ltd., London.

ISBN 0-941533-78-6

This book is printed on acid-free paper.

Printed in the United States of America.

But now I am returned, and that war-thoughts
Have left their places vacant, in their rooms
Come thronging soft and delicate desires . . .
                    Shakespeare: *Much Ado About Nothing*

For Penny and Nigel,
Sarah and Trevor.

I

Frost and thin mist afflicted the street outside.

Henry Fairfax let drop the corner of the curtain, thankful that he could nurse his fire. High pressure in January had brought sunshine during the day and freezing fog at night; bushes and grass in that part of the garden shadowed by the house remained ashen, frost-bound through the daylight hours. Fairfax returnd to his kitchen, took to a cushioned chair and with his back to the central heating boiler laid two books on the table, deferring the moment of opening and reading. The room shone; kitchen units were neat, matching, highly polished; the few items of crockery on show glistened. No cooking smells distracted. Clean warmth and brightness cut off the bleak winter beyond drawn curtains.

Fairfax eyed a title: *A. E. Housman, The Scholar Poet.* On the cover of the paperback unleaved trees rose above squat, dark conifers on Wenlock Edge patterned against the fields below. No wind troubled them now. He considered the title page, began to read through the list of illustrations. His evening's occupation had begun.

The telephone rang.

Fairfax shrugged, almost with pleasure, reclosed the book, squared it with the edge of the table and went out into the hall.

'Fairfax.'

'Oh, Henry. It's Molly.' His sister-in-law.

'How are you?'

'I'm all right. Thank you.' She sounded tremulous. 'It's James. He hasn't come home.'

Fairfax glanced over to the grandfather clock. Seven thirty. He waited for more information. None was forthcoming.

'Not from work?'

'No.'

7

'What time did you expect him?'

'About five. That's his usual.'

Again the awkward pause, as if she listened for a key in the door.

'Is he often late like this?'

'No. I didn't get back until after six. There were one or two things I wanted to finish.'

'He hadn't been home and gone out again?'

'No. Why should he?'

'If for some reason he had, would he have left a note?'

'I don't know.'

Molly sounded uncharacteristically vague, as if she was immersed in problems remote from her husband's non-appearance. Henry Fairfax wondered why she had rung him. She seemed capable of looking after herself; she always had.

'He wouldn't be attending a meeting, would he?'

'He didn't mention it at breakfast.'

'Would he have done so?'

'We talked about what we were going to eat this evening. He said nothing about meetings.' They paused. 'Can I come round to see you now?'

Fairfax swallowed his surprise.

'Of course. But wouldn't you do better to wait in for him?'

'There's something I'd like to talk about. To you.'

'You're welcome to come at any time. But if you're worried now, you stay there at home. I'll tell you what. Give me another ring at nine o'clock if he's not returned. Right?' She agreed, in a reluctant murmur. 'Does Jim seem well? In himself?'

'He's not happy.'

'I shouldn't think too many teachers are these days.'

'It's not the pupils. It's the head and the head of department.' Molly sighed, theatrically. 'Nothing suits him.'

'Why doesn't he look around elsewhere? He's well qualified. He'll easily find another post.'

'He doesn't think so. Besides I'd have to go with him.'

'And don't you want that?'

'No. I'm just settling.'

8

Molly had trained in art at the local polytechnic, and at the end of the course had held a successful exhibition of the jewellery she had made. This had caught the eye of an antique dealer, Martin Fowler, who had taken her into a kind of partnership, finally providing her with a studio and successfully selling her work over his counter and by catalogue. She taught two afternoons and an evening at a college of further education, and kept an eye on the shop when Martin was out at sales, but the arrangement meant that she had at least three full days a week at her bench in a warm, well-equipped place. Now the name Mary Dennis-Maguire began to have weight. Fowler claimed that he could sell twice over every item she made, up in London, at metropolitan prices.

'It's all happened more quickly than I expected,' Molly had explained to her brother-in-law. 'I'd expected the odd commission now and then. And no more. But Martin's a smart operator. And it's so much more convenient to work away from home, and in a properly set-out shop.'

His wife's success had not altogether pleased James Fairfax. He disliked, said he did not trust Martin Fowler, who stood to make an unreasonably high profit from Molly. James's own adversities darkened his judgement.

'Why should he go out of his way to spend money on Moll?' he asked his brother.

'There's cash in it for him.'

'You've no need to tell me that.'

'It is just possible that he really admires her work and wants to advance her reputation.'

'It is just possible,' James mocked his elder brother, 'that I'm the angel Gabriel. I don't trust him as far as I can throw him. Bloody pervert.'

'He's given her her chance.'

'But what's the price, that's what I want to know, what price does she have to pay?'

'She's satisfied. That should be enough for you.'

'You're one to talk.'

Presumably this was a reference to Henry Fairfax's divorce. Certainly neither he nor his wife had earned much satisfaction from marriage. Perhaps both he and Jim were poor choosers.

Molly rang off and he returned to his Housman. Within five minutes he had forgotten family troubles, caught up in the poet's adversities. From time to time he switched from biography to the complete poems, read and reread carefully as if it mattered that he misunderstood nothing. Sometimes he stood, repeating a poem out loud:

The heart with many wild-fires lit,
Ice is not as cold as it.

He made and drank tea, comfortably reading about another man's sorrows. Exactly on nine o'clock the telephone rang again.

'Hello.'

'It's Molly, Henry.'

'Hasn't he come back then?'

'Oh, yes. He has. Over an hour ago. But I thought I ought to ring you to set your mind at rest.'

'Where had he been?'

'Round to a friend's.'

'Until eight o'clock?'

'He said,' Molly's speech was cold, its pace measured, 'that he tried to ring me just after five, but I was out.'

'That's true enough. You were.'

'I don't believe him, Henry. He could easily have tried again. He knew I should be worried.'

Fairfax made no comment. Molly waited for him.

'Where is he now?'

'In the spare bedroom. Marking books.'

There was a sound of movement, footsteps, a mild burst of music. He heard Molly say, 'I'm ringing Henry to tell him you're home,' and the clear reply, 'What the bloody hell's it got to do with him?' She covered the mouthpiece for the next exchanges. Suddenly there was clearance and James Fairfax spoke.

'Is that you, Henry?'

'Yes. Molly was just letting me know you'd returned.'

'Why?' A strangled shout rather than a request for information.

10

'She phoned earlier to say you were late. She was anxious.'

'She didn't think I'd be with you, did she?'

'I don't suppose so. She was worried, wanted somebody to talk to, I guess.'

'She's a silly whore.'

On that James Fairfax put down the phone.

Henry stared at the instrument in his hand with distaste. He disliked his brother's uncouth words, and cursing he packed away his books. Not yet ready for bed he decided to go out.

Orange lights clashed vilely with the cold shadows of the street. No one else was about; his footsteps clapped loudly. For twenty minutes he walked hard, reaching the golf course. A path skirted the edge, rising and falling shallowly. Up here, above the town, though surrounded at a distance by houses, he could see the stars in a velvet of darkness; the valley below lay in silence, garish with sodium light. In the distance strings of pin-point lamps marked main roads. His face froze; he blew his nose sorely. Making haste, he legged it towards the first exit and out into a suburban street. Three cars passed in quiet succession, headlights furious. Henry Fairfax had just paused by the house where a schoolfriend had lived twenty years before when he was suddenly pushed, pummelled backward. Staggering, heart battering his chest, he clawed behind him, then prevented himself from falling by pawing flat-handedly against a front-garden wall.

A man stood in front of him, in a pool of darkness, his hands held forward.

'Come on.' A rough voice. 'Hand your money over.'

'Eh?' A grunt of fear, not a question.

'Your wallet. Quick.'

The robber took a step forward. Fairfax hit him angrily in the face. The blow landed on nose and upper lip, jarring the right arm. He had struck powerfully, ferociously, without thought, surprising himself by the impact, and with a low cry the other man seemed now to sway.

11

Fairfax advanced, fists clenched.

'No,' the assailant said, low-voiced. Suddenly he flapped his arms, turned, began to run, with silent speed.

Fairfax leaned on the wall, breath short.

'Bloody hell,' he warned himself. The robber had reached the brow of the hill. Fairfax followed uncertainly, not thinking, instinctive aggression paramount, but unable to hurry. The other had made no sound as he ran.

Exhilarated, if afraid, Henry Fairfax reached the summit, and looked down the deserted slope. Either his assailant had turned into the one side street or into one of the houses or entries. Now, in the distance, Fairfax could make out two figures advancing towards him, on the same side of the road.

He stopped; perhaps the robber had gathered an accomplice for a second attempt. Unlikely. He looked round for means of escape, decided that his first move would be a diagonal rush across the road. The two dark figures approached, shoulder to shoulder; they appeared to be talking.

With fists bunched, furiously ready for flight, Fairfax walked on. He trembled, his breathing rapid. The men came level.

'An' I said to this feller, "Yo' can please your dead a'nt, but . . ." ' On the dramatic pause they were past, about their own business, fifteen yards on up the hill before conversation was resumed. Fairfax did not diminish his pace until he reached the lighted porch of the Newstead Abbey. From within, nothing; no murmur of pleasure, music, social intercourse. The pavement was starkly illuminated; glass doors displayed oblongs of frosted brightness, but the coldness of the night remained, undismissed.

Henry Fairfax had begun to recover. He would have claimed, reasonably, that he had in no way expected to go round the streets hitting people in the face. At the same time, the punch, the jarring of knuckles on bone, however unrehearsed, had gratified him. In a time of trouble he had stood up for himself, defended his property. He had, moreover, struck an opponent who had been put

12

to flight by a single blow. At thirty-six Fairfax was fit, walked, jogged, exercised, but could not regard himself as an expert in street brawling. It must have been nearly twenty years since he had loosed such a blow. His speed of walking, his displeasure with his younger brother, surprise or fright had combined with a snap judgement, that here was someone he could physically beat and get away with it, to the successful delivery. Now striding homewards he felt no pride, only minor satisfaction, and wondered what his reaction would be if another challenger emerged from the shadows. He did not know.

Five minutes later near the open market place, deserted and disfigured with litter, he saw two policemen. Waiting until they came up to him he explained what had happened. They listened, young and wooden-faced.

'You can't give any description of him, then?'

'No.'

'But he took nothing from you?'

'No.'

He offered them his name; they noted it, complacently grumbling about the increase in amateur bag-snatchers. The younger constable said, 'I only hope, sir, that you hit the bugger good and hard. That might discourage him.' Fairfax added his own grouses. 'Well, at least, sir,' the voice held neither comfort nor encouragement, 'you can walk about most days of the week in this part of the town fairly late at night without being murdered or mugged for certain.' All three laughed in reciprocal misunderstanding.

Henry Fairfax felt a spurt of anger. These young men lacked sympathy; he wasted police time with his boasting. His punch made them suspicious, perhaps his presence in the street. They wished him good night without warmth, swaggered officiously away, forgetting him. He was a pariah, a nuisance, one stepping out of line.

He reached Victoria Avenue without mishap. His neighbour was bolting the gate across his drive. Hatless, without a jacket in spite of the cold, he greeted Fairfax.

'Keeping the damned dogs out. They've scratched great holes in this front lawn.'

13

'That's sensible.' The man jerked his hand back at the answer.

'People let them run loose at this time of the night. Or can't get them back in. I don't know . . .'

'No.'

'Not many about now. It's too chilly. Men or dogs.'

Fairfax resisted temptation, said nothing about the attempted robbery. His neighbour, a retired house agent, a widower, muttered that he was about ready for 'the wooden hill'. 'No late-night telly for me these days. If I stop up, I fall asleep in my chair. So I might as well do it in comfort. 'S a sign I'm getting old.' He clucked tongue on palate, leant comically over the closed gate to look both ways along the street.

Indoors Fairfax pulled off his gloves, examined the hand that had done his violence. It was unmarked. He touched it with his left. Nothing. Unbruised. He laid out his breakfast utensils, walked round the house, securing the locks. He decided against further drink, took a bath, and read the Housman slowly until midnight.

14

II

Henry Fairfax considered the sentence he had written.

'I can't think why I ever deceived myself into believing that I loved you.'

He now spoke the words out loud. Though he managed them without difficulty he felt dissatisfaction. They had a literary, stagey, stilted sound, as if the speaker, a woman, was propounding a statement she did not exactly hold to be true, and was tricking herself once again. Fairfax rubbed his chin. The fault lay outside the psychology. That sentence, however subtly or musically delivered, or even if mumbled in words bitten back, had the artificiality of the theatre about it, of life transformed into a clueless, limelit code, an implausible utterance making all clear except the red cores of feeling and motivation.

Bristles rasped under his fingers.

Henry Fairfax was writing a radio play, and knew that now, at eight thirty-five in the evening, he had reached the point where he'd do nothing more of use. He had worked hard for nearly two hours, and, resting, nit-picked amongst his lines. He felt by no means disheartened, encouraged himself pencil in hand by scribbling question marks or wavy lines at the edge of the text. When he was composing he rattled away at the typewriter, hearing and copying down the words in his head, almost at the speed of some poor reader murmuring it aloud. That was not right. 'I can't think . . .' his character orated, and he heard the sharp, well-articulated thrust. Had she such control over her emotions that she could mould them into a complex sentence of this sort? Complex? Yes, grammatically. With two subordinate clauses. But merely a line in length. 'Deceived' – 'believed' clashed. 'Kidded', vulgar, not in her vocabulary, or not at high moments of drama. 'Cheated myself', 'defrauded, misled, cozened'. He underlined the word, nodded towards his Roget, deliberately declining to fetch it down from the shelves. He'd play with other words, entertain himself, and if by this time tomorrow he had doubts, the sentence would go, a strong line through it and a handwritten first correction above.

He saw the woman, Honor by name, straight-backed in her chair, patrician, Roman-nosed, enunciating his words. She might have chosen the rhyme, past tense half-untangled from present participle, to express not only contempt for her former lover, but scorn for her own weakness. Inside his head, Fairfax considered a murder, but refused to make up his mind. Sleep, meals, a day's work, with their interstices of conscious or unconscious literary attention would help him decide. He would be sorry to rid his play of Honor so early in its composition, and against the original conception, but he wrote best when he set up a problem, put himself on his mettle.

'I can't think why,' he repeated out loud, and left the sheet in the typewriter.

No sooner was he on his feet than he heard the rattle of his back-door knocker.

Surprised, for he did not expect visitors, he opened the door on the chain after hesitation and an unhurried progress downstairs in the direction of the kitchen. There had been no second knock.

'Hello, Henry.' A female figure, fur-tipped black hood in place, feet stamping. 'It's beginning to snow.'

Molly, his sister-in-law.

'That's better,' she said, once inside, still thumping her booted feet. 'It's icy cold.'

'Why didn't you come to the front?'

She considered this, pulling off her gloves.

'Yes. Front.' She spoke slowly, as if she needed to thaw the words out. 'Front? Oh, I'm a relative.'

He considered that, his mind still engaged at his type-writer, as a possible line in a play. He was not sorry to see her.

Molly's cheeks glowed as she pulled back the hood from dark, curly hair.

'It's trying to snow.' She pulled off her duffle-coat, scarf;

16

kicked off her boots. In a daffodil yellow sweater she looked attractively athletic. 'Are you busy?'

'No. Just finished.' She moved with speed from one end of the kitchen to the other. Henry dodged out to fetch her a pair of moccasins. 'A bit big for you. Shall we go into the sitting room?'

'This'll do me.' She laughed, eyes light blue, white teeth regular.

'Coffee? Are you hungry?'

'Now you ask me, yes. To both.'

'Cheese sandwich?'

'Please. Nasty dreams later.'

She took his usual seat by the boiler while he dashed about, slicing bread, lacing the cheese with pickle.

'Do you bring work home?' she asked, from behind the evening newspaper.

'No. Hardly ever. I stay behind if I haven't finished. I need the computer and the files.'

Henry Fairfax worked as a manager for his former wife's brother, Conrad Le Jeune. He had read English and Law at the university, and had done three years in an accountant's office when Le Jeune, whom he had met at the Arts Club Dramatic Society, had offered him a job, with the promise of a share later in his road-haulage firm. Fairfax had been doubtful, until his father, an old fogey, a solicitor, a law lecturer, had encouraged him to take the chance.

'Le Jeune's doing well. He's got a great deal going for him. He'll never be short of either work or money. Don't let his Flash Harry performance put you off. He's got an eye for the main chance, and if he thinks there's something in it for you, there's something in it, I'll be bound.'

His father's unexpected enthusiasm had convinced Fairfax. The son would not have been so sure now. The old man had little real judgement outside the limits of his work; he was a blinkered, agnostic puritan, quiet, Conservative and provincial. But in this case he had been exactly right.

Le Jeune had prospered; his every venture proliferated; he chanced his arm often, and invariably succeeded.

17

Nothing went awry. Fairfax's promised share in the partnership, duly delivered, small as a proportion, now had grown quite frighteningly valuable. He himself had worked hard, arriving in the office at eight fifteen each morning and never out before five thirty, putting in late hours and Saturdays if necessary, taking or cancelling holidays at the firm's convenience, but it was Le Jeune's flair that made the large profit. Conrad was the entrepreneur, the man of incandescent ideas; but his common sense remained massive. Henry Fairfax modernized the office, appointed efficient staff, assisted in the opening of new branches, but never saw himself as other than a journeyman, a tidier-up with his humdrum dust-pan and brush behind the boss's whirlwinds. Why Le Jeune had taken him on in the first place Fairfax never understood; he'd given his employer value for money, but there must have been two dozen young, local, qualified accountants who would have worked as hard, done as well.

Henry often wondered if his father had offered Conrad Le Jeune a helping hand early in the meteoric career, but he had no notion how this would have come about for his father hated both wagering and boasting. Perhaps the assistance had taken the form of legal advice; the old man would have as soon favoured wasting his hard-earned capital on a race-horse as on an untried business. There was, in his view, always plenty of steady interest in safe investments; his life held enough excitement in the classroom, the courts, the social worker's office, the broker's counter and the financial pages of his newspaper. And yet both men spoke well of their opposites to this day.

Henry completed the cheese sandwiches with a flourish, as the percolator delivered. Molly had not spoken a word, but sat brightly drumming on the table top.

Fairfax often occupied spare minutes with Le Jeune whom he saw nowadays only about once a quarter though the two spoke regularly on the telephone. Now that the London, Bristol and Manchester offices were established and throve under energetic Le Jeune clones, Henry Fairfax puzzled exactly what place he occupied in the hierarchy and for how long. He told himself that he wrote

18

radio plays to try to convince himself that human motivation was infinitely variable, so that he might just continue to occupy a niche in the expanding Le Jeune empire.

'That looks delicious.' Molly holding her plate up to the light. He matched her gesture grandly as he passed her a coffee cup. 'I hope I'm not disturbing you.'

'I said not. I've finished my night's labour. I'm doing another play.'

She made noises of approval, then bit into the sandwich.

'What's it about?'

'Adultery in Hampstead.'

The phrase meant nothing to her.

'Are you an expert, then?' she asked, but did not allow a reply. 'What's the difference between adultery in Hampstead or in Bulwell?'

'Financial.'

'Does that affect the emotional trauma?' More jargon.

'Could do. Very easily. Lawyers harassing over division of the spoils. On the other hand in a poor community with very strict rules about marriage, an Indian village, let's say, there'd be shattering pain even though very few rupees were involved.'

'Is that your line? In the play?'

'Not really. I'm worrying myself at present about a single sentence. Or I was until you rapped on the door.'

'Go on. Let's hear it.'

'If I can remember it: "I can't think why I ever deceived myself into believing that I loved you." ' He spoke with solemn clarity.

'Well?'

'If you heard that in a play, would it put you off?'

'No. Why should it?'

'Doesn't it sound like a piece of factitious, cobbled-up English? Straight out of Wardour Street?'

'Say it again.'

He repeated the sentence, without intensity this time, like a disappointed shopkeeper reiterating an unacceptable price.

19

'No. It's all right for me. I can understand it. It just about sums up what I'd say to Jim.'

'So you might well use those words?'

'It depends.' She cleared her mouth of food, scratched her face. Her fingers were short, capable, not altogether clean. 'If I wanted to get my own back on him, I'd try to make out I'd never loved him.'

'And it wouldn't be true?'

'No.'

She concentrated on her sandwich as if that held more importance for her than the breakdown of her marriage. In no way did she appear distressed.

'But the words, the language? Didn't they strike you as facile, unlikely, overdone?'

'No. I never thought of them as words you had chosen. It was just somebody hurt or getting her own back. It was a woman, wasn't it?'

'Why do you say that?'

'I don't think you'd make a man talk in that way.' She stared, almost rudely, as at an inanimate object. 'Or perhaps you would.' Now she grinned. 'I'm too simple for you. I listen to what people are saying, not to how they're saying it.'

'Oh, no, you don't.'

'Perhaps not. Who knows? I don't. But this is only a play for the radio.'

'Only. Only.'

They ate their sandwiches in comfortable companionship.

'Another?' Henry asked when she had picked up the last crumb.

'I wouldn't mind. It was delicious. It's only greed, though.' She slapped her hips as if to indicate surplus weight. Henry cut and spread with pleasure, glad of his guest. When Molly had finished eating and had accepted more coffee, he suggested that they move to another room.

'No, thanks. This is exactly what I want. It's neat and tidy. I can't lounge on these stools. I feel at home.' She grimaced. 'As I don't in Ravensworth Road.'

'You wanted to talk to me about something?'

20

'Don't rush me. Let my creature comforts settle me down first. It's about Jim, as you can imagine.'

Molly did not rush but sat fondling her coffee cup.

'How's the weather?' she asked. 'I wonder if the snow's settling?'

'No. Clear again.' He reported from under the lifted curtain. 'How did you come down? Car?'

'I always do. I ought to walk more. I ate too much at Christmas.'

'The streets aren't safe at this time of night.'

He succinctly told her about the attempted robbery. She listened with animation.

'And you hit him?'

'I did.'

'I would never have believed it of you. Jim, now, yes. But you . . .' She laughed out loud.

'I'm stronger than Jim.'

She weighed that up.

'It's nothing to do with physique,' she answered. 'Or not altogether. It's temperament. Jim would have his fists whirling before he considered whether the other man would be capable of any retaliation. He'd take a swing at a heavyweight champion.'

'Is that good?'

'What do you think? Though usually I'm the one within range. He might easily get hurt. Still. That's when he's normal.'

Henry did not press her as she sat pert, unperturbed at his table. Molly swept the crumbs on her plate together and rolled them into a doughy ball between finger and thumb.

'He's very down at the moment,' she began.

'Is there any good reason? People suffering from depression are often at their worst in January and February. Or is it just school?'

'That does him no good. But I think he's taken up with another woman.'

'How long have you been married, Molly?'

'Nearly four years.'

Henry did not know why he asked the question. He

could easily have worked it out for himself. He remembered the early summer brightness at Edwalton village church, the reception where he had made a speech, the desperate quarrel he had fought through with Laura on their return home.

'Who is she?' He asked this, grudgingly, to keep the sluggish conversation moving.

'A girl on the staff.'

'Do you know her?'

'Her name, yes. Christina Brown. And I could pick her out at an identification parade.'

Again the awkward silence.

'What do you feel about this, Molly?'

She blushed, blew out breath harshly.

'What the hell do you think?'

'No. Just a minute. You misunderstand me. Things have not been right, on your account, between you and Jim for at least a year, if not longer. I wondered if this might not be a convenient, er, moment to, to call it a day.'

She scowled, still moulding the bread, not looking at him.

'There comes a time, as I know only too well, when the best thing is to decide that enough is enough. Laura and I had reached such a pitch that we couldn't see each other without scratching eyes out. It's odd when you consider that nine years earlier we were people who were so attracted to each other that we could not do without marriage. How did you find out about Christina Brown?'

'An anonymous letter-writer. Presumably a colleague. Typewritten. Said that their behaviour was the talk of the school, that they spent every spare minute of the day, breaks, lunch-time, after-four together, "sitting like love-birds", that was the expression.' She pulled a sour face, having this time noticed the cliché.

'Man or woman?'

'I don't know. Somehow I put it down to a woman. I don't know why. Now you ask me, men can be just as catty, and malicious, can't they?'

'What does Miss Brown teach? It is *Miss* Brown, isn't it?'

'Biology and maths.'

That seemed wrong or unaccounted for.

'How old is she?'

'I don't know. Younger than I am, I conclude. She's not been there long.'

'And she knows Jim's married?'

'If somebody bothers to spend eighteen p on a first-class letter to me then they'd let her know that.'

'Did you show Jim the letter?'

'No.'

'When did it arrive?'

'Less than a week ago. The day he didn't come home and I rang you.'

'And he was with her?'

'I know he wasn't. He was where he said he was. But at the time . . .'

She shrugged. They both looked up.

'Are you going to show it to him?' Henry began.

'What do you think?'

'What good would it do? To you? Or Jim?'

'Or Miss Brown?' Molly mocked his pretension. 'What would you have done if it had happened to you?'

'That's easy. Just as you did. Put off doing anything about it.'

'You're not much help.'

'No. I can listen to you and hope it does you a mite of good talking about it. But I don't know enough. Why is Jim so unhappy?'

'He sees himself as trapped. In his job, his marriage, oh, everything.'

'And whose fault is that?'

'His own. Mine. Yours. His parents'. God's.'

Her flippancy annoyed him, made up his mind.

'Show him the letter.'

'Why do you say that, Henry?' Slowly.

'It can't do any harm. It could bring things to a head. It might make Jim's mind up for him.

'Yes, he could decide to poison me or cut my throat.'

23

Again he felt anger.

'I see there's no helping you, Molly.'

'I'm afraid not.' She frowned, thinking or giving that appearance. 'And now I've annoyed you. I do seem to get across the Fairfax family. I don't suppose you like Jim much, do you?'

'He's my brother.'

'You mean you're lumbered with him whatever happens. He's not over-fond of you. I'll tell you for nothing. "Trouble with our Henry," he says, "is that he's too bloody sure he's always right." '

'There's some truth in that.'

'Only you don't believe it. Anyway, thanks for listening to me. I shall have to make my decisions for myself in the long run. Were you serious about showing him the letter?'

'I'm not sure.'

'Neither am I.' Molly was standing. 'What's wrong with Jim may be pathological, nothing really to do with his circumstances. Some chemical imbalance.' She tapped her thighs with her flat hands, so like a rapt child that he half expected her to break into a skipping rhyme in time to the beat. 'My mother said/I never should/Play with the gypsies/ In the wood/ If I did/She would say/Naughty little girl/To run away.' Nothing. She ceased to tap, straightened herself up.

'Has he been to the doctor?'

'That's one quick, direct route to a flaming row. You suggest it, this time.'

'So he's not been?'

'Yes, he has. More than once. But he won't do as he's told and follow a course of tablets. And as Dr Taylor said to me, "I can't find him a more congenial job." What about Christina Brown? Should I ty to see her? Or write to her?'

'Not without saying something to Jim first.'

Molly made her way out to the hall where her coat was hanging.

'Thanks for the sandwich. It's all a bloody mess. But I'll keep in touch.'

When her coat was on she tapped him with a gloved

hand on the top of his head, livening his brain. Demeaned, he broke away, opened the door for her. She stepped through in a rush.

'It's not snowing,' she reported back. 'Thank God for small mercies.'

Henry Fairfax shut the door with careful quietness, appeasing somebody.

III

Conrad Le Jeune ordered Fairfax over to Zürich.

This was so unusual that Fairfax found himself fretting about the peremptory summons. On arrival he, on instruction, booked into a comfortable hotel by the lakeside. Le Jeune, engaged by day in some high-powered conference, deposited several thick box-files of accounts into his room and asked for an audit.

'Do it carefully,' he gritted. 'There may be some hanky-pank.' It might have been the opening of a television thriller.

Henry settled to the table and worked. As the day went on he became increasingly puzzled. Here were the balance sheets of two small Swiss firms engaged in the import and export of light machinery. They were meticulously straight, entries matching receipts, nothing omitted, and could have been put before an accountancy training course as an exemplar of how to present financial transactions. Even the German presented no great difficulties after an hour and a good dictionary.

Le Jeune had instructed Fairfax that he would see him that evening, probably at dinner, but it was not until nearly eleven thirty that the tycoon put in an appearance at the hotel.

'Are you in bed?' he shouted, entering. Fairfax, now in dressing gown, had in fact been asleep before the phone call from the foyer. Le Jeune, cheerfully wide awake, accepted a vodka from Henry's refrigerator, and parked himself in an armchair.

'Have you been through them?' He pointed to the folders on Fairfax's desk.

'Yes.'

'And?'

'Perfect. Models.'

'Nothing untoward about them, then? Out of place?'

26

He held his vodka up to the light, tipsily. 'Nothing troubled you?'

'Just one thing.'

'Go on.'

'These were so straightforward that you could have vouched for them yourself after an hour or two's work. And if you hadn't wanted the fag, there are competent firms here who would have done it for you. Why send for me?'

'Two reasons. I already employ you, and secondly, I thought it was time you had, or I gave you, a break.'

'My holiday allocation is quite generous.'

' "Here's Henry slaving away in my service," I told myself. "And I do nothing for him." '

'Except pay me and increase the value of my shares in Le Jeune's.'

'Ye', ye'.' Le Jeune considered this, tokenly chewing his thumbnail. 'I just thought a day or so off in foreign parts might suit you. The weather's not perfect, I agree.' It had recently snowed. The sky still threatened with cloud while the temperature stood two below zero. 'But it's comfortable in here. The meals are good. The drinks. It costs the firm next to nothing. It flutters the dovecotes when I announce I'm bringing in my own high-powered expert from England. And it makes me feel like Santa Claus.'

Conrad Le Jeune no longer raised his voice, nor attempted to disguise his regional accent. He dressed well, but quietly, rarely smiled, narrowing the brown eyes in his pasty, sagging features. Sometimes he bared his yellow teeth or dashed his hands nervously about in contrast to the stillness of the rest of the body, the almost total lack of expression on his sallow face. In movement he gave the appearance of a man in his early thirties; his hair was thick, dark, boyish. Next year he would be fifty.

Now he attempted sociability.

'Aren't you going to join me in a drink?'

'No, thanks.'

'Not at the firm's expense? You bloody puritans. We're doing very nicely, I can tell you. Especially these last

27

weeks. And so I thought, out of character and all that, I'll drag that brother-in-law of mine over here to enjoy the fleshpots with me. But then I knew you'd expect to do a bit of work for your keep, so I laid on an audit for you. Useful, but not really necessary. You're singing for your supper in a quiet way.'

Fairfax thanked him.

'Yes, we've made a bob or two.' He held up his vodka as if he'd sooner look at it than drink it, but offered no further comment. Then he sighed, sneezed, wiped his nose. 'Have you seen Laura lately?'

'No.' Fairfax grew suspicious again.

'No. I suppose not. Do you ever see her?'

'No.'

'Not even by chance?'

Fairfax shook his head.

'Pity. I always thought you were good for her. She needed somebody like you. Still does, in my opinion.'

'She didn't think so.'

'No. She wouldn't, would she? How long were you married. Ten years?'

'Nine.'

'Pity there were no children. I fancied myself as an uncle.' He looked in no way avuncular, yellow left hand exploring his face. 'Did you try?'

'Laura didn't want a family, well, after what . . .'

'You let her have too much of her own way, Henry. Doesn't do to let the likes of Laura rule the roost.'

'I don't know.'

'I do.'

There was no emphasis about Le Jeune's voice, which sounded not much above a whisper, and hoarse, like a smoker's.

'That's it, then, Henry. That's how it is. Stay here until Friday. I shall put one or two extra little jobs in your way. Otherwise enjoy yourself, as you like. You don't fancy a night club do you? I thought not.' He'd not waited for an answer. 'Here's a ticket for a concert tomorrow. All Beethoven. Daniel Barenboim. Rock solid. It'll suit you.' He placed it on the desk by the neatly stacked files.

Again Fairfax thanked him.

'Forget it. I've done myself well this week, and last, and I thought I'd spread the happiness around a bit. Though by the look on your face I don't know whether I've succeeded.' He threw his head back with a bray of laughter. The movement seemed inhuman, the jerk of an ill-coordinated mechanical toy.

'I'll do my best for you.'

'You're a funny bugger, Henry. I like you. I don't understand you, but I like you.' Le Jeune pointed at the box-files. 'I'll have them collected first thing in the morning, and leave you another similar chore. Have my money's worth.' Now the man seemed to be chuntering to himself, absolutely sober but concentrating on some unknown concern. 'I'm sorry I spoiled your beauty sleep. I don't need much myself. If I go to bed now, I shall be up and wandering about at five tomorrow. Bad conscience, perhaps.' He laughed again, awkwardly.

'What would you do if you saw Laura again? Would you speak to her?'

'I think so. It's two years now since the divorce. I wasn't pleased at the time. I was sore. The lawyers made it nasty. But the worst's over. I'd speak to her if that's what she wanted. We're civilized.'

'You may be. I don't know about me.'

'You've got nothing in mind, have you?'

'About what?'

'About Laura?'

'Oh, I see. No, not a thing. You don't trust me, Henry, do you?'

'We've worked together for nearly eleven years, and this is the first time you've invited me abroad.'

'A whim, that's all it was. A generous impulse. I'll know better next time.'

'I'm very grateful.'

As Conrad Le Jeune quitted the room he stopped with a large hand on the door.

'You seem to me, Henry, a man satisfied with life. Would that be so?'

'Well, yes. Ye'. That's about right.'

'But your wife has left you, and your job's dull. You make up to yourself with these radio plays of yours. I've never heard one. Why don't you try for the television?' He interpreted Fairfax's expression. 'That's just what I'd say, isn't it? Laura was very proud of the plays.'

'That wasn't my impression.'

' "Henry's a real talent," she told me. "He brings out all sorts of surprises. And when I think I can guess their origin, I'm always amazed how cunning he is with the changes he's made. He's clever." '

'We never talked about them.'

'No? Why was that?'

'Once I had finished a play I didn't want to. It was done. And even less when I was working on it. Basically I was confident that she wasn't really interested in what I was doing, subject matter or anything else.'

'You were wrong.'

With that Conrad let himself out.

The rest of the week Henry Fairfax traipsed willingly round the wintry city, enjoyed his concert and excellent meals, carefully examined the accounts Conrad left with him, but did not come to terms with an unexpected congé in a foreign town. He talked easily to people, in the streets and hotel, but was glad to board the Swissair plane for Heathrow. It had all been a mildly interesting waste of time.

It had snowed in England during his absence, but his house was in good order thanks to central heating. The bath scales showed he had put on a pound and a half in Switzerland. He went to bed early, and slept well.

On the next evening his brother telephoned.

'I've been trying to get hold of you all week. Where have you been?'

'Zürich.'

'Have you, by God? Some people are lucky. I want a word with you.'

'Go on, then, I'm listening. About what?'

'Not over the telephone. Can I come round Sunday morning about eleven?'

'If you don't stay too long.'

'What are you doing then, that's so important?'

'The week's washing and my lunch.'

'Bloody hell. The model housewife.'

James put the phone rudely down.

He arrived twenty minutes late on Sunday morning, hail-fellow well-met. Henry provided a mug of coffee.

'You're late.'

James sucked at his coffee, crossing, uncrossing his legs.

'Well?' Henry said at length.

'My wife, Molly.' He stopped.

'Yes, I know her name.'

'Christ, you've got it on you this morning. She's been to see you, hasn't she?'

'Yes. Before I went to Switzerland.'

'What did she want?'

'You must ask her that.'

'She was complaining about me, wasn't she? I know she was. She told me herself she'd been here. About Christina Brown. What did she say?' Small pauses punctuated the jerk of each sentence.

'I've just said Molly's the person to ask, not me.'

James picked up his mug again, squeezing it hard in one hand. He replaced it, and eased himself forward.

'I'd just like to know what she said. We're not getting on well. It'll do no harm for you to tell me, and might even do some good.'

'You won't get anything out of me, Jim, on that score, so you might just as well give up.'

'Bastard.' He delivered the word without rancour, almost comically, then scratched the crown of his head. 'She thinks I'm having it away with a girl on the staff called Christina Brown.'

'And are you?'

'I am not.'

'What makes her suspect you?'

'Somebody at school has written her a letter accusing me.'

'Have you seen this letter?'

'Yes. She showed it to me.'

'And you've no idea who sent it?'

31

'No. I could guess, but I might be wrong.'

'And was there any truth in the allegations in this letter? Did it actually accuse you of adultery with Miss Brown?'

'Not in so many words. It said we spent a lot of time together in the common room.'

'And is that the truth?'

'Well, yes. There's something in it.'

'You spend sufficient time with this lady to make somebody think it proper to inform your wife?'

James considered that.

'That school's full of cranks and bloody-fool crackpots. Silly, nosey bastards who'd do anything to cause trouble.' Paranoia bubbled.

'Let's admit that, for the sake of argument. But how do you stand with Miss Brown?'

'That's none of your fucking business.'

'Exactly. End of conversation.'

'I don't like this big-brother tone of yours.' James waited for an answer he did not get. 'I need some help.'

'And you're not going the right way about getting it. Either from me or Molly. I can't speak for Miss Brown.'

James's head sank; he stared dully at the floor between his feet. Now and then he shifted as if to find a more comfortable position. His misery was blatant, almost palpable. The red mouth puckered like that of a child about to cry. Hands hung limply over corduroy knees.

'You tell me about it when I've made you another cup of coffee.'

James clung to his mug, not allowing his brother to wrest it from him. He shook his head in hopeless vigour.

'Leave me alone, can't you?'

Henry sat down again. He remembered his young brother eleven years ago at the age of eighteen, handsome with his fair, close-cropped curls, his blue eyes, quick movements, his rapid stutter of speech as if he had too many ideas to handle one sentence at a time. Jim had been a fine runner, county cross-country champion, head boy of his school, a position his brother never held, and was about to go to university. They all admired him: his father, his mother especially, Henry, the school friends he

32

brought home, his teachers, bright-eyed girls who hung on his words. Now here sat a ruined schoolmaster, a failure who had lost self-respect.

During Jim's first year at university his mother had died, quickly, almost desperately with cancer. She had kept quiet for too long, it seemed, serving her husband, children, church and charities, so that diagnosed illness and death came suddenly. Even their father, a careful observant man, knew nothing, it appeared, until his wife's comfortable belly swelled into distortion and she could hide her pain no longer. She was dispatched into hospital but died within the month, stoical, aghast, frightening them all.

James had raced back by train for the three weekends. It had cheered his mother, though she confided to her husband that she did not want the boy to neglect his work. That was important. Ill as she was, they were never certain whether she knew she was about to die. The word 'cancer' was not mentioned. Louise Fairfax grew weaker by the day, but never lost her hold on a kind of reality. She could joke; she made out to Jim that he was really coming over to see not her, but some sweetheart. Whatever mortification the sleepless nights, the pain, nausea, weakness, degradation inflicted on her, she put on a show for her visitors. Drugged to the eyes, she saw their grief clearly and helped them towards hopeless hope.

James was most affected.

His boyishness, his dash disappeared. He wept openly at the funeral, standing next to his bewildered sister-in-law. Yet his work did not suffer; he took a First in Part One, and a high Upper Second in Part Two. He still ran hard; he was seen about with pretty girls, but there were periods of blackness, of blank depression when he seemed to be locked inside himself, selfishly fighting against, wrestling with his own desperation. His father wished him to take up a study of the law, but he set his face against it and went back to the university at the last minute to follow a post-graduate certificate course in education. He did two years of teaching in Southampton, successfully, it was understood, and then returned to Beechnall to a large

33

comprehensive school. Shortly afterwards he had married Mary Maguire as soon as she had finished her final year, in a blaze of publicity, at the polytechnic.

On his return to the home town, James had seemed extraordinarily subdued to his brother. The young man who had gabbled so volubly at school, who had sparkled in school debates, hectored sluggish rugby and athletic teams, charmed parents and visitors on speech day and the governors' feast now sat apathetically for long periods, staring out at nothing, locked inside himself. His fluency reappeared for complaints alone.

Henry mentioned the change to Laura, his wife, but found no help there.

'He's been quiet ever since I've known him.' There was an element of truth there; Jim had never found much to say to his brother's wife. Their father was more forthcoming.

'He had a bad time at university after your mother died. I had to go up several times. They made him see a psychiatrist.'

'You said nothing about this to me,' Henry objected.

'You were busy, very busy at the time, and wrapped up in Laura. Besides, I didn't think Jim would want his troubles trumpeting all over the county.' His father shook his head. 'And he threw over that Mortimer girl I thought he was serious about at much the same time. It was all very unpleasant. That's one reason why I thought it a good idea for him to try the law. These difficulties hadn't affected his studies, as far as we could tell. And I could have taken him into my office, but he wouldn't have it.'

Now James Fairfax sat uncomfortably in his brother's house.

'I'd help if I could,' Henry answered.

'Moll's more interested in her jewellery than in me.'

'She's the right to take her career seriously. You must admit that.'

'Working with that poofter, Fowler?'

'That's hardly sensible. Molly is a gifted woman, and you have to accept it. You should encourage her.'

'You think I don't?'

34

'It doesn't sound like it.' Silence lay soddenly between the two men. Henry roused himself. 'Do you want to tell me about Christina Brown?'

'No. You're as bad as that set of poncing clowns I call my colleagues. I don't want to talk about her. Why should I? It's none of your business.'

'I hope you don't take the same line with Molly.'

'Moll can look after herself, believe you me. I'm a bit of furniture about the house to your favoured Molly. She doesn't care.'

'That's not true.'

'You'd know better, wouldn't you?'

'I'd hardly say that. But you won't be helped, and I don't know what's wrong with you.'

Again the sullen hiatus. James fidgeted with a cushion.

'You're not prepared to tell me, then, what Molly said?'

'If it's any help, pretty well what you've come out with this morning.'

'And the letter? Did she show you that?'

'No. She told me about it. She was worried as far as I could make out, and that was the last straw. I don't think you're being fair to her. I take it that things are rough between you at home, and then the letter arrives. She rang me because you were very late back.'

'What in hell did she think you could do?'

'Nothing. Except listen. It gives you some idea of her desperation that she had to tell somebody. She always struck me as being pretty self-contained, not the sort to go crying on the first shoulder she came across.'

'She thought I was out with Christina, didn't she?'

'I expect so. But by the time she came here she seemed to have accepted your, your innocent explanation.'

'Because it's true.'

'That's what she said. I know what it's like, Jim, when things begin to go wrong in a marriage. I've been through it. And usually both parties are to blame. But as far as I could make out Molly was genuinely concerned.'

'She's a silly bitch.'

Henry Fairfax shrugged, giving argument up as hopeless.

35

'I'm haunted.' James threw himself about in his chair. His brother hated watching.

'By what?'

That question angered, but James struggled inside himself for a reasonable answer.

'This feeling. Depression.' Words suddenly burst on him. 'This intolerable conviction that nothing in this world can ever go right for me again.'

'Is all this recent?'

'No. But it's worse now than it's ever been.'

'Is it the result, do you think, of what's happening at school'

'In part. But that's not the whole.'

'And your relationship with Molly?'

A sneer disfigured James's handsome face, before he rallied himself.

'That makes it worse. But it's not the cause. That aggravates the tension.'

'And Christina Brown?'

'She's a pretty, decent, innocent girl who likes me, God knows why. She listens to me. And it does me good to talk to her. It makes time pass. I look forward to seeing her. I go to that rotten school eagerly now because I know I shall see her.'

'Are you in love, Jim?'

'What does that mean in a bloody case like mine? I don't even express myself properly. I hate that school. Nothing can make it bearable. Christina's the only bright spot. She keeps me up.'

'Why don't you look for another job? You're well qualified.'

'What makes you think one school will be any better than another? Come on, let's hear your reasoning.'

'If this one is so unsuitable, it would be the barest common sense to try another.'

'Molly wouldn't move. She's too well established in Fowler's workshop. I'd have to leave her the house, and live in digs. No Molly, no Christina, no comforts.'

'But a job, we hope, that would offer you more satisfaction.'

36

'There isn't such a thing. I've had enough of teaching. It's ill paid, run by incompetents, supervised by ambitious idiots and by ham-strung, ignorant political mobsters or thick-headed parents.'

'Have you thought of doing anything else?'

'It would mean re-training. Molly would have to keep me.'

'Have you discussed it with her at all?'

'It's six months since I discussed anything with her. She's incapable of rational argument.'

'Look, Jim, your language is hardly a model of moderation.'

'Model, bloody model.'

James rose, stepped towards his brother, fists clenched. His face, patched with pallor, twisted, uglifying itself. He led with his left, hitting Henry, who now stood, on the shoulder. Henry, though surprised, easily checked the right cross which followed; the blow seemed delivered without conviction. The elder, broader, heavier, stronger, shoved on his brother's chest violently with both hands so that James staggered back into his chair, which shot away on smooth casters, dropping the uncontrolled body to the floor. James landed on the carpet face downward. He pushed himself up to his hands and knees.

'Brawling's no help,' Henry managed. He found difficulty breathing, but he felt anger without excitement. He calmed himself by standing quite still.

James now stood, bending, feebly brushing his knees.

'Sit down,' Henry ordered. He pushed past James, recovered the chair, set it in its usual place. 'Sit down. You won't take up so much room.'

James obeyed, still batting at his trouser-legs.

'I didn't much like that,' Henry said, squaring his own chair to the hearth. James made no reply. Now he sat motionless, as if his spine were broken, but stiff, like a wrecked umbrella. 'What can punches achieve? Even suppose you'd knocked me out where would that have got you? Eh? You might have felt better, perhaps. Or guilty? Or frightened?'

James sat unspeaking.

'I hope,' Henry began again, 'that you don't take your fists to Molly.'

Nothing.

Henry felt his temper rising again.

'For God's sake go down to the doctor and see if he can sort you out. You need help. I wish I knew what to do or say.'

'You leave me alone,' James muttered like a punished schoolboy.

'You're my brother, Jim. I'd do for you what I could. I always liked you. Admired you. You had more about you than ever I had. I was a plodder, a stick in the mud. You could run. And shine. Our mother thought so. You were her favourite. I never held that against you.'

James lifted his head, eyes like those of a chidden dog. Henry moved across, sat on the arm of his brother's chair, put an arm lightly across the shoulders. James leaped up.

'You leave me alone.'

James shuffled across the hearth-rug. His arms hung as if held in place by his sleeves. His shoes had not been cleaned.

'If you want me to do anything for you, just let me know.' Henry, upright again.

'What makes you think you can?'

'Jim. Jim.'

'You just name one thing you could bloody do.'

'I could ask Conrad Le Jeune if he could fit you in somewhere.'

'Driving a lorry?'

Henry gave up.

His brother hunched his shoulders, slouched out of the room, fumbled his coat off the pegs in the hall, let himself clumsily out, leaving the door ajar. Henry followed him with his eyes along the garden path. The shambling figure left the street gate open, but drove off neatly enough.

38

IV

'And how are you keeping then?'

At the annual dinner and dance of the Le Jeune (E. Midlands) Transport Ltd, Henry arriving, cheerfully prepared to overeat and spend the evening refusing drinks, was greeted by his ex-wife.

How well he knew that voice, a bright mezzo-soprano. Laura looked healthy, youthful in red and silver, finger-nails scarlet, hands heavily ringed, hair held in place by a small tiara. She lifted her face to be kissed. Henry swooped briefly, stood upright, nostrils provoked by her perfume. Laura was smiling, a glass of champagne in her left hand, a presence. Le Jeune had said nothing about his sister's likelihood of attending. She lived in London now.

'I can't grumble, thanks.'

Henry kept his voice flat. He'd not show surprise.

'And you?'

'I'm really very well. Don't I look it?'

'Perfect.'

It would not be long, he thought, before they'd be niggling, scoring off each other if not openly quarrelling. He pulled himself together.

'What are you doing in this part of the world?' he asked, pleasantly.

'Con asked me if I'd like to come, and it's more than a year since I was in Beechnall. It's a place I'm very fond of. I was born here. You knew that, didn't you?'

'Yes. I did.'

'Are you all right, Henry? You look very glum to me.'

'It's all this dressing up.'

Laura looked him over.

'I hadn't noticed it,' she said.

She moved away with an ironical wave of the hand. Fairfax, as head of the Beechnall office, began his round of hand-shaking with colleagues and wives. Already the party grew noisy, punctuated by bellows of laughter. Drink flowed; unmarried ladies simpered or looked bored. Jokers and hearties congregated, sometimes deserting their wives in favour of cronies and places near the bar. Henry always knew middle age at these affairs; people seemed glad to see him, but smiled quietly, lowered their voices, told no risqué stories, searched round for topics of conversation. Perhaps he put a damper on the function. Certainly they would all have noticed his passage with his divorced wife, but would not mention it to him. The wet blanket raised tomato juice.

At eight o'clock the head waiter, in tails, struck a gong and announced that they were required to sit in the dining hall. He advised them to consult the seating plan at the door to save time and added that the quicker they were settled the sooner they would be fed. He did not smile; he wore white gloves and spoke lugubriously.

'He doesn't seem a bit pleased to see us,' the wife of a chief clerk told Henry. 'Why must he look so superior?'

'He's giving us a sense of occasion.'

'Oh, that's what it is. He's wasting it on me.' Relenting, she laid a hand on Henry's forearm. 'I always look forward to this dinner. It's such a good idea to hold it at the end of January, in the dark of the year.'

'Come on, Sal,' her husband chided. 'Don't keep Mr Fairfax from his food.'

'Onward to indigestion,' Henry countered. All dutifully laughed.

A glance at the seating plan showed Henry that he was at the top table, as he expected, and between Laura and an accountant from Manchester, new to the firm, known only by name and reputation. Henry introduced himself to the man, who looked about sixteen. Laura had not yet arrived. The Manchester visitor, Dr Newbolt, made a few guarded, complimentary remarks about Henry, claiming that Conrad had often said in his hearing that whenever he was in a real dilemma he asked himself what Henry Fairfax would do.

'And does the opposite?'

They laughed. Newbolt gave some account of his career so far. Henry, interested, encouraged him. When the hall was full, Laura arrived with Conrad, was helped to her chair by the head waiter. She bowed slightly in the direction of her ex-husband before concentrating her attention on the man on her right, a Canadian. The toastmaster banged with his gavel, called them to order and grace.

Service was good and swift. As the soup plates were being cleared Laura turned towards her left.

'It really is lovely to be sitting next to you again. Hen.'

She had never used the abbreviation during the period of their married life. Free with endearments, she had avoided his name. He often wondered if she did not like it. As she leaned towards him her perfume played delicately, and he had the impression, wrongly as reason corrected him, that since they had last spoken half an hour ago she had taken a bath, revisited the hairdresser and completely changed her clothes. She had made it new; striking, powerfully attentive, quite beautiful, she disquieted him.

'We're friends again, now, aren't we?' she inquired.

The notables sat on a dais on one side only of the high table. Slightly below, the employees enjoyed themselves, feasting eyes on the MD and his party. Wives asked questions; characters were sketched; hoary anecdotes were given another airing. Mr Fairfax, quiet Mr Fairfax, sitting there next to his stunning divorced wife, like a cat who had got at the cream, came in for his share of comment. Henry thought it would not be long, two more glasses of wine, say, before the bawdy began. He did not mind, he decided. Laura's leg touched his, accidentally, he was sure.

'What are you doing while you're up here?'

'Visiting. Sightseeing. I'm using Con's house. His housekeeper's looking after me.'

'Does he still keep Mrs Edwards on? He's hardly ever here.'

'It gives her somewhere to live. He sets her against tax, I guess.'

'Is she here this evening?'

'I think so. Somewhere about. Con looks after her.'

She turned to the other side, graciously, and did not claim his attention until the plates for the main course were being cleared.

'That was delicious,' she said. 'Roast beef can be boring.'

'Conrad knows where to get value for money.'

'Is he interested in food, then?'

'Not really. But he can get good advice.'

'From you, for example?'

'Not about meals.'

Laura played for a moment with a spoon, using it as a mirror.

'I think,' she began, then stopped, twisting the spoon, 'I think that while I'm here you should invite me to your house.'

'I'd be delighted.' Courtesy covered surprise.

'Do you mean it? I don't want you doing what you don't want.'

'You name an evening.'

'Tuesday.'

He took out his diary, knowing it empty on that day, inquired a time and made an entry.

'I shan't feed you quite as well as this evening.'

'I don't want a meal. You can ply me with a drink or so.'

Laura made an inquiry about the best way to find his house. He explained.

'That's the place you took after our débâcle? Why didn't you stay in Avalon?'

'Too large. And conservatives like me need a change. This seemed a good opportunity.'

'So you can say I did you good in a way?'

'It didn't feel like it at the time.'

She laughed, laying a hand on his arm. He settled to his fresh fruit salad, the plainest fare on offer, while Laura's spoon chopped at the piled, creamy confection before her. After the loyal toast, a witty succinct speech from the professor of banking at the university and a telling response from Conrad, also short but unintelligible

42

to any outside the workforce, the guests retired to the bar so that the room could be cleared for dancing. Henry Fairfax, alone, watched from the door the efficient bundling away of flowers, decorations, starched cloths, long deal tables. Husky men scattered powder on the floor, polished it with vigour, sprayed air-freshener, set small tables, chairs by the walls. The whole operation took twenty minutes, by which time the band had assembled. Conrad would approve of the efficiency; Henry wondered if Le Jeune owned the place.

Fairfax enjoyed ballroom dancing, did his share and did it well, though he sat out specialities, pop-style or over-energetic romps. He invited Laura to a slow fox-trot; within seconds they were at one, in a performance, worth watching, paragons. At the end of the first stretch she said, 'That was superb. I'd forgotten how good you were. It always seemed out of character.'

'Sign of a misspent youth.'

'John King,' that was the Canadian, 'thinks that walking forward flat-footed is the way to dance.'

'And Professor Dench?' She looked up. Henry had noticed with whom she had danced.

'He's like a man pushing a supermarket trolley.'

They concentrated on steps rather than conversation. As he led her back to her table she whispered, 'Bags I the next quick-step with you.' She smiled broadly at her brother, King, the Denches; Fairfax slipped away. He danced three times in all with Laura without learning much. She was friendly, said all this made her young again, because apparently she had learnt ballroom dancing at school. 'We thought it suitable only for the aged and decrepit. And now I might be fourteen or fifteen again.' Her sentences were neatly delivered, but she did not talk readily, hesitated. How they would make out when there was no music or cross-chassé-and-lock to distract them, he did not know. Laura looked no different, no older. She was without argument the most striking woman in the room. When after the second dance Conrad invited him to sit down at their table, Henry made his excuses: he had promised a dance to Mrs Slater, true enough; he'd left his drink elsewhere; he needed to spruce up. Laura was already engaged in a laughing exchange with John King, stroking his lapels.

By midnight Henry had reached the bearable level of social enjoyment. He said good night to no one, took hat and coat from the cloakroom and drove sedately off.

V

Henry twice telephoned Jim's house but found no one at home. He took comfort from this, deciding that his brother and sister-in-law must have found some sort of accommodation in their domestic life. He recognized this conclusion as moral idleness on his part, forgave himself and prepared for Laura's visit.

She arrived, dressed more soberly than he expected, offered her cheek for kissing, and settled down comfortably enough in an armchair.

'Before we start are you sure you wouldn't like to have dinner out? There's a very good trattoria not five minutes away. I can easily ring for a table.'

'I prefer to stay here, thank you. Don't fuss.'

'Drink, then?'

'Vodka and tonic, if you please. Not too strong, for a beginning.'

Laura looked about her, bright-eyed, and while he played with tongs and the ice bowl stood and made a tour of inspection.

'I remember that clock.'

'It was a wedding present to my grandmother.'

'I never liked it.'

'Then I'm sorry.' He spoke more sharply than he intended. Laura, placing her glass, found no offence, comfortably observing him.

'Tell me,' she used an actressy, social tone, 'what you're doing with yourself these days.'

Henry did his best. She interrupted the account of his time at Le Jeune's.

'I work for Conrad, in the London office. On the publicity side. I think I know what you're up to down here.' She looked pleasant. 'Are you still writing?'

'Yes. To the best of my ability.'

'I haven't heard anything recently.'

45

'Radio Four did *Nightingales* last month.'

'I missed it. I look in the *Radio Times*. But you were working on that when I lived with you, oh, four, five years ago.'

'That's so. Was it called *Nightingales* then? It must have been.'

'About a holiday in Greece?'

'That's it. I couldn't get it right. I kept putting it aside. And when I finally sent it in, the script editor wanted it doing all over again.'

'You were always a bit of a perfectionist.'

'Yes and no. It's usually a quicker business than that. I wasn't myself. What with one thing and another.'

'You mean the divorce?'

He nodded, gravely.

'Our last good holiday was in Greece. I remember it with a great deal of pleasure.'

'Yes. I enjoyed it.'

'It was just after that,' she spoke normally, 'that we began to get across each other.' She laughed, behind a polite hand. 'I blame myself as much as you. I do now. I didn't then.'

'No.'

'Still, it's no use going into all that or we shall be at one another's throats. You were always too private for me. You went your own way; not that you weren't considerate. You were. But there seemed some part of you I was never allowed to know.'

'Wouldn't that be so with everybody?'

'Yes. But the part I wasn't allowed near in your case was the important bit.' Her tone was light. 'Don't you agree?'

'What you say doesn't apply to me at all. Or at least in my opinion. I don't see myself as secretive in the least.'

'You think I've made it up, do you? That all this springs from some misjudgement or inadequacy of my own?'

'I've no idea.'

'Of what?'

'Why you hold such views.'

'That's what I mean.' She spoke glumly, as if compelled

46

by logic to propound unpalatable truth. 'You were never willing to argue things out. You were kind and generous and you would give me my way if you could.'

'We raved at each other, as far as I can remember.' He refused to be rattled. 'Made all sorts of accusations. Opted for character assassination in a big way.'

'That was once the marriage began to break up. Before that we never seriously discussed anything.'

'I don't remember.'

'Oh, come. You don't want to remember it.'

'I seem to recall considerable argument about holidays, about furniture and decorating the house. And on a more serious note we often talked about the advantages and disadvantages of having children.'

'We said things to one another, true. But the conclusions were left to me. I had to make my mind up. I had to decide. You seemed to make a principle of not having any strongly held views.'

'I deferred to you. About a family, for example. You were the one who had to bear the children, carry the main onus of bringing them up. It still seems proper that you should be the one to make the final decision about that. I would willingly have had children, but I knew I'd be out of the house eight and a half hours every day of the week, and so . . .'

'I had absolutely no idea, Henry, whether you wanted a family or not. Not a clue. Not an inkling. You'd hum and ha until I could have screamed.'

'If I had laid the law down, you wouldn't have liked that, either.'

'No. You're probably right.'

'You didn't want a dominating male figure for a husband, did you?'

'I certainly didn't get one.'

Laura sipped her drink.

'Do you never think of marrying again?' she asked.

'I think about it. I'm not completely put off marriage.'

'But take no steps?'

'Not so far.'

47

'Oh, so you have someone in mind?' She laid a hand playfully on her mouth.

'No. No. I'm in no hurry.'

Henry wished they had gone out to dinner. Then there would have been plenty to occupy them. Clearly Laura needed conversation; wordless warmth and comfort were unacceptable.

'We quarrelled a great deal,' she said. 'It seemed inevitable at the time. And cruel. We went out of our way to squabble. We couldn't help it, I suppose.'

'An inquest now won't be of much use.'

'Oh, I don't know about that. Might put us on guard for next time.'

'I doubt it. I'm quite pleased to see you, really. I mean, we have some good things to remember. But I notice that, polite as we are, we're beginning to argue. That's an advantage perhaps, makes for an interesting evening. But if we felt chained to each other, or angry with the world, or dissatisfied, these differences would soon be fights.'

'You're a funny man, Henry.'

'With respect.'

'What's that mean?'

'It's a lawyer's ironical way of telling the judge he disagrees with him. I'm attributing the phrase to you.'

'Goodness.'

Laura put the vodka to her lips.

'But tell me,' she continued. 'Are you really pleased to see me?'

'Yes. I've admitted it.'

'You wouldn't have said so just after the divorce, would you?'

'True. The lawyers made it worse. I never wanted to see you again.'

'And now you do?'

'Yes.'

She sat solemnly.

'I'm sorry,' she began. 'But I had to get my pound of flesh out of you. I'd no idea whether I'd be able to get a job, or keep myself. And the cost of property and living in London's beyond all sense.'

48

'But it worked out well enough.'

'For a start Conrad took me on in his London office. And found me a flat. I wouldn't say he was exactly generous, but at least it kept me off the streets. He wasn't pleased when we split up, you know. He said it was my fault.' She stroked her face. 'Conrad thought very highly of you.'

'Why was that?'

'You seemed a different sort of person from him. I mean you did your work properly, sure, or you'd have been out on your behind quick enough. But he admired the way you spent your spare time on writing. He told me, oh, often enough, that I was lucky to have married someone like you.'

'That's flattering.'

'To Conrad, I was an ignorant, useless little woman with a pretty face. I think, I hope he sees me differently now I work for him. We didn't know each other very well when we were young. He was seventeen years older, and he'd left home before I started school, even. I think he realizes now that I've inherited some of the Le Jeune drive.'

'That's good.'

'I enjoy my work and find plenty to do. In a way, it's an advantage to be single again.'

'So if you decide to remarry, you might have to give up your career?'

'It would be a consideration, certainly.'

Laura held out her glass. Henry jumped to his feet to replenish it.

'I sometimes regret that I have no children,' she told him, vodka lifted for inspection. 'I think if you had kept on at me when we were married I'd have come round to your way of thinking.'

He said nothing.

'No need to be sad about it,' she said, pertly.

'You're not too old now.'

'I'm thirty-three this year. I suppose not.' Laura looked her ex-husband over. 'I did take up with a man when I first went to London. He was younger than I was. But he didn't measure up in the end. He'd plenty of money; he was a stockbroker, but he was a wimp, really. Cultured, a wine buff, very amenable, quite active sexually, but, no, he wouldn't do. In the end.'

Henry knew a pang of jealousy at her frankness. It silenced him.

'How's that brother of yours getting on?' she began again.

'Jim? Not happy. Hates his work.'

'And his wife? Mary Dennis-Maguire, wasn't it?'

'She's doing well with her jewellery, I believe. Sells most of it in London now. But she and Jim are at loggerheads.'

'Why's that?'

'Nothing pleases him these days. He's depressed. And her success, and the fact that she's not always there at his beck and call doesn't suit his book.'

'He was a nice-looking boy.'

'Still is. And clever. He ought to make something of his life, but he's failing. I sometimes wonder if I should ask Conrad to find him a place. He hates working in a school.'

'You do that. Con would be glad to do you a favour.'

'No. For one thing, Jim would accuse me of interfering where it doesn't concern me, and secondly I'm not sure he'd do any better with the firm. This depression seems ingrained in him.'

'Pathological?'

'Yes. I don't know. Chemical imbalance, perhaps. It started at the time my mother died, when he was at Cambridge.'

'That was the cause?'

'A trigger mechanism.' He smiled wanly at his expression. 'I don't like to say. To tell you the truth I knew little of it at the time. We hadn't been married long. And we were expanding at work, if you remember.'

'I tell you what did strike me at the time, and that's how easily you seemed to take your mother's death. It was almost as if she didn't mean anything to you.'

Henry shrugged, unwilling to contest the point.

'It couldn't have been so. You always seemed very close to her. More so than Con and Jack and I were with our

50

mother.' Laura spoke dully as if the subject held little interest. 'She had you running about after her even when we were married.'

'We saw eye to eye in some things.'

Laura cocked an ironical brow at the answer, and waited head on one side. How often had he noted the position.

'Of course, Jim was her favourite. She made that quite clear,' Henry said drily.

'Why so? It's usually the first-born who's most highly regarded.'

'He was more handsome, and cleverer. More attractive. I don't blame her.'

'You still run yourself down, do you? I don't think you see yourself as others see you. Not as I do. You're a survivor, if ever I knew one.'

'And you?'

'I manage.' She sat straighter. 'But I'm really glad you're pleased to meet me again. It would be a shame to throw those nine years away.' She waited for a comment which was not forthcoming. 'How did you find Zürich?'

'Puzzling. There was no need for me to be there. Conrad put a little work in my way, and sent me to a Barenboim recital one evening and even offered to show me the night-life. But, at bottom, I was not there for any good reason, not anything connected with business, anyway.'

'Con likes to distribute patronage. Oh, I know you think he should let you choose your own venue or means of pleasure, but. I guess he'd want to terrify those firms whose books you looked over.'

'An expensive way of doing it. Besides, their accounts were perfectly above board.'

'I don't think you quite latch on to Con. He thinks there are facets of life he's missed. And you, employee, brother-in-law, represent one of them.'

'He's rich.' Henry Fairfax's voice demonstrated his dissatisfaction with the answer.

'And getting richer by the minute. He's really minting it now. But I suppose you know this?'

'My little neck of the woods is . . .'

'No. It's abroad. It's marvellous, especially when you think he didn't cross the Channel until he was nearly thirty, even on a day trip.'

'Will he get married?'

'Not he.' She laughed and drank. 'Though one never knows with men like Con. Making money is his life. But he might run across some little woman who traps him into matrimony. He might just try it himself out of devilment. An optional extra for the very rich.'

'I see.'

'You're a bit glum, Henry.' That was the first time she had used his name. 'You're not going to allow yourself to grow into one of those dull, pudding-faced bachelors, are you?'

'Likely, very likely.'

Laura settled back into her chair, hitching her well-cut skirt, crossing the admirable legs. The relaxation seemed to signify, he thought, that some kind of test period was now over. Her aggressive questions had prodded him into a mood of restrained anger, but from this moment she could take it easy, as if some point had been made. She began an amusing account of a holiday she and a friend had spent in Tenerife. They had enjoyed the sun; she and Lisa, a commercial lawyer, had been both energetic and argumentative. They had decided to read Lawrence's *Rainbow* while they were there, and though they did not get far with the project, they had hilarious bouts of verbal all-in wrestling over the few pages they had managed. They drank too much, so that serious discussions soon deteriorated into laughter, but that had been exactly what they needed.

'We'd come in at night, and start on Lawrence, and inside ten minutes we'd be wetting our pants and squealing with laughter. It would have been the same if it had been the Lamentations of Jeremiah we'd have been talking about. When I think of it now, it seems absolutely silly that two grown-up women with highly responsible jobs, and Lisa's a real intellectual at that, should have acted like schoolgirls. And yet it rested us. I came back full of life. It was the most restorative holiday I've ever had.'

'Good. Laugh and grow fat.' She indicated mild dissent by her expression.

'And men didn't seem to matter. Not that Lisa's very interested. It was great, a revelation at my time of life. And all due to sunshine in January, and drink.' She raised her vodka, and sipped.

'And do you see much of Lisa in London?'

'Now and again. I'm too whacked at night to be racketing round, though we sometimes have a meal out, now that Con's beginning to pay me something near what I'm worth to him.'

Here Laura began a disquisition on food. When they were married she had prepared excellent meals, consulted cookery manuals, encouraged him to blunt the conservatism of his taste in Indian, Italian and French restaurants, but now her interest seemed almost academic, obsessive, well organized, directed into topics, with themes, schemes, sub-headings, and, as her voice ironically made clear, footnotes and appendices. He admired the performance, the richness of the lore, the colourful, ingenious, supportive details. And yet Laura at thirty-two was as slim as when he had first met her.

He said as much.

'It's the amount one eats.' She dismissed him imperiously, as if he should have understood this. 'If I have one meal a day only, that's three hundred and sixty-five a year, with plenty of room for variety.'

'You need a strong will.'

'Which I have.'

And there he was put in his place.

'How old is Lisa?'

'About your age. Thirty-seven. A clever woman. Con employs her from time to time; that's how I first got to know her.'

'Is she married?'

'No. But very attractive. A small, dark, lively person. Had a long-standing live-in affair. Even when she's being serious, discussing legalities, you can see what a fireball she is. But bi-sexual.'

For the next quarter of an hour Laura dissected Lisa's character for him, amusingly, admiringly.

Again, as with her interest in culinary matters, her stress seemed too great, as if she must convert her ex-husband to her way of thinking. Sentences rattled out; her eyes flashed; her hands danced. Henry did not remember Laura as excitable as this; she seemed now to have learnt a rôle, to be practising it, though quite beautifully.

She refused all food, accepted a third vodka, but no more.

Her decision to leave came in a hurry. She looked at her watch, pointedly, and stood.

'I've enjoyed this evening.'

'It's not very late.'

'No. You've a job to go to tomorrow. I shall probably return. But it's been great to see you again.'

'I'm no different.'

'I didn't expect you to be. That's one thing I counted on: that the same old Henry Fairfax would be here.'

'With his ha'penny.'

'I beg your pardon?'

'Oh, a local expression meaning "making the most of the very little he's gifted with".'

'Very good.'

She dismissed the phrase, his explanation, him, but when he had helped her on with her coat, and rung her taxi, she kissed him on the mouth, held him to her. He attributed her warmth to the vodka.

'How long will the cab be?'

'Five, ten minutes.'

'Let's sit down again.'

They returned to their chairs, saying nothing, on edge, welcome outstayed. She stood, placed herself squarely in front of the clock she disliked. With both hands, delicately, she altered its position, cocked her head to one side in dissatisfaction, straightened the clock and smiled an apology at Fairfax.

'Will you come to see me in London?' she asked.

54

'I don't often visit town.'

'You could make an effort. We could go to see a play. It might encourage you to write for the theatre proper.'

He shook his head.

'I'd be wasting my time. Writing, I mean. You look out a play you'd like to see, and I'll get tickets. It might do me good.'

Laura sat down again, in an awkward silence. The taxi-man rang, and she leapt to her feet.

'Thanks again for the hospitality,' she said. She did not kiss him this time. He felt, and it rankled, that he had missed an opportunity.

VI

One morning, a week later, still in the coldness of early spring, Conrad Le Jeune telephoned Henry from London. He had just returned, he said, from the Caribbean and tropical luxury. He sounded pleased with himself as he made routine inquiries, and instructed Fairfax about the plan for a new line of heavy transporters to be controlled from the Beechnall office. As usual, he briefly offered Henry convincing reasons for his proposal. When he asked if Henry's office could manage, he listened, laughed short as a cough, and instructed his underling that if he needed to set on new employees that would not be considered amiss.

'What I want you to do, Henry, is think about it. I shall send you an outline of plans so far and ask for your comment. I'll try to get somebody to cost it accurately.'

'Space will be the snag.'

'Good boy. Glad you see it. It may mean a new depôt up there. But where? Big time. But we'll think. I'll send the papers up today.'

'I'll do my best.'

'There's just one thing, Henry.'

'Yes?'

'Laura mentioned it. It's about your brother. She said he might like a job with us. Would you recommend him?'

'He's clever. Has an excellent appearance.' A gap.

'What's wrong with him, Henry?'

'Why do you ask that?'

'Oh, something Laura said. And you're not exactly forthcoming, are you?'

' "Clever and excellent appearance"? What more do you want?'

'What's wrong with him?'

'Depression.'

Silence.

56

'I see.' Conrad had re-emerged. 'I see. Laura thought we might use him in publicity. She wants to enlarge her empire. The snag about it is this: you've got to believe in the job, in your skill at it, your wits. You needn't care much about the product, but you've got to be sure you can sell it. And depression's not much help. Not anywhere, but especially there where you need Cheerful Charlies verbalizing all bloody day. See what I mean?'

Henry made no attempt at argument.

'I'll organize an interview,' Conrad said, 'if that's what you and Laura want.'

'I don't know whether he'd consider it.'

'Well, ask him, man.'

'He might not like that either.'

'Sounds awkward. Please yourself.'

Henry troubled his conscience about his own lack of enthusiasm, blaming himself. This might be the cure that Jim needed, and he'd already prohibited it with his half-hearted response.

Guilty, he called at his brother's house on his way back from work.

Molly opened the door, said Jim was in, that they were due to eat in half an hour. She disappeared into the kitchen. Jim barely raised his head from the *Independent*, but asked Henry to sit down.

'What can I do for you?'

Molly came in to ask if they'd like a cup of tea. Henry refused.

'I rang you about an hour ago,' he apologized, 'to ask if you'd be in, but there was no answer.'

'We've not been back long.'

Molly slid out. Jim looked up either bored or hostile.

'Well?'

'I saw Laura the other day. She wondered whether you'd like a job with Le Jeune's. She spoke to Conrad about it, and he asked me.'

'Doing what?' Bright-eyed.

'Publicity. Public relations. That sort of thing.'

'You don't know any more than that? It's pretty vague, isn't it?' Why so grudging?

'No. I'm sorry I don't.'

'Have you a publicity side to your office?'

'Not really. I mean we do some little advertising locally. And subsidizing, sponsoring for publicity. Chap called Dexter handles it with a thousand and one other things. We're very much a subsidiary branch now. We do as we're told. The firm is expanding terrifically, but at the London end and on the continent.'

'Not here? Not at all?'

'There is talk of expansion.'

'It would mean I'd have to live in London, then, would it?'

'I don't know. But that's quite a possibility. Anyhow, think about it, talk it over with Molly, and let me know. Conrad said he'd give you an interview.'

Jim seemed animated, asked questions, rubbing his hands together, stood up, straddled the hearth.

'I don't dislike the sound of this,' he pronounced in the end.

'Talk it over with Molly.'

'Oh, I will, I will.'

'He's a good employer, is Conrad. Slave-driver. He's like all these whizz-kids.'

'He's hardly young, is he? Over forty?'

But Jim was smiling as he accompanied his brother to the back door, expansive and humming to himself. Later the same evening he telephoned to ask his brother to put his name forward. Henry passed the message on at once.

During the next fortnight he heard nothing until Laura rang.

'We've arranged for Jim to come up for an interview. He'll be with us for two days. Has he said anything to you?'

'Not a word.'

'Does that surprise you?'

'No. Though he seemed excited at the prospect.'

'I've spoken to him on the phone, and sent him the job specification as well as a good deal of material, and some things to try his hand on. We've fixed the date for the interview. It's up to him now.'

'Molly might tell me what's happening this end. She's usually a bit more forthcoming than he is.'

Molly, in fact, called round one Saturday morning before nine o'clock.

'I thought I might just get you before you go out. Are you working today?'

'I shall put in an hour or two at the office from about ten onwards. Somebody has to do something.'

'You've plenty on hand?'

'Too much, if anything. We'll fit it in.'

'What do you know about this job Jim's applying for?'

He told her the little he had learnt from Laura.

'Yes, yes. Thanks. We knew that. Laura has been to a great deal of trouble. We've had two or three big parcels of past features they've done, at various stages, so Jim can see how they finally agreed on the line they took. And she's sent him the material for something they're working on now, and asked him to let her have his ideas.'

'And has he done so?'

Molly narrowed her eyes.

'Yes, he has. He's putting a great deal of effort into this.'

'Does he discuss it with you?'

'Yes, he does. Pretty well every night. It's astonishing, really. We've not talked so much to each other for months. It's been marvellous. He's a different man altogether.'

'Does he show any talent at the job?'

'Oh, yes. Jim's clever when he sets his mind to anything. You know that.'

'Does he listen to your advice?'

Again the suspicious pause.

'Yes. And he's taken it a time or two, incorporated what I've said into his schemes. I had an art training after all. Of course he worries that he doesn't know any of the technical details. His ideas might cost the earth to put into practice. He'll have to learn the ins and outs of that. But he is good. And he's a changed man.'

'I can believe it. No mention of Miss Brown?'

'He never said much about her to me. Not even after the letter.'

59

'Did he send you round to quiz me?'

'How did you guess?' Molly laughed, delighted at his question. 'Just nip round and see if Henry knows anything we don't.'

'Why doesn't he come himself?'

'That's not quite ethical.'

'But you can show up and do it for him?'

'A good wife would do that in any case. If she had thought of it.'

'Which you didn't.'

'You're nearly as sharp as he is.' She waved contention aside. 'Anyhow, I'm very grateful. It's made a different man of him. He's happier, even at school. He's let them know that he's considering going into commerce, and I guess that's impressed them. Schoolteachers are pretty conservative creatures, to judge by those I know. They want security in a known environment. The thought of taking a job in a concern that might fold up or give you the sack at the snap of the fingers terrifies them.'

'But not Jim?'

'He's been so despondent lately that any change would be for the better.'

'And what do you think?'

'I'm delighted.'

'But you might have to move to London. Would you go?'

'Yes. I'd have to.'

'Could you continue with your work?'

'There'd be difficulties. I'm nicely settled now in Martin's. He's spent some money and time on me. But it'll come to an end. I've always known it would.'

'In what way?'

'He'll lose interest. He's a bit like that. He's enjoyed his time setting me up. Most men enjoy showing women the way. Even fags. And he's done me well. I've made some good contacts in London through him. But it will be up to me from now on, I reckon. And if I'm going to work for myself I might as well do it in London. The opportunities are greater. It'll mean leg-work and letter-writing for me, and I shall resent this because it'll take me away from my bench. But it will have to be done some time, so it might just as well be now.'

'I see.'

'I'm not ungrateful to Martin. Don't think that. But he takes a very good proportion of the profits. I know he's provided a workshop, and heat and light and power and openings and all the rest of it, but he's doing very nicely out of me now, thank you very much. He's worked on it, I'll say that for him. He's given me a chance to do my own thing rather earlier than if I'd taken another sort of job.'

'Teaching, you mean?'

'That's what it would have boiled down to. And then I would have had to do my tinkering at the weekend. And what you really need for any sort of artistic work is plenty of time. Day after day. So.'

'Are there, oh, changes of fashion with your sort of product?'

'To some extent. There are crazes. I've not hit one yet. But I kid myself that's to my advantage.' Molly grinned, answered his unspoken question. 'What I need is to learn to do something original, and yet be paid at the same time.'

'I see.'

'Too much success at the beginning would not do. So I tell myself. As I gnash my teeth.'

'So a move to London might be advantageous?'

'Could easily be. Even if Jim gets the job he wouldn't start before the summer, so we have some little time in hand. Housing's going to be a problem. But I tell you, Hen, anything will be an improvement on the way Jim's been these last few months. He's driven himself scranny, and me.'

'Scranny? I've not heard that word for long enough.'

'My father used it at one time. This Laura of yours seems quite a power in the land?'

'I don't really know. We're a backwater here.'

'But isn't this where Conrad started?'

'It is. But he's gone far beyond us. I'm not saying we're not a profitable concern. We are. He'd close it down in no time if we weren't. But quite what Laura's place in the larger scheme of things is I don't know.'

'Don't you ever see any of her work?'

'To tell you the truth, yes. We receive a whole lot of publicity, mostly posters and what-have-you. I decorate our places with them. Good for morale. I hope. I'm not sure. I've this old-fashioned notion that if we have a product or efficient service that people want and it's at the right price then we're in business. It's not so, apparently. We need hype.'

'You have to let people know that your firm exists.'

'So they say. It seems a waste of money.'

'You don't altogether approve, I gather?'

'I live in the past.'

'Look, Henry, you're thirty-six, nearly thirty-seven, not ninety.'

'Thanks for reminding me. I'm just showing you how little I know of Laura's doings or status and importance. We've even had telly adverts. I won't say what they cost. It staggered me.'

'Did Laura tell you?'

'No. Chap from Manchester. At the annual dinner. He didn't seem either surprised or put out.'

'And you didn't argue with him?'

'In a refined way. Laura was sitting on my other side. She didn't utter a word. Maybe she didn't hear. I ought to have raised it with her, but I didn't. That's the way businesses are run these days. I'm just an old-fashioned accountant.'

'Accountants always carry the blame for the mess industry's in.'

'Somebody has to. Conrad's a genius in his style. He was good at my sort of level, a largish local concern. But he saw the way up, and that's where he's really outstanding. He knew who to nobble and who to join.'

'Is he ruthless?'

'I imagine he is. I don't suppose he minds if he tramples on a few rivals. But he must study the field and know what's worth doing and what's not. Or can buy the best advice. And he must have the right sort of steady nerves.

Wouldn't do for me. They'd have to lock me away inside a fortnight. But if he cares to employ a fuddy-duddy like me and his sister and my brother, well, he must know what he's about. Or it's of so little importance that it really doesn't matter.'

'He's an interesting man?'

'Very. But I don't know what drives him.'

'But don't you watch him?' Molly's eyes were wide. 'I mean, he'd be useful for your writing, your plays. It's not everybody who's got a millionaire to study at first hand.'

'I hardly see him these days. He used to ring me up, oh, practically every day at one time, but not now. This concern is a very small corner of his vineyard.'

'Jim says he runs betting shops.'

'And supermarkets. And property. Office blocks. If they told me he owned the North Sea or the oil under it, I wouldn't dismiss it.' Henry coughed. This interview was too long-drawn-out. 'But that doesn't mean he's interesting to talk to. At least, not very. Not to me.'

'Didn't he ever talk to you about his wider plans?'

'I suppose he did in the early days, when he lived down here. But it didn't mean much. To me. I put it down to imagination. He was doing well in the Midlands, chasing business, scaring off opposition, making money, and so I thought it, I was going to say proper but I suppose I mean endearing, that sometimes when we were together he'd boast of feelers he was putting out, or men he was meeting, or nation-wide schemes.'

'You weren't involved.'

'Not really. Once or twice he asked me to check figures for him. But he was tearing about day and night, and the phone bill was unbelievable. But it wasn't cloud-cuckoo land. He was actually arranging and concluding deals, fixing and asset-stripping, making takeover bids.'

'On the profits the firm here provided.'

'Originally, yes. Later, he'd need a lot, lot more than we had.'

'How would he do all this?'

'Attract backers. Borrow money. Basically.'

63

'But that's quite different from running Le Jeune (E. Midlands) Ltd? Or isn't it?'

'Yes, I suppose it is. I don't really know. They both need tremendous commitment and energy. And risk-taking. Sometimes he'd accept some job here that couldn't possibly make a profit. He knew that. But he'd see it was done properly and promptly so that people came back for more. We had to be efficient at our end. Workmen who didn't do as they were told, or who couldn't turn up on time, were given the sack, no messing. They either did exactly as on the schedule, or they didn't have a second chance.'

'Did that include you, Henry?'

'I suppose so. I always thought it did.'

'Were you frightened?'

'Yes. Sometimes. Yes. I think I was. I had to take decisions I wasn't sure about. Nothing tremendous. Ever. But I had to guess how big or little to make the profit margins. As a reasonably small firm we could often arrange to do the job much more quickly than larger concerns. That was an advantage. But if we wanted the work, we had to decide how far up or down the scale our charges were to be. The donkey work, the early progress, getting over inertia had all been done before ever I joined the band. They were doing nicely when I arrived. That's why they needed me. But they'd already acquired some largish steady contract and sub-contract working. What you football-pool addicts would call "bankers". And it all seemed to snowball. I don't really know why to this day.'

'That's fascinating, Henry. You could make a marvellous play out of it.'

'Do you think so?'

'That means you don't, I take it?' Molly's face grew into seriousness. 'How will Jim fare in this high-powered world? What do you think?'

'He'll do as I did. I managed my sort of work, because I'd had a good training and put a lot of time in. He'll have to do the same. I don't suppose for one minute that Conrad wants somebody to show him how to run Le

Jeune's. Though he's attracted some high-fliers into the firm. And he'll know how to use them.'

'But Jim?'

'It's not the same as schoolteaching, as you've already told me. But Jim will be an understrapper, at least for a start. He won't be allowed to rule Laura's roost, never mind Conrad's. But if he does what's required of him, they'll pay well.'

'But they'll tell him if he's making a hash of it?'

'I suppose so. I'm in no position to make a fair judgement on Laura. We tangled too often. I think she has a sharp tongue. And an eye to her own ambition. How good she'll be at bringing Jim on, I don't know.'

'But you'd advise him to put in for this?'

'Surely. He'd be a fool not to.' Henry paused, biting his lip. 'There's one thing *you* should remember, Molly.'

'What's that?' Brightly, ignoring his tone.

'Jim may not get the job. And that may set him back. "So the last error shall be worse than the first." '

'Is that a quotation?'

'The Bible. There are some people who are flattened by even the smallest setback. I'm one, I think.'

'Rubbish. And as to Jim, at least it's livened him up beyond all telling this last few weeks.'

'Good. We'll hope for the best.'

'You don't think he'll get it, do you, Henry?' Molly stood, suddenly grim yet vulnerable.

'I've no idea. When I see Jim, and can forget all I remember of him as a little brother, he reminds me of the young masters at my grammar school. Big strides and college scarves. Bags of confidence. And yet you tell me Jim's been hopeless.'

Molly shrugged, giving it all up.

'You need to be off to your office. Thanks, Henry, for putting him on to this. At least it's kept him from murdering me.'

Molly stepped across to her brother-in-law, kissed him full on the mouth, hugged him, hugely. She had never acted like that before. He did not understand.

'Aren't you at work today?' he asked.

'After lunch.' She buttoned her coat. 'I'll do an hour or two.' She examined her hands, for dirt or fitness, and marched out.

VII

Conrad dispatched experts to report on the possibilities of expansion. First two grey-suited men, smiling, not friendly. Then a quick-talking young woman, who looked not much older than a schoolgirl, but who probed.

Henry Fairfax felt under pressure or suspicion. The men worked for two days in his office, their computer hard at it. They took lunch with him on the first day, but refused his offers of hospitality in the evening, saying that was when they consolidated and planned. He could not understand why they took two days over his files; they could have plugged into his computer from London. Perhaps they needed to see the effect of their inquiries on him. They asked questions often, and once they began visiting estate agents about possible sites, they canvassed his opinion, and that of his under-managers. They were polite, Mr Marshall and Mr Kelsey-Thomas, but threatening, looking for something behind his transparent answers, his adequate balance sheets, his day-to-day accounts, his contingency plans. Their questions to the workforce caused some offence, so that Fairfax felt bound to explain to his people that the probable result of this inquisition would be expansion and promotion, not redundancy. At the end of a week and two days the two wished Henry goodbye. He asked them if they had enjoyed their stay. They looked at him in distaste, but thanked him for his cooperation.

'We shall make some small suggestions for the improvement of this place,' Marshall answered pacifically enough. 'We've already hinted at them to you.' Spring sunshine garishly hit the brickwork outside, burnished the daffodils on Fairfax's desk. 'But the real question we've been addressing ourselves to, as well you know, is whether there is the potential for a really large expansion of the Midlands concern . . .'

'You think there is?'

'We do. We've not hidden it from you. We couldn't very well, could we?' Man to man. 'And secondly whether the whole business should be moved to a new site, or whether this,' Marshall waved a pudgy hand, 'should be retained, and two other areas be utilized. I suppose, if our proposals are accepted, and you remain in overall charge, it's more likely than not that you would have to remove to one of the larger sites, though we do detail how the main administrative headquarters could remain here. That might well save money, but of course within a very large extension of services it could have drawbacks.'

Both men, in a cross-talk act, outlined the reasons for their decisions. They emphasized the careful costing that would be required of them. Had he seen any major objections to this general outline? The two consultants seemed no more friendly now, distant, clear in their own minds but regardless of human consequences, their effect on him.

'Shall I see the full report?' Fairfax asked.

'Not unless Mr Le Jeune provides you with a copy. We can't.'

'And will Mr Le Jeune take any steps as a result of your report?'

They smiled, thinly, hostile to his naïvety.

'That's his decision,' Mr Kelsey-Thomas muttered, smilingly, and closed the interview. Handshakes all round concluded the meeting, thanks again, a march together through the sunlit activity, the industry in the yards, warehouses, hangar-sized garages.

Fairfax stood shaking his head.

The young woman, Mrs Menzies, seemed even more threatening. She was young, small, a chatterbox, who donned large tortoise-shell spectacles irregularly. Immediately she arrived she issued all senior management, Fairfax not excluded, with a long questionnaire, over which they grumbled. 'How in hell am I expected to answer this in two lines?' Dexter, the second-in-command, fumed. It asked if it was possible to save any large sums of money in day-to-day transactions. The next teaser demanded to know whether such economy had major drawbacks. 'What's she after?' Dexter grimaced, affronted. 'What's she ever been in charge of? She's hardly out of her cradle. How the hell does she land this sort of job, and what's she being paid? I've a bloody good mind to put down it would save money if they didn't send round highly-salaried, scented young busybodies asking damfool questions and stopping me from working.'

'Ummh.' Henry Fairfax rubbed his chin. 'Ummh.' Dexter would never queer his own pitch.

'What's that mean? Look, Henry, we were both here when Con Le Jeune was. This doesn't seem like him.'

'I don't know.'

Dexter stared, red-faced.

'He had me out in Zürich,' Henry spoke slowly, 'to check the perfectly good paperwork of two super-efficient Swiss factories. Why? To keep them on their toes. Or at least that was my conclusion. So, here. We're being chivvied, Harry, harried, hustled.'

'But think of the expense. That's what narks me.'

'Narks?'

'You know what I mean.' Fairfax did, indeed.

Mrs Menzies made him uncertain. She seemed so innocent and vulnerable, as if a gruffness or impolite word on his part would slap her into tears. On the other hand her volubility annoyed him. The constant rattle of her consonants about his head, her demand to know this and that, the ins and outs of unimportant matters caused him to look on her as both silly and devious. The shotgun spatter of questions would in the end wound some vital spot. She declared that her remit was to study the management of the expanded concern: how many men, of what calibre and experience, to be paid what, to live in what houses? Fairfax remembered his rôle in Zürich, that of bogey-man. But this girl was a professional, felt herself morally bound to come up with conclusions. Out of all the blether, glances and rush she would write steely recommendations, in confidence, for her employers. And Henry, old-fashioned, a dusty ledger in an age of computers, would stand condemned. On edge, half ready for redundancy, he flicked at his keyboard and glowered suspiciously at the green screen.

Laura rang on the evening of the day when Mrs Menzies had said her goodbyes. She asked after his health, almost with ferocity. He reciprocated, mildly.

'What I really wanted to talk to you about was your brother.'

'Oh, yes.'

'I take it you've spoken to him? About his interview?'

'No, I haven't. I've seen neither Jim nor Molly.'

He explained how he had been tied up with Conrad's consultants. She knew nothing about them. She'd heard that there was talk of expansion, but the names of Marshall, Kelsey-Thomas and Menzies meant nothing to her. They'd be outsiders; Con generally used Howarth and Wright or Mansell's. Fairfax could have told her that. He asked how much notice Conrad took of these experts. She descended to vagueness, proverbial expression and confident assertion about character. 'You know what it's like. He certainly won't keep a dog and bark. But Con will do what he wants. He always does.'

Henry smiled to himself, said his own piece about the consultants, realized from her answers that Laura had no idea how worried he had been. Now those preliminaries were over.

'Yes. About Jim.' She called the meeting to order. 'You are interested, aren't you?'

'Of course.'

'He made a very favourable impression.'

'So you're going to employ him?'

'I didn't say that, but yes, probably.'

'And you're having a last-minute consultation with this expert?'

'You could say so.'

Laura paused, though he could not deduce why.

'He'd prepared himself well,' she declared. 'He'd done marvels with the material I sent him. He wasn't short of ideas. He'd no experience, but I couldn't expect otherwise. When he came up here, he spent two whole days in my office. He was personable, receptive, quick on the uptake, got on well with people here.'

Again she stopped, waited. Henry said nothing. She was forced to resume.

'You, Henry, had reservations.' The use of his first name as well as her tone warned him.

'Not really. Jim's something of a depressive, but so are many successful people. He dislikes his present job, which doesn't stretch him. I felt bound to tell you this. But new challenges may be just what he needs.'

'This job is stressful. And it's not nine to four. What about his wife?'

'She seemed to think the exodus to London would suit them both.'

'Are you quite sure?'

He repeated what Molly had told him. Laura kept the conversation on the boil. The same questions were repeated, rephrased, wrenched into different contexts as though she suspected he had hidden something from her, but would give himself away before long. Henry grew bored, said he was busy.

'It's like this. I shouldn't really be . . . It's all very hush-hush for the present.' She rattled on like a girl offering thanks for an over-extravagant present.

Laura, it appeared, had done well for the firm, and Conrad had suggested that she set up on her own. He would provide money, and would put work in her way, even allow her to stay on his premises. It would need energy, time, total commitment, and though she would have offered Jim a position in Le Jeune's she wasn't sure that he was the right partner for the new enterprise. What did Henry think?'

'Look, Laura, I don't know any more than you. It's possible that you'll strike sparks out of him. He's clever enough, and he's not afraid of work. But you put it to him in the same plain way you've set it out for me. Let him agree to a probationary period long enough for you to test the water but not too long to ruin your plans if he doesn't come up to scratch. He can always go back to

71

teaching; he's well qualified. He knows that. Put him on his mettle for three, six months.'

'I see.'

'He needn't sell his house here. I realize it will mean big changes for him, but if he's not prepared to make them then he's not the man you want.'

Laura thought, whistling tunelessly in her teeth.

'Will you put that to him?' she asked, suddenly, unexpectedly.

'If you want it. But why not you?'

'Because it will come more,' she searched for a word, 'seriously from your end. In your rooms, or his, in his streets. He'll see his furniture round him, and the trees and shrubs through his windows, and hear your homely voice, and not be over-excited as he would with me.'

'It sounds like poetry.'

'You can be a sarcastic devil when you try.' Genuinely angry? He could not guess. 'You'll do it for me? Yes? Right. There's one more thing, Henry. I'd like you to come to London and stay with me for a day or two.'

'Why?' He had been caught out by the snap in her request.

'That's rude, Henry Fairfax. I could question you about your brother. We can make that the pretext if you must have one. But I have a yen to see you again. How's that for a poem? I could show you round. We could dance.'

He remembered the voice of the girl he had met at aa party twelve years ago. That had not changed. Nine years of marriage had ended in shouting matches, violence on her part, near hysteria, and now she begged him to visit. It made no sense. They had tried each other out long enough; they had been found wanting. She knew it better, more savagely than he. Then why this nonsense?

'That's kind of you, Laura, but is it wise?'

'Explain yourself,' she snapped, then softer, 'explicate.'

'The end of our marriage was a shambles, and,' he fumbled, 'extremely painful to me. It's perhaps some weakness or failure on my part, but when I think about us, it's the rows, the fights, the squabbles that come into

72

my mind, not the earlier, good times. I'm sorry, but that's how it is.'

'So you want to keep out of my way?'

'Within reason.'

'That's not very kind. After all, we were married for nearly nine years, and it was only the last twelve months that things went wrong.'

'Laura,' he'd lay the law down, in honesty, 'if it had been left to me, we'd be married still. In my book, you wanted the break.'

'So you had no faults?' She spoke without rancour now, thoughtfully.

'I didn't say that. I don't doubt I got on your nerves. But you wanted an end, not I.'

'You didn't want a divorce? Is that what you mean?'

'I didn't. Not until you made it inevitable.'

'I see.'

Immediately, sentimentally he felt sorry for her, but waited for her next assault. It did not come.

'Look, Laura, it does no good to go over these old arguments. Let's drop it.'

'That's what I'm saying. Listen. You come and have a couple of days with me. It's what I want. It'll be a holiday. For both of us. But especially for me. I really mean it when I tell you it's what I want.'

'I don't see it at all.'

'That's because you're an old stick-in-the-mud. Or because you've been hurt and frightened. Now forget all about that. Ditch the past. You come along up here and have a mid-week or a weekend break with your Aunt Laura. It makes sense. You know it makes sense.'

'I don't understand you, not one bit.'

'Not from that distance. But you just turn up here and complete your education.'

'You're not serious about this?'

'You think I'm taking the piss, do you, my friend? Forget my jargon and the jingles. I want two or three days of your company, unadulterated.'

'Why?'

'Because we were married for nine years before we

made a mess of it. All right, I made a hash of it. But I owe you something. I've just come round to seeing it. So. Report up here and I'll try to recompense you, if that's the word.'

'No, Laura. Many thanks, but . . .'

'Don't start your Holy Joes, for God's sake. Think of me, for once.'

'I just do not understand . . .'

'You've said that before. I'm serious. I'm not out to make a fool of you. I want you to myself for two or three days.'

'Why?'

'Why, why, why? I don't bloody know why. If I said I thought perhaps we'd made a mistake, what then? You wouldn't believe me.'

'Is that the reason?'

'Something like that. I'm not sure. I don't want to mislead you, whatever else I do. But. I just want you to come. Perhaps it was seeing Jim. I don't know. He reminded me of you in some ways. I know you don't trust me over this, but I'm trying to speak the truth. I don't . . . I. We are . . . Look, Henry, I have this strong feeling that I'd like your company for a day or two. I may be wrong. I admit it. I don't think so, but . . .' She spoke with a breathless speed. 'After an hour or two in each other's presence we might be at loggerheads again. It's very possible. You're suspicious. I can see that. And I don't blame you.'

'This feeling of yours? Has it come on you, over you in the last few days?'

'Oh, Henry, don't be like that. For God's sake. Just give it a run. That's all I'm asking. I can't tie you down, or lock you in. You can walk out any time you like. You don't believe me, do you?'

'It seems, oh, unlikely, You weren't given to whims of this sort.'

'You think I'm trying to get at you?'

'Possible. I don't see why, but, yes, it's a possibility.'

'I could shake you.'

'That's what I mean. I enjoyed our meeting at Le

74

Jeune's dinner because there were other people about, and anyway we could eat or dance. But while you were at my place I felt all the time that we were on the edge of quarrelling.'

'That's not true.'

'That's how I felt it.'

'I enjoyed arguing with you, and differing. Not that we did very much, as I remember it. If you imagine that I enjoyed the end of our marriage, or all that wrangling in court, then you're wrong. But that's behind us. You can't perhaps forget it. Neither can I, but . . . No, Henry. I'm slightly surprised at myself. I'll admit it. Perhaps it's because of this new venture, and I feel the need to touch wood, and there you are, an old block, all ready with your good luck.' She gasped for breath, giggled. 'I'm babbling, aren't I? You think I'm cracked. Oh, that's enough. If you won't come, you won't.'

'I'm not averse to doing you a good turn.'

'So?'

'Why are you so excited, Laura? Excitable?'

'Am I? I didn't know I was. If I am it's because of the launch of this new company. Make allowances for that, will you?'

'Very well.' He stopped. 'I'll come.'

'Against your better judgement?'

He did not answer the jibe, and quietly they discussed dates, made a decision. Almost effusively she thanked him, but broke off the call not trusting her luck.

Henry's exhilaration at his pact soon disappeared. He did not trust his judgement. This Laura was new to him, or he had made a bad mistake. He worried himself unmercifully as he had over Conrad's consultants, though that did not lack sense. Those people might have outlined alterations which did not, could not include him. He gave value for money in his present capacity, but a brand-new, streamlined organization might well make him and his like unemployable. That wide-eyed young woman, Miss, Mrs Menzies, might already have written him off the company's concerns. Perhaps Laura knew it, and was making some reparation to him, preparing him for

75

personal disaster. He did not see it intellectually. Those experts, Marshall, Kelsey-Thomas, Menzies did not speak a language so unintelligible to him that he was left deaf and dumb. Nor were they so bright that he was left floundering. He was, he considered, as clever and careful as they were, and knew more about road transport than they. He would be able to cope with larger issues; he was nobody's fool. But his anxieties accumulated: he muttered to himself at work, found himself shredding his underlings for minor errors. He had no one to consult; Dexter blithely followed his usual path, saw no danger signals. Fairfax accused himself of not attempting to impress the assessors; he'd come over as a dull, grey, efficient nonentity, faithful over a few things but incapable of mastery of the many. The joy of his lord would shortly be denied to him.

He slept badly, neglected meals, nibbled biscuits, took to early evening whisky, hating his occupation or his lack of it. Conrad and his understrappers had frightened the life out of him. He looked for disaster.

VIII

Henry Fairfax visited his brother.

'I hadn't heard anything from you about this interview,' he excused himself.

'Neither have I,' Jim answered. 'They're in no bloody hurry.'

'How do you think you shaped?'

'Laura seemed satisfied. And the other people I talked to. They praised my ideas.'

'Did they not say when they'd let you know?'

'No. I had the impression it would be a matter of days. But it's three weeks now. They enjoy pissing you about, these people.'

Molly, who was listening, supported her husband's complaints. Jim made no demur, but went on to give a detailed, lively account of the two-day interview, the work he had prepared, its reception, his suggestions to the principals, their comments, his criticisms, their attitudes. Again Molly was allowed to intervene with corrections or questions. They were certainly in alliance over this. Jim's disgruntlement vied with the certainty that he'd shown up in a good light. He'd expected early acceptance.

'Laura phoned me.'

The eyes of husband and wife stared accusingly.

'What did she say?'

'I had the impression that you'd done well, that they'd offer you the job.'

'When was this?'

He told them.

'Why hasn't somebody rung me, then?'

Henry asked if they knew about the formation of a new company. They did, though neither had mentioned it. That surprised.

'I take it that there might be some snags or delays

about arrangements. Doesn't that seem likely? I mean you've been there. You've actually seen them at work.'

'It's possible, I suppose,' Jim glared. 'She didn't send you round, did she?'

'What for?'

'To make a final assessment, to find out how I'm coping with their silence; I don't know.'

'No. She wants me to visit her.'

Molly, interest immediately afire, bombarded him with questions. He explained that he had been amazed at the invitation. The exchange between the two was listened to in impatient silence by James.

'It's not to ask you further about me, is it?'

'No. I can't say, but I don't think so. How did you find Laura?'

Jim scowled, bit his lips, slapped a thigh.

'She rules the roost all right in her little empire. There was another man called Rex Drummond I had a bit to do with, and a Tony Beasley, and two or three assistants or secretaries, but she's the boss.'

'You didn't see Conrad?'

'No. He left his apologies. He's in America.'

The actual office space they occupied had been smaller than he expected. They used freelances from time to time. The secretaries, if that's what they were, were encouraged to make suggestions. One of them was a graduate. 'Sussex, I think.'

'What was the atmosphere like? Pleasant? Relaxed? Were you rushed off your feet?'

'There was plenty going on. Both Rex and Laura and Beasley as well, took work home the night I was there.'

'What sort of person would she be to work for?' Henry asked the question of his fingernails.

'She seems to know her mind. But as she was full of ideas, one couldn't complain. She kept her distance. She wasn't sour, ever, or discourteous, but she wasn't all over me, either. She was a teacher, wasn't she? When you were married?'

'Yes.'

'Did she enjoy that?'

'I believe so. She grumbled, but she was good at it. She was always, well, spirited.'

'Did she teach all the time you were married?' Molly.

'No, she had eighteen months off. She had a bad miscarriage, and didn't recover very quickly. But they asked her to go back and she did.'

'Did she teach art?'

'No. English and French.'

'Was that the cause of the breakdown, the divorce?' Jim, eager, angry, putting his brother down.

'The miscarriage?' Henry found he could answer without vindictiveness. 'No, I shouldn't think so. I'm very loth, anyway, to attribute catastrophes to any one single event, however traumatic. We had three or four good years together after she'd recovered.'

'You didn't try for another child?'

'We were very careful for a time. That's true. She had gynaecological difficulties. Did she mention anything about me, or her time here?'

'Yes. Not much.' Jim's face was lit by a sudden smile, so that he looked like a bright eighteen-year-old again. 'She talked about it as if it were a good holiday she'd had.' He smiled again. 'She prefers living in London. This is a bit of a dump to her.'

'I guess that's right.'

'Wasn't she born here?'

'Yes. And Conrad. They're an old Beechnall family.'

'Are her parents still alive?'

'No. Both dead.'

'Were they old?' Molly.

'I remember them at your wedding.' Jim.

'Early seventies, I'd guess. He was some kind of minor civil servant. Worked at the Carrington Drive headquarters.' The two digested that. 'What will you do about living quarters if you get the job?'

'I shall be on probation. So it would be wise to seek something temporary. Laura said as much.'

Conversation petered out. The younger Fairfaxes made no attempt to detain him, except that Jim asked him to speed up the decision if he could. He left them at the

door. They were talking volubly, forgetting him immediately. He felt envy at their concentration and their
closeness.

In the days before his London visit, Henry found
himself more settled. There had been no word about reorganization, and he and Dexter had landed a contract that
both occupied them and boosted their confidence. Nobody
could accuse them of idleness or inefficiency. Their tenders
had been masterly, superbly tailored to acceptance and
large profit, and all without guidance from the London
end. These two locals had acted in the Conrad class.
Henry wondered how success in one sphere could affect
the unrelated. He now felt he could handle whatever
mischief or tomfoolery, even pleasure, that Laura was
preparing for him. One of the consultants had expressed
scepticism about this new contract; so much for the value
of his opinion.

The London visit was arranged to last from Thursday
evening to Sunday afternoon. Henry packed on Wednesday night, worked until noon the next day, bathed and
changed at home, made a leisurely lunch, took a taxi to
the Midland station. He felt pleased with himself, at ease,
in no hurry. He found a seat in the train, he would not
travel first class, prepared *Guardian*, *Times* and *Independent*
for perusal, enjoyed the sunshine and the dash of a
shower.

He made his way from St Pancras to North London by
tube, arriving about seven. He took pleasure in the trek
along the underground corridors, humping his suitcase,
trying to remember when he'd last been away without his
car. Nights were lighter; the clocks had gone forward;
London gardens were a week or two ahead of his own.

Laura's flat, tracked down from his *A–Z Guide*, was in
a not-straight street of Victorian buildings. He puzzled
himself over their date, and oddities. What accounted for
Beechnall would not do here. A regency house, much
battered, stood back from the rest behind a tangle of
laburnum and lilac. No. 114, Laura's was in a three-
storeyed terrace, bow-windowed, behind small walled
gardens, a line of rectitude, but to his surprise shabby,

the paint peeling, brickwork crumbling and discoloured. He mounted steps and in a short passage under a gothic arch pressed Laura's bell, L. E. Fairfax. He read the other names: T. Winckelmann, R. B. Sharma, E. T. Gordon, M. I. F. Rhodes, Lake Turvey. Laura opened the door.

'You found it?'

'Without difficulty.'

She kissed him on the cheek, led him upstairs in light and shade. The impressive wooden balustrade creaked when he put a hand to the rail. The stairs were uncarpeted but clean. The second set were narrower, leading to the servants' quarters. A pale door cut Laura's apartments off from the rest of the building. They stepped along into a narrow passage, brightened by a strip of red and blue Axminster. There were no windows, but three prints decorated the wall. Laura opened the door of her living room, which faced the road, curtains already drawn, welcomingly warm. He had left his case, on her instructions, in the passageway.

'Now sit down,' she welcomed him. 'Drink?' He asked for coffee. She prepared that, dodging in and out of the kitchen on the other side of the corridor. He looked round the large room, with its bright furniture, matching carpets and curtains; Laura had carefully failed to fill every corner; spaces were wide and irregular, suggesting grandeur under the high ceiling. What had been a dormitory for the servant girls was now a place of comfort, even luxury. But she had not thrown her money away; the furniture was beautiful without being expensive. Silver-framed prints decorated the walls; she used no bric-à-brac; the only antique was a small, highly polished eighteenth-century table which had stood in their Beechnall house. This room spelt out quiet, harmony. He'd expected noises from the flats below, from the streets; shouts or a distant piano, a quarrel or slammed car door. He commented on this calm.

'Double glazing,' she smiled. 'Useful. I sometimes hear Emma Gordon's typewriter from below, but on the whole we're not riotous very often.'

She described the other tenants, amusingly emphasizing

81

that three-quarters of the information she handed him was fictional. Mr Sharma was a headmaster; Mr Rhodes, retired or redundant, visited the library every afternoon. Mrs Gordon worked for an architect. Mr Winckelmann was rarely in residence and Lake Turvey, new, never seen, offered mystery, with sex unknown. Conrad had bought the house some years ago, several houses in the terrace; she ought to invest in property herself now she was beginning to make money, but she was comfortable here, had decorated it herself, had grown fond of it.

Over the coffee she outlined the programme.

'Tonight we shall stay in. We've both been at work. About nine I'll go down to a takeaway, Indian, Chinese. Two minutes' walk.'

'Let me . . .'

'No, thanks.' She dismissed his invitation before he had the chance to formulate it. 'You're here for a rest. And to do as you're told. Do you mind sleeping on a camp-bed?'

He did not. She explained that it was in her workroom.

'I won't touch anything.'

'You'd better not.'

Both seemed nervous. They had been married for nine years, but the divorce had made strangers of them, or put a strangeness between them. He remembered movements of head or hand, tones of voice, but she was wearing striking clothes and her hair was short, cut fashionably. When he had met her she had just begun to teach, and wore student mufti, jeans and shirts. Then she had been nervous, telling him at his importunity of the year she had spent in Alsace as part of her language course. Then she had appeared shy, not short of words, but genuinely modest. He had just begun to work for Conrad Le Jeune, and had expected something of the boss's brashness about his sister. He had learnt later that Laura had a mind of her own, a will, but on that first occasion she had affected the persona of a young girl.

'Tomorrow evening, Friday, we'll go dancing, and on Saturday to a concert. In between, you can do as you think fit. We needn't get up early. I'm not going in to work. We can walk out, or drive, or stay in and yap. It depends on the weather, or on you.'

Henry hardly felt comfortable. He could not believe that Laura had enticed him here out of the kindness of her heart.

She asked about Jim. He gave his impression of his brother's present state. Laura laughed, guiltily, he thought, but insisted that Jim had certainly done well, though the one or two snags to be ironed out would be dealt with before the letter offering an appointment was sent off, probably at the end of next week, or the beginning of the following. 'I wouldn't say anything to him, if I were you,' she warned.

'He's certain to make inquiries.'

'You don't know anything, then. It may be things will not work out as I want them. Anyhow, it'll do him good to have to wait. And you to sit on the glad tidings.'

Henry felt more at home with this aggression. Laura showed her proper colours, laying down the law, putting him into place. Coffee, whisky, high-spirited talk from Laura first about her life here, then the prospects of her new company soothed him, so that he could easily have dropped asleep. At the suggested time she asked him about the meal.

'I'm not hungry,' he said. 'Don't go out for me. If you must provide me with food, cheese and a water biscuit will do.'

She pulled a wry face at his austerity, but filled up his glass and her own, settling back.

He congratulated her on the décor and she inquired after his plays. She led him round the apartment which consisted of her bedroom, a kitchen, offices and the work-room where his camp-bed stood disguised by a pink duvet; the rest of the rectangle was occupied by a huge desk with Anglepoise lamps, piles of paper, an executive's swivel chair, a stool, a table with a word-processor, a second with three layers of music centre. A filing cabinet stood in one corner; amplifiers were hung high; there were no pictures on the walls, but three posters roughly pinned to a big rectangular baize-covered, old-fashioned notice-board. The floor had been stripped of paint and glistened with polyurethane, without benefit of carpet.

'This is where it all goes on?' he said, foolishly, whisky working on him.

'You could say so.'

Laura splayed a hand on her table among folders, squared piles of loose sheets, drawing instruments, a complicated tray of pens. She had obviously tidied it.

'Odd room,' she said. 'Just that one little window. And I always keep the blind drawn.'

'A place of secrets.'

'I don't court distractions.' For a moment she looked sour, almost grim, but taking him by the arm piloted him first to the kitchen and through to the bathroom. 'I should be sorry to leave this hideaway. I've managed a great deal of work here.' She wheeled him back to the sitting room. 'I'm glad you've seen it,' she said, 'so you can imagine where I am and what I'm up to.'

He did not understand that.

Laura's ideas on cheese and biscuits were expansive. A great bowl of salad, five kinds of pickles, three of brown bread, three of white, pâté, a cheese-board, a presentation tin of assorted savoury biscuits. The low table, the hearth-rug were laden.

'Would you like wine?' she asked.

'No, thanks. I'm nearly drunk now.'

'Oh, good. You need to relax. You've never done it properly.'

He ate wholemeal bread, yellow butter, blue Stilton and felt more sober and no less cheerul. By the time they had cleared away and washed up, it was half past ten, and Laura was pouring more whisky. They had chatted about the theatre, about some new prints she had bought and which had arrived that morning, about her plans, and once, not at length but not dodged away from, their married life. Laura had been in good spirits, glad to see him, friendly without affectation, welcoming.

'May I look through your curtains at the street?' he asked, returning from the kitchen.

'Do.'

84

He peered out into the mixed darkness and orange of the lamps. Tree branches, stationary cars, one cat caught his attention.

'Not many people about,' he reported back.

'The pubs haven't closed.'

When he had re-sealed the gap in the curtain, she patted the seat alongside her.

'Come and sit here. I shan't bite you.'

'I shan't see you so well.'

He did as he was told.

'You're still suspicious, aren't you?' she chided. 'Never mind, another glass of whisky and the world will seem a better place.'

'It's remarkably comfortable just now, thanks to you.'

'You know the right thing to say, Henry, but you don't mean that.'

She did not torment him, and he began to talk about a play he had in mind. A student, lonely and homesick in Cambridge, met with the ghost of A. E. Housman, still walking out from Whewell's Court on fine afternoons. Spirit and human worked through 'the world as God made it'.

'Housman wouldn't talk easily to a student, would he?' Laura asked. 'Unless the boy was very attractive, and Housman was drawn sexually to him.'

'That's not what's stopping me from getting on with the thing. Or even starting it seriously.'

'What is, then?'

'The ghost. I don't believe in the supernatural.'

'It's only a convention,' she argued. 'Just accept it, and all your listeners will. Then treat the apparition as if he's alive. I take it that you're writing a conversation piece between a lonely old man and an isolated young one who find they've something interesting to say to each other.'

'No, I can't accept it. There's some headway to be gained from the fact that one of them is dead.'

'That's an advantage, surely?'

'But I don't see it. I can't convince myself.'

Laura looked him over, comically, leaning back.

'You do make it awkward,' she pronounced. 'Just set

85

it back in history, then. To the nineteen-twenties. Then you're between two wars. Think of the charge from that. The shell-shock, the disillusionment. The boy might have had a time in the trenches. Or he could be a scientist. The possibilities are endless.'

'I ought to have you there to write my plays for me. Or to smarten me up.'

'You never allowed me to help you when we were married. Not that I'd the confidence to butt in. I was a bit, not suspicious, no, diffident about it all. As if you were in a different world. Like a clergyman at the Eucharist. Performing a rite. I can tell you this now; I can feel a freedom I couldn't then. And when I read or heard what you'd written I was always surprised. It seemed good, but odd. As though you had insights you never showed in your ordinary life. I didn't always agree. I thought some of your women were far too neurotic, but I couldn't help thinking to myself that you were working out of your system all sorts of trouble you never mentioned to me. There.'

'Go on,' he said. 'This is interesting.'

'There's nothing more to be said. That's it.'

'A pity.'

'You were an accountant. A nice accountant. Handsome and quiet and decent, but good at totting things up, and costing schemes to put lorries and buses on the road. Not that you talked about that very much. I wished you had. I wanted to know about business, especially as that was where Con was getting on so fast. You wouldn't say much, any more than he would. You used to encourage me to talk about school, and you picked up bits and pieces from my chronicles to use in your plays, but changed.'

'This isn't the cause of our break-up?' Whisky permitted the foolishness. Laura stroked her chin.

'No. It added to your attraction. This secret life of yours with a pen in your hand. Annoying from time to time, I'll admit that. No, the reason, well the main reason among several dozens, why I couldn't stand our life together any more was that I lacked day-to-day satisfaction. Teaching was tolerable, but I spent my working hours amongst

86

nonentities. Don't get me wrong. They were decent, the majority of them, and some of them were clever. But they had no idea of their quality. They instructed and marked and prepared and talked to parents, but they accepted society's valuation of them. One old chap, Maurice Millsome – do you remember him? – always used to complain, "Laura, I've been a poor bloody usher all my life. And always shall be." He taught classics until there were no pupils left to teach and then they made him take general studies and do the entries for examinations, clerk's work. And he was a learned man, quick and witty, *Times* crossword every morning inside half an hour, but nobody cared, neither the DES nor the local authority, nor the headmistress, nor the pupils and their parents about the waste. He would have been marvellously occupied in my office.'

'Selling bus rides?'

'Yes. And a hundred and one other things. And getting paid properly once we saw how good he was. And if we didn't cough up, he'd have been off like a shot to somebody who would give him what he deserved. But there he was, stuck in his rut, pleased to be able to afford a fortnight in Greece or Italy once a year.'

'And you weren't having it?'

'Not if I could help it. That's why I'll give Jim a hand-up if I can.'

'Do you know, Laura,' now Henry spoke slowly, fighting against his comfort, his pleasant lassitude, 'I can't remember your saying any of this when we were married? I honestly cannot.'

'I probably didn't know myself what was wrong with me. I lost our baby. That knocked me about, but . . . I didn't want to do housework all day. I quite liked, enjoyed making our rooms look good, but that's not a full-time occupation. No, I had to try something else, and until I did, and found out I could do it well, I harassed and worried myself to death and blamed you for it, and everybody else. Once the disease was diagnosed, and I came up with something that I could give my mind to and make money . . .'

87

'Money.' Mournfully.

'. . . and gain status and have power, I was worth living with. I was a human being again.'

'I see.'

'It seems very sad to me now that our marriage broke up because I wasn't finding job satisfaction. I know you think it's pretty well impossible to pin down any disaster in the human condition to one simple cause. But that's about the long and short of it. Of course, if I'd have had a different temperament then I'd have spent my time looking after you and the home, but I'm not like that. You married the wrong woman.'

'It sounds as if you've done overtime thinking this out.'

'Since I saw you at the dinner, and then talked to your brother, I've thought about it, certainly, and often enough.'

'Any conclusions?'

'It seems a pity that I've ruined your life, or sabotaged it, just because I was in the wrong job.'

'All that means,' Henry spoke slowly, 'is that we chose wrongly in the first place. Or changed too radically.'

'That's so. When we were first married I thought I loved you so much that I could put up with anything. I was an innocent, then. Now I know how selfish I am, but after all we've only one life. I wish now I'd stayed with you, if you really want to know, but it would have meant your putting up with my chasing off after this contract, or working myself crazy for days on end. It wouldn't have been fair. Not to you.'

'I don't know. It would have been an unusual marriage. I'd have stopped at home to scrub the floors. But there's more of that nowadays, I guess.'

'Could you have accepted it?'

'There you have me. I think I'd have been proud to see you achieving so much. But when I came home and there was no dinner on the table and the bird had flown then I expect I would have sulked.'

'You're a good man.'

'I shouldn't count on that.'

She topped his glass up, then hers.

'Would you like some music?' she asked.

'Depends what sort.'

'You choose.'

Henry thought.

'I don't know,' he said. 'The decision's too difficult.'

She chose a Handel Concerto Grosso.

'There you are,' she answering, naming and numbering it. 'Just like you. Old-fashioned and good.'

'There is the truth.'

Laura frowned at him comically, but he, uncertain of the exact words, gave no explanation of his quotation. His head spun pleasantly; he stretched his legs; Handel added to the pleasure. Laura laid her head on his shoulder. They made love easily, tipsily, and fell asleep naked in her bed.

IX

Laura and Henry rose late, ate heartily at noon, spent the next two hours walking the streets together in bright sunshine, congratulating themselves at playing truant from work on Friday.

'Can they get on without you?' she asked, arm linked in his.

'Harry Dexter'll be in his element. Especially as he knows I'm back on Monday.'

'Is that kind?'

She talked with real eagerness about her plans, and questioned him about his estimate of her work.

'You think it's a waste of money, don't you?'

He explained how his view had changed. At one time he had wanted to produce objects, he explained; it had seemed more important to manufacture lorries than to send them about the roads, but now he saw the value of a service, and this he provided. 'God might want it otherwise,' he concluded, lamely, uncertain what she demanded of him. She squeezed his arm.

They returned to a light collation in her flat; she would not allow him to take her out for a meal. 'I don't want to sit waiting about in a restaurant,' she said vigorously. 'There is no excitement in it for me.' They made love again voluptuously before they prepared to go out to dance. The light, inside and outside the room, gleamed springlike, encouraging to energy.

They drove to the 'club' where she parked in the minimum space between a Mercedes and a Jaguar. Their destination was a large house, of much the same period as Laura's, uniformly curtained at each window, and with a glass notice lettered in chaste gold: The Grenville School of Dancing. A smartly dressed young woman admitted them, leading Laura upstairs to a cloakroom.

Henry Fairfax stood in a rather narrow hall, square-

90

tiled in black and red, decorated with three ornate gilt mirrors. Laura, as usual, was in no hurry. Canned music played; it sounded like Victor Sylvester. He heard the faint scuffle of drums or of feet on a dance floor, the chatter of inconsequentiality, the scattered applause between each number. His impression as he stood in this thin hall, by a newel post, having got rid of his coat in a cupboard-sized cloakroom, was of old-fashioned formality. He had had no idea where Laura intended to take him when she said they'd spend Friday evening at a dance; he certainly would not have guessed at a place like this. He'd not spent much time on thought or anticipation, but had expected a night club, with a neon signature, a cabaret, expensive drinks, no room to do more than shuffle. This looked and sounded utterly provincial, a bit of Beechnall.

Laura made her descent.

'Glorious things of thee are spoken,' he said.

They entered. The room, rather two big salons and a kitchen now opened out, was brilliantly lit. White chairs were set round the walls, the only furniture; walls and high ceiling lacked all pictures, sacrificed to the brightness from oddly shaped, shallow chandeliers. There were no fireplaces, but low radiators under the windows. The polished floor reflected light; five or six couples skated through a quick-step. Another dozen occupied the chairs. Two pillar-like loudspeakers provided the music. Laura at once seized Fairfax's hands and they joined the dance. As they spun, Laura acknowledged greetings, encouraging Henry to a dazzle of activity. They clapped, danced again, dropped down to the nearest chairs delighted with themselves.

'You've not forgotten,' Laura laughed.

'Do you come here often?'

She was just beginning to give a real answer to the old cliché when an elderly overweight couple joined them. The woman sat down; the man, with thick curling silver hair, stood, bowing slightly as he mopped his forehead. 'John and Inez de Courcy.' Henry rose to shake hands. 'Colonel de Courcy's an associate of my brother's.' The couple, smiling damply, claimed that Laura had warned them of his coming and his prowess on the dance floor.

Inez talked non-stop, praising Laura. She spoke quite loudly but at a speed which made much of her talk unintelligible against the background of conversation. Fairfax nodded politely in the right places. The colonel, who had made a ball of his handkerchief, dabbed at his head, saying nothing, breathing heavily and humming a deep note. Henry, overwhelmed by Mrs de Courcy's verbal floodtide, was glad when the next dance, a slow fox-trot, was announced from the kitchen end by a man in a white tie and tails.

'What on earth was she telling you?' Laura asked. Henry would have preferred to concentrate on his steps, to refurbish rusty skills, to enjoy the woman in his arms. Not more than two hours ago they had been lying naked in contentment.

'God knows. Something about an estate agent in Hampshire.'

Laura kissed him, a mere snatch at the cheek. True, the lights were lowered, but it seemed daring, adolescent. Nobody noticed. They locked and glided. 'She's always the same,' Laura said after a time. 'I don't think she knows herself what she's talking about. But they're a nice couple.'

It appeared, Henry learned later, that they were there as guests of the de Courcys. Laura had told them of her ex-husband's pleasure in ballroom dancing, and they had suggested this evening in the Grenville School. 'There'll not be more than thirty or forty there; they keep the numbers down so that there's room on the floor. They're mostly our sort of age, the sixties, but all good.' Laura, apparently, had been once or twice before. There were more ladies' excuse-mes or Paul Joneses than was usually the case, to let the experts try their skills with different partners. Henry, who wanted to do no more than hold Laura, danced with eight or ten other women before the night was out.

The kitchen end formed a kind of cross-piece, a transept, the middle of which they used for dancing. On the right, as one faced the garden, were small tables and chairs, painted white, suitable for the lawn outside and the striped parasol. On the left more chairs were arranged in rows so that people sat with their backs to an improvised bar, a long table with glasses and a refrigerator. As well as an entrance fee, he learnt, each dancer provided a bottle of wine. Orange and lemon squash, ice and tonic water were on offer at the proprietors' expense.

Mrs de Courcy described the gathering, in breathless monologue, during a long interval, as the *crème de la crème*. The Faulkeses who ran the school – who or what Grenville was Inez did not know – arranged this function on the first Friday of each month except August and twice 'in the run-up to Christmas'. One qualified by attendance and performance at advanced classes for an invitation. Fairfax understood at once the honour to be allowed to attend with the aristocracy of talent, and even, when one was especially well regarded, to be permitted to bring two, no more, guests. Henry felt grateful, appreciating the hierarchical principle; he determined to dance to the top of his ability, to show that grace and favour was not wasted on him. The de Courcys, the colonel muttered, attended here at least twice a week unless they went on holiday. 'Preferable to bridge.' 'Or solitary drinking,' said his wife. 'Or adultery.' The colonel laughed at his own drollery.

They introduced Henry to Mr and Mrs Faulkes; Madame danced an old-fashioned waltz with him, on her invitation; she gave the directions, stepping delicately fast, but with a guiding eye and hand. She probably marked him at the end; eight plus out of ten, he judged. Mr Faulkes, he in white tie and tails, was enjoying his turn with Laura. People talked freely to the 'young couple', made inquiries, offered information. There seemed a dichotomy of opinion about the value of a formation-dancing competition to be held next month at some Mecca or Palais. All approved, agreeing that standards would be raised, but half were certain that the team would be beaten by more lithe, more competitive, less aged

93

entrants. The Faulkeses were putting in and training one such team; their loyalty was questioned.

Between dances, Fairfax tried to adjudicate on the social level of the dancers, but without much success. One man had been back last month to his Oxford college to encourage students to join his firm; another spoke with a Cockney accent broad as a pearly king's; a third, a bald, foxy-faced man with a wispy beard, was, according to de Courcy, a clergyman and a professor of theology. All would be moderately well-to-do; the entrance fee, never exactly mentioned, but vaguely complained about, appeared to be steepish, whatever that meant in these circles. He wondered whether Laura or de Courcy had paid for him, but never found out. The evening filled itself with such interesting, unanswered little teasers. A visit to a Bushman, Inouit or Hottentot festival would not have been more entertainingly mysterious.

During the twenty-minute interval beginning just after ten they and the de Courcys were joined by another couple, grey-haired in their fifties, who after the social preliminaries were over seemed content to listen smilingly to Inez de Courcy's monologue and applaud the colonel's bluff interjections. Fairfax sat at ease; nothing was required of him but the appearance of attention; Laura's presence offered silent benediction. Mrs de Courcy's account of the fruitless attempt by a tout to sell them a time-share in a holiday flat on the Costa Brava seemed endless. The young man, English from Edmonton, Middlesex, had talked unstoppably, with a range from flattery to angry obscenity; he offered them lunch, which they refused. 'Our trouble's avoirdupois not starvation,' the colonel managed. They then drove round to the place, which was dusty, unattractive, three concrete prison cells, where the argument had become lively. They had demanded to be driven back to their hotel; the salesman had refused until such time as a bargain had been clinched; this had suited his opponents. 'Better than sweltering on the beach,' the colonel snarled. The battle of Titans had lasted another hour before the young man had acknowledged defeat. Ungraciously he had returned them.

94

'John wanted to buy him a drink, but I wasn't having that. He hadn't been polite enough.' Moreover he wasn't smart, either. 'He could have seen if he'd had anything about him that we weren't greenhorns.' The word delighted them all. Mrs de Courcy went on to expound the principles underlying commercial advancement. She bared her false teeth, shook her bosom, her face growing red under its layer of powder.

In the first quick-step after the interval Laura explained why she liked the de Courcys. 'He's an old sweetie, and very sharp, or else Con wouldn't employ him. She's the grand-daughter of a peer, the Earl of Ulverston, and John kowtows to her in every way, except at work. She's nice, really, very good-hearted, but she can't stop talking. They drive about in a Silver Shadow.' And the other couple? 'They're both dentists. Run a very lucrative practice.' Henry Fairfax, feet obeying him now, knew an interesting comfort, aesthetically satisfactory, with Laura as the presiding impresario.

At 11.25 the last waltz was announced. All crowded on to the floor, the Faulkeses leading off. On completion, with polite becks, people approached the proprietors, like children and their hosts at a birthday party, to shake hands, thank them, express appreciation. No one delayed proceedings, or stood about talking once they were through the salon doors. Laura and Fairfax sat together in the car quite silently.

'What did you think of that?' she asked, in the end.

'I didn't realize such places existed.'

'Humankind is infinitely various.' She laughed. 'They're on a nice little number. Hard work. But the bank balance's handsome.'

'How old are they?'

'Sixties. Oh, just a minute.'

She swung open her door, jumped out and tripped along the street to accost a couple who stood by the Mercedes in front. The man rounded his car to return to the pavement and the three laughed together, the woman pawing Laura's sleeve with a gloved hand. The reunion was animated, exaggeratedly cheerful, all three talking at once. Fairfax could not recall seeing Laura's companions inside. He could not hear what they said, but their postures, facial expressions, their liveliness gladdened him.

He lounged patiently, pleased with the evening's outing. The occasion seemed lifted from some old-fashioned, politer world. Of course, these people could afford to pay for the kind of pleasure they wanted and they had chosen the dances of their youth, of forty, fifty years ago, in the war when they were energetic and important and capable of everything. The picture delighted him.

But Laura had brought him, to disport himself with people almost twice her age, and he had enjoyed it. The entertainment had been temperate and formal, and he had, though lacking recent practice, been proficient enough both to be accepted and to make the most of it. To hold Laura formally dancing would have been enough, but the rest of the company provided a sufficiency of subject matter and the elderly ladies whom he had partnered had an admirable deftness or easy reply to any new steps he had tried. Lightness of foot, so great as to seem intelligence, was universal amongst these silver-haired. It surprised.

On the pavement Laura and her friends had now reached such a pitch of spirited hilarity that he expected them to join hands to dance ring-a-roses. Another bonus. Laura would tell him when she returned what had so enlivened them. He watched; they talked, touched, sidestepped, changed positions, trunks never still. Once they threw back their heads, all three, so that he could hear their laughter and Laura looked towards the car and raised her hand to him, as an overflow of vivacity or an excuse for exceeding propriety. Mildly fascinated, the phrase 'transport of delight' entered his mind, and he eased himself up from the seat, smiling.

Laura kissed the couple, the woman hugging her, and returned. She sat down breathless. She blew out her last puff of air, and took his right hand with her left, in exhausted silence.

'Oh, well,' she said, looking about for her keys, already

in the dashboard. She flicked them, disparaging her forgetfulness, with finger-ends.

'Who were they?'

'The Kings. I wanted to ask them about Wimbledon, but their daughter has suddenly decided to get married. They thought she never would.'

'They looked pleased enough about it.'

'I ought to have introduced you. They're the nicest couple in London. He's some sort of executive in British Telecom, and she runs a florist's. Helen's the only child, clever, and smart, and pretty. And she's told them the good news. By telephone. She'd been living with some unsuitable man. And now it's this boy they approve of. Helly's known him all her life.'

'How old is she?'

'Twenty-nine. She's no infant.' Laura laughed out loud, applauding with her free hand on the steering wheel. 'They're delirious. Can't believe it.' She turned round. 'And they wanted to tell me all night, but didn't come across because you were there.'

'Why not?'

'They're very proper, socially. They didn't know who you were, or what, and so just wouldn't burst in on us to break the good news.'

'You told them.'

'What?'

'Who I was. Your ex-husband.'

She gave his left hand a violent toss, knocking it on the hand-brake. 'You miserable sod.'

But she was laughing still as she turned on the ignition.

She occupied the five minutes' drive in comparatively empty streets with an account of the de Courcy house, a small gem in Hampstead. They had been most kind to her when she first arrived in London. 'They're boring, but marvellous. Can you understand that?'

Laura parked further down the street, at least a hundred yards from her house.

'First come, first served,' she said, locking up. 'That's the principle.'

'Is it safe?'

'Let's say nothing's happened yet.'

They walked arm in arm along the street, in the mild air. Downstairs lights shone in many of the buildings. He asked how one could distinguish flats from family houses.

'Bells and cards on the doors, I'd think. You never see matching curtains these days. Most of the people here are nomadic.'

'They don't own their own places?'

'I'd guess not. You occasionally see a flat up for sale.'

They paused outside her house; light touched the new green of leaves, an irregular, huge mass of berberis blossom.

'It's all quite beautiful,' he said. She kneaded his shoulder-blades with a knuckled right hand. 'And so quiet.'

'It's midnight.'

They moved up the steps; the outer door was open.

'Not usual,' she said. 'I wonder if someone's nipped out.'

He thought of the word, the speed, the twinkling shoes. They heard a noise, as if a heavy body pressed creaking timber. Somebody groaned.

'Who's that?' Laura called.

A louder groan answered. She turned back, away from Fairfax, to click on switches. The result disappointed. In half-light they could see a man on hands and knees. He lifted his head to them before he collapsed.

'Mr Rhodes,' Laura called.

The man's head, bald, streaked with hair, bled from a wound. The face was black in the half-light, with blood, one eye completely closed. They lifted him, gently.

'Mr Rhodes,' Laura asked, 'what is it? Did you have a fall?'

The man groaned again, began to breathe stertorously. They could make out a trail of blood from the door, great spots.

'Stay here,' she said. 'I'll ring 999.'

Laura sprinted upstairs. Fairfax held the man upright, pressed a handkerchief to the head wound, murmured comfort. No one else stirred; doors remained obdurately shut, though Laura had turned on more lamps up above.

He could hear nothing of her; the wounded man leaned heavily on him, groaning and snuffling alternately.

'What happened?' he asked, not for the first time. No answer. 'Did you fall? Were you run over? Did somebody . . . ?' He realized that he was merely keeping his own spirits up. 'Don't worry,' he continued. 'We'll soon get you seen to. You'll be all right.'

He listened for Laura's return. In vain. Perhaps she was having trouble getting through to authority.

'Don't worry,' he continued. 'You'll be all right.' The man seemed out now, unconscious and immobile. 'We'll soon have the ambulance here.'

Their cramped position pained Fairfax's limbs. He wondered if he could, or should, put the man down. He had read of a safe position, so that an injured person would not choke on his own vomit, but he had no idea what it was. The victim stirred and groaned. The rescuer ventured further comfortable words. The handkerchief on the head blackened bloodier.

Laura approached, clattering downstairs.

'Can we straighten his legs, do you think?' he muttered. They managed it between them.

'I've called police as well as ambulance,' she said. She seemed nine feet tall to him as he crouched. She peered down. 'That coat of yours will be in a mess.' True, blood splodges darkened the near-blond mac. She had brought down a torch which she shone into Rhodes's face.

'God,' she said, directing the beam elsewhere. She took two or three steps in the space, her shoes clacking on the tiled floor. Then she stood impatiently. 'I wish they'd bloody hurry up.' He could hear all three breathing; Rhodes snorted, weakly and rough. Laura sniffed. He dragged air in through his mouth.

'You go and put the kettle on,' he ordered.

'Shall I?'

'Yes. I'll see to him. They shouldn't be long.'

'We hope.'

She went upstairs at a cracking run. He heard her fiddle with the keys at her door at the top of the second flight.

She muttered to herself. Nobody else heard anything, or poked a face out of a door.

Laura was coming down again when he heard the car outside. A young policeman entered, without hurry, peering about.

'Hello, over here,' Fairfax called.

'What's happened then?' A northern accent. The constable bent, knelt, used his torch, stood again and relieved Fairfax of the burden. 'Was it an accident?' He laid the body on the floor, arranging it. 'Is the ambulance on the way?'

'They said so.' Laura, upright, very clear.

Fairfax could barely stand; knees and thighs ached. He straightened himself, rubbed and began to explain. The policeman listened. 'I shall have to take a statement.'

'There's blood all along the hall floor,' Laura said. She and the policeman mooched together, flashing torches, heads lowered. Fairfax held his place alongside Rhodes who suddenly groaned. The seekers opened the front door, ventured out, talking. When they returned Laura reported that it, accident or mugging, had taken place on the pavement. Rhodes must have been checking the doors of his Mini.

'I didn't notice anything on the steps when we came in.' Fairfax.

'Quite big splashes.'

The policeman asked Laura for her account. The ambulance arrived. Again there seemed no hurry, men on top of their job, unflurried. They examined Rhodes, brought in a stretcher, made a note, removed the injured man, drove off.

Laura invited the police officer upstairs for coffee while he took statements. Half an hour in pure light. When the constable had finished and gone, Laura and Fairfax sat with another cup and a glass of whisky. Twenty minutes to one.

'We could have done without that.' Laura, shuddering. She cried a little, tears dampening her cheeks, as she had when first the disagreements which led to divorce had appeared. She dabbed her face, stood up, cleaned his coat, sat down. She became taciturn. When he told her how much he had enjoyed the dance, she nodded sadly. He made a few inquiries about Mr Rhodes, but she knew little. He had retired, she thought, spent most afternoons in the library, carried books about, occasionally patronized the Mason's Arms.

'There were no books about tonight,' he ventured.

Laura shook her head, dazed.

In bed they clung together, and Laura wept again in the dark. They made love, but without much pleasure or excess; they were glad when it was over.

They lay late on Saturday, and drank tea in bed until eleven, wasting the sunshine. They felt more cheerful, rang the hospital where Rhodes was said to be conscious, very comfortable and likely to be out within the next day or two. Fairfax accompanied Laura to a local market from which they bought apples, oranges and a copy of the *Penguin Book of Greek Verse*. They ate a light lunch after Henry had made a presentation to his ex-wife.

He had acquired, two days before his visit in the euphoria of his firm's new contract, a small brooch: three gold leaves, deeply incised with veins, mounted on a thin bar. He had noticed it in an antique shop he visited irregularly, admired its delicate solidity. 'English, 1908,' the dealer had said, 'but I've no idea who made it.' 'Would it be local?' Henry asked. 'Could be, at that. I've no idea. Came to me as a part-payment. Not my line.' 'It's very beautiful,' Henry argued. 'Is it? Three leaves. Beech leaves are they? Aesthetically, yes. Perhaps so.' 'How much?' The man named his price. 'That's not cheap.' No,' the shopkeeper grinned. 'Eighteen-carat gold never is. You have to be able to afford it.' Henry paid up and looked pleasant.

That it was beautiful he had no doubt. The shape of the trinity of leaves satisfied him, exaggerating nothing and yet achieving a uniqueness, almost as if by chance, as if the understatement, the small provincial attempt at realism had culminated in a universal. Fairfax laughed at his fancy, and cleaned up the shabby little case. It would be an ideal present for his hostess, he decided, but had felt, once in Laura's house, a reluctance to hand over the gift. He did not want to keep the gew-gaw for himself, but he did not wish to appear to be buying her favour. A bribe. Gew-gaw, a belittling word.

When they returned from the Saturday jaunt, he slipped out to the bathroom, then his bedroom for the brooch. Laura had emptied her two shopping bags, he had carried both, on to the sitting-room table, where she stood staring as if the extent of her purchases baffled her. Why had she not unpacked in the kitchen, near the fridge and cupboards? Her face was thoughtful, as if at a decision, or at an attempt to recall some omission. She smiled absent-mindedly at him, picked up a packet of sugar, turned it over, read it, replaced it.

'Have we forgotten something?' he asked.

'No,' she answered. 'No. I don't usually do my shopping in dribs and drabs like this. I take the car and have a big burst at a supermarket.'

'This was a little outing for my benefit?'

Laura frowned again, mildly, not despoiling her beauty, still preoccupied.

'Let's take them into the kitchen,' she said.

'Just before we do, I've something . . .'

She put her head on one side like a small girl.

'. . . I'd like to give you.'

His hand went into his jacket pocket; he pulled out the case, and presented it to her on the flat of his hand.

'What is it?' She seemed suitably delighted.

'Open it.'

'No. You.'

He hesitated, then obeyed. Now he held the brooch out towards her. She took it, lifting it from its case, quite silent. Then she twirled it.

'It's beautiful,' Laura said, 'beautiful.' She leaned forward, kissed him on the mouth, immediately stood back, held the brooch nearer to her eyes. 'It's lovely.'

'Good. I hope you'll wear it sometimes.'

She looked abashed, or affronted, as if he had made some immoral suggestion or discourteous implication, then she smiled.

'You still surprise me, Henry.'

She returned the brooch to its case which she laid on the mantelpiece, before she hugged him again, her pleasure palpable. He explained the little he knew about the brooch. She recovered herself.

'You shouldn't have given it to me.'

'It's pleasure for me.'

'Henry Fairfax, sometimes you're nice.' She stood tongue-tied. 'I don't deserve it.' A tear slopped on to her face and she dashed it away with the back of her hand. She wore no rings, no jewellery.

'Shall I cart these into the kitchen?' He pointed at the groceries.

'Please. We shall never get round to lunch at this rate.' She dabbed another kiss at him.

After lunch, they talked, walked hand in hand round the streets in wind and sunlight. Laura wore the brooch, patted it, drew his attention to it. In the evening, after high tea, they bathed, dressed, made for the Barbican and Beethoven.

'The Le Jeune family nourishes me on Beethoven.' He told her about Conrad's ticket in Zürich.

'Good for him. I didn't think he knew a piano from a banjo.'

They listened to Egmont, the Fourth Piano Concerto, the Seventh Symphony; the music appealed to a kind of heroism in him, unlike the everyday man. He was silenced, stern, while Laura seemed released, gamesome. The tube stations, grubby with litter, walls scrawled over, dark with the Saturday crowds, shone and sounded for them. They laughed, sitting opposite, children on an outing. She had won. They made cocoa; they emptied the whisky bottle, opened a second, they stripped in the sitting room, achieved orgasm easily. She put on Mozart, a violin concerto; they drank, listened, laid hands on each other.

Next day over lunch they were subdued, preoccupied by his departure.

'This has been marvellous,' he said.

Laura was dressed in a simple dark blue frock with a narrow white collar; she wore the brooch, had primly dressed up for Sunday. She looked young, fresh, as if in a school uniform. Nothing of Friday's experience showed in her demeanour. Rhodes was in hospital still.

Insistently she questioned him about his plays; he had no wish to answer. Secretive by nature, he saw in the imminent parting a warning. He explained his plans without enthusiasm. She listened with a serious air.

'My writing,' he said, 'is the equivalent of Scrabble, a means of passing the time, with a slight intellectual content.'

'But luck plays a part in Scrabble.'

'As in writing. And the arbitrary numbers. Some genres are acceptable, some out of fashion.'

'You're running yourself down again.'

'No. I'm speaking the truth. I couldn't make a living out of my plays.'

'What if you had to?'

'The DHSS. No. I seriously clean out my provincial corner and put the findings on exhibition. There are enough horrors there for my talent, such as it is. I don't need the holocaust or the nuclear bomb, though they loom, they must, behind what I'm saying. For all the treacheries and adulteries and Mr Rhodes's muggings in my streets, my characters are at least alive and capable of improvement. The gas chamber, the nuclear winter effectively burn and freeze literature to death.'

'You mean we shouldn't write about them?'

'No. I don't. But. Somebody must deal with these major catastrophes so that they won't happen, or happen again. I think people are just beginning to realize what nuclear wars mean. Only just. They talk about nuclear missiles as if they were merely bigger Lancasters or nastier Boeings. But . . .'

'You seem to argue exactly against yourself, Henry.'

'I know. I write more tellingly about life as it is than about its ultimate destruction. My plays for all the foolishness and wickedness in them, and there is plenty of both, at least make out something, something squalid or unacceptable perhaps, about human dignity, decency. If I wrote about the lacerated, impotent dying survivors of a nuclear war I'd despair myself, drive myself crazy. I'd do better, I think, to go round with a CND banner on a demo.'

'But you don't. Or do you?'

'No.' He smiled, rubbing his chin. 'I'm a poor fish. I haven't even got the courage of my convictions. But,' he pointed a straight index finger at her, 'it's by such warped, crippled, non-action men that the best of literature is written.'

'You're a funny soul, Henry Fairfax.'

Laura came across, kissed him and returned with renewed appetite and relish to her salad.

He ate silently, both discouraged and enlightened. His grumble approached the truth, but he felt he was missing the heart of his present situation. This day or two with Laura had comforted, or changed him, so that he ought to make some large statement to her. This was not the Laura of nine years of marriage, though habits, gestures, tones of voice, turns of phrase, manners, quirks of mind remained, like ghosts, to warn, to caution. He should open his arms to this new woman, but he could not. He had shared warm company, sexual enjoyment, the talk, drink, food, a sickening good deed, but that was all. The world had not been turned upside down. He knew it. With infinite care he spread margarine on his cob, exactly to the edges.

They parted soon after lunch.

'I can't tell you how much this has meant.' He was right.

Laura hugged him violently. She showed her real strength.

'Will you come up to see me?'

'Yes, please. I think I will. Let's not rush it, though.'

'I daren't have said that.'

'You understand yourself better than you did.' That disfigured his image for him.

Laura did not come to the station, but fluttered about the room and sat down after their last embrace. He wondered if she would creep over to the window. His face seemed stiff, set in a deliberate plaster of unfeeling. He turned back, but he could not make anything out in the small dark sector of her bay. He waved, foolishly. The case handle dug into his hand. He must buy something more comfortable. Why had she not accompanied him to the tube station? It was a compliment, he decided. A child on a cycle hurtled past on the pavement. No bell or shout. A side step and he would have been felled. He shook his head. He had walked straight.

By the time he reached St Pancras he had regained normality, could cope with the internal maelstrom. He settled to the Sunday newspapers and the rush of the countryside. His house, sunshine notwithstanding, felt damp so that he turned on the central heating. Tomorrow morning he would be back in his office, slaving to earn an honest copper or two for Con Le Jeune. Everything stood extraordinarily still; nobody shouted in the streets; neighbours had deserted their darkening gardens. He walked round his small patch, admired the blossoms on his two pear trees. Rushing back he telephoned Laura to announce his safe arrival, to thank her. She was out. He allowed her phone to ring, wondering if Mr Rhodes, returned from hospital, could hear the sound. Laura had started life again; he crouched in an armchair, clinging to a cup of coffee.

X

On Monday evening he wrote an enthusiastic note to Laura, went out to post it and continued the walk for half an hour to his brother's house. He rang the bell, slightly annoyed with himself; he did not like off-chance visits.

Molly invited him in. Jim, it appeared, was not at home.

'I visited Laura this weekend, so I came round to report what she had said about Jim's interviews.'

'So she was impressed?' Molly said, when he'd finished.

'Yes. Very much so. It all depends now on the arrangements that are agreed for the new set-up.'

They talked that over for a few minutes; Molly produced the sherry bottle, poured, took a thirsty sip.

'Where is he tonight, then?' he asked, raising his glass, ironically.

'I don't honestly know.' She drank again. 'Lady love, again, I expect.'

'Christina Brown?'

She shrugged, an ugly movement.

'I thought things were better between you?' He would have done better to have kept quiet, but he could not bear her restlessness. She kicked at the air.

'We did talk more. When the job was in the offing. While he could make use of me.'

'I'm sorry.'

Molly angrily refilled her glass. Glum silence divided them. Henry tried once more.

'How's the work?' he asked.

'Plenty on hand. Too much, if anything. Martin wangled me quite a big set of commissions, and I've an exhibition in Cardiff in June.'

'On your own?'

'Don't talk daft. Modern British Jewellery, it's called. Five of us. I'm lucky to be invited.'

'Have you got enough pieces ready?'

'I shall have to, shan't I?' She blew out breath. 'It's a bloody good job I have. I go down and slave, and it stops me thinking what's happening to me here. And I don't care what time I come home. He can look after himself.'

'Is that wise?'

'I thought about . . . what you said . . . about it being a good time . . . to break it off.'

'Do you want to?'

She could contain her physical unease no longer, but sprang from her chair, stalked across the room, back, back again. He guessed she had no idea of the frantic impression she created.

'Want?' she panted. 'I could kill him sometimes.' She stood, back to the empty fireplace, legs apart, mannishly.

'Is that how you felt with Laura?'

'I suppose so. Towards the end. We'd quarrel over nothing, and make no effort to please the other. Deliberately. I'd delay myself at work. She'd arrange to be out. We felt so sore, we could barely help it. It seems silly now. As if we cultivated hurt, went out of our way to wound each other, but worse, ourselves.'

'Were you jealous?'

'Yes. Though there was no other man, as far as I know. We made ourselves hate each other. I can hardly believe I behaved so badly. It was, I was abominable.'

'And she was as bad?'

'I suppose so. She blames herself now, says she'd no satisfactory job and so took it out on me.'

'Is that true?'

'Could be. I was losing interest, really. I'd have said that we'd got out of the relationship all that we could. We'd run dry.'

'Was there another woman in your case?'

'Yes, though I would have said "no" at the time. A young woman at the office was making eyes at me. It was nothing, really. She's happily married to someone else now.'

'Does she still work with you?'

'No. She has a child.'

108

'You surprise me. I always thought of you as a model of rectitude.' Neither irony nor humour lightened the sour tone of voice. 'You're as bad as he is.'

'Yes.'

They did not speak, shiftily quiet. She stood still, aggressive, but partly pacified by his confession.

'What shall we do then?' she barked, suddenly.

'Look,' he spoke emolliently, 'is there anything that's going to set this marriage straight?'

'What do you mean?'

'Is it a total wreck as far as you're concerned?'

'That's how I feel about it. And yet. And yet.' The repeated phrase rang strong, without hesitation. 'I'd make it work if I could.'

'Why?'

'I don't know why. I don't like change. I meant my marriage vows. I could still love him. He might go utterly wrong without me. There are a thousand and one reasons.'

'Is pride one of them?'

'You mean that I don't like losing what I consider my property?' She thought, sidestepped, slapped right fist into left palm, turned. 'I suppose that's true. I'm no different from anybody else. What do you expect?' She straightened herself. 'Another drink?'

'I tell you what. Let's go out for a little stroll, and I'll buy you a drink in a pub.'

'Why?'

'Fresh air will do us good.'

'I'm not dressed for going out.' She dashed a hand down on to her skirt. 'Oh, all right.'

She spent ten minutes beautifying herself, refused to leave a note for her husband, changed her mind, scribbled a line or two, sealed the sheet in an envelope and threw it on the kitchen table.

'We'll probably be back first.'

They walked smartly in the dusk, and her mood changed immediately for the better. She decided they'd make for the Duke of Cambridge, but deviously, round the back ways.

'It's not too cold.' She seemed surprised. They passed along a street of terraced houses, which petered out into a road built up on one side only. On the other the pavement was bordered by a hawthorn hedge, eight, ten feet high, behind which they could make out in the gaps greenhouses, garden sheds, apple trees.

'Allotments,' she told him. 'I come down here and buy flowers and tomatoes sometimes. Runner beans.'

'Cabbages.'

'And kings.' High spirits brightened her voice. 'This is nice.'

'Walking the streets?'

'I'm talking. Not arguing. Exchanging ideas. Working the inches off my hips. You know, Henry, you're quite different from Jim. He's never settled. The genes must be the same, though, mustn't they?'

'Not necessarily.'

'And the environment?'

'There's a difference of seven years.'

'Had your parents changed in that time? Jim never says anything about it. He never mentions . . .'

'You surprise me. He was very shaken by his mother's death.'

They had stopped and were peering through a white gate. A straight, flagged path led uphill past brick shed, long greenhouse to a small orchard. Great ranks of daffodils stood ready for cutting, lit by the high street lamp.

'Good man for flowers,' Molly informed him. 'I often drive down. Treats it like a municipal garden. Plants in and straight out when they're done. He's got control over three or four allotments together. Nice chap. Brother runs a flower stall somewhere.'

'Must be a full-time occupation?'

'Don't think so. But I don't know what it is he does.'

'How old is he?'

'Hard to tell. Sixty, perhaps. Your parents were old, weren't they, when they had you?'

'My mother was thirty. They'd been married six years. End of the war.'

'Why doesn't Jim talk about his father?'

'Doesn't he? Doesn't Dad write occasionally? He sends me news at Christmas with his card.'

'I have this impression Jim hates him. I may be wrong. He doesn't say anything. Did your father not treat his wife properly?'

'The very opposite, I'd have said. But he's a quiet man, Doesn't show his feelings. Never did. I wouldn't say he was without them though. Would you? You've met him.'

They walked faster after this exchange. Henry's father had retired to a bungalow in Penarth soon after his wife's death, because he'd once enjoyed a holiday there. A solicitor, he'd taught part time for a period at the poly Laura had attended. She'd told him that he was known as 'Killer', this quiet, unassuming man, that the law students feared him.

'Who ruled the roost?' Molly was asking. 'Your mother or your father?'

'My mother was much the livelier. But you never quite fathomed my dad. At least I didn't. He could blow his top. Not often, but impressively.' Henry felt pleased with the expression. His father had once hurled him clean across a large room crack into a wall, brutally knocking every atom of breath out of him. He didn't hold it against the old man. His father was entitled to get his own back on a world that didn't regard him highly. Few knew how well off he was. The old man never boasted, but looked after his own interests.

'Are you like your father?'

'In some ways. A bit of a loner. Didn't like to give himself away. He wasn't easy dealing with people en masse. He was good though, still is, with money. Gambling on horses he hated; on holiday he wouldn't risk a brass farthing on a fruit machine, but he invested with real care, studied to improve, and has made a pretty profit. Or so he claims.'

'Jim's hopeless.'

'With money? You surprise me.'

'He's more like his mother, isn't he?'

111

'That's about right. Insofar . . . Does he ever talk about her?'

'He did. He doesn't talk about anything much to me now.'

They were climbing a hill at a speed which kept them quiet. At the top they turned and looked back. Not a soul in the street; both kerbs lined with parked cars. One failed overhead light procured a patch, a sinister ball of darkness.

'I wonder what they're all doing?' Molly asked.

'Watching telly.'

'I always imagine I'm viewing on my own. Odd, isn't it? I was at school with a girl from this street.'

'Does she still live here?'

'I don't suppose so. Her parents may. It's not much more than ten years ago. I never meet any of my school friends. One girl wrote to me when I had an exhibition at the end of my course at the poly and there was a photograph in the newspaper. She wrote from Carlisle. Her mother had sent her the cutting. We didn't keep it up. Were you a prefect at your school?'

'Oh, yes.' He was amused by her switch.

'Do you approve?'

'Of children looking after children? I'm not sure.' He wasn't interested enough to pursue the argument. Molly took his arm and they set off again.

'What if we meet Jim and Christine in this pub?' she asked, cheerfully.

'Would you be angry? Would he?'

'I don't know what I'd do. I've never met her. I don't know that I've ever even spoken to her. I think she's pretty.'

'Does that make any difference?'

Molly withdrew her arm from his. Slowly, deliberately. He felt the disgrace.

By the time they reached the Duke of Cambridge her good humour had been restored.

'Who's this duke?' she asked.

'Wasn't he some sort of royal Victorian soldier? It's about the right date.'

'I hated history. And the man who taught us. He was the idiot who christened me Molly.'

'Go on.'

'They were a kind of Irish mafia. The Molly Maguires. In Ireland, and then in the USA I think.'

'Have you any Irish antecedents?'

'Not recently. All good middle-class nondescripts. Sunday school teachers. Temperance advocates. They'd hate to think of my creeping in here.'

'We'll turn back, then.'

'No fear. I can't even spell the word.'

'What word?'

'Temperance.'

'With an "a".'

'Thanks. We do see life.'

They turned in at the street door of the lounge. The place was dull, with darkish paint and strips of unbright mirror. He sat her at a table, obtained immediate service at the bar and returned with her gin and his half of bitter.

'Your health,' he said, lifting the glass.

'I need it.'

Though she smiled, he could not miss the volatility of her mood. It would not need much more than a wrong word or a loud noise to bring her to tears. He hoped for help from the gin.

No music sounded and the drinkers were quiet. The room, its furniture offered little by way of comfort. Cleanliness prevailed; the green floor had been scrubbed that morning, and the large glass ashtrays were empty. No spare utensils littered the tables; cardboard beer mats were almost mathematically arranged; signs, he concluded, of lack of patronage. She finished her drink before he was a quarter of the way down his.

'Let me fetch you another.'

'There's no bursting hurry.'

She passed him her glass.

'This is good,' she told him on her first sip. 'Being out, without responsibilities. The trouble with working for yourself is that you never let go. Or I don't. I'm frightened of idling.'

She began to explain her present preoccupation, with necklaces and bangles. She'd been to an exhibition in London, at the same time he was there, of Indian and Persian jewellery and this had set her head racing. 'It's only on paper yet, but I spent the whole of yesterday sketching and all today.'

'Does Jim mind?'

'He hasn't noticed. I provided him with lunch, and he did a bit in the garden in the afternoon. Or so he said. I was busy all day.'

'You can keep out of each other's sight if you want.'

'We use a spare bedroom. He marks, and I draw.'

'He doesn't try to interrupt you?'

'No. Why should he?' She frowned. 'Oh, dog in a manger. I see what you mean. To work his frustrations off by stopping me. No, he didn't. Not yesterday.'

Molly described the exhibition and the expensive catalogue she had invested in. No, she had no commercial ideas of breaking into lucrative Arab markets. She had no notion if such existed; she had been excited by what she saw, and was now modifying her own view, translating Mogul to Maguire, she said, playing variations. 'One thing gives rise to another, I can't stop myself. I spent all day today filling sketchbooks and drinking black coffee. When you came I hadn't been home long, and I was absolutely knackered.'

'You didn't say so.'

'Wouldn't it have been pretentious? "Please excuse me, but I'm worn out by my creativity." ' She laughed, and tried to explain, out of affection or apology, the nature of her inspirations. She failed, lacking all clarity. The designs, it appeared, led her fingers to sketch patterns, and these she shaped again, and again, until she found a basic aesthetic satisfaction, which could be translated into metal or precious stones. She spoke with speed, spluttering, never at a loss, while her hands circled in traceries of emphasis, but he did not follow her.

He told about the brooch he had bought for Laura, defining its appeal.

114

'You should have supported modern art,' she chaffed.
'Meaning me.'

'I saw this by chance. Just when I was considering the visit.'

'How much did you pay for it?' He told her. 'You could have bought three of my things for that.'

'I was very taken with it.'

'How do you choose? Is it as an investment? Or do you do it on aesthetic grounds?'

'The second, though I'm ignorant on both counts. We never know what will appeal to the next generation, and I'd be very pushed to establish criteria of beauty.'

'You know what you like?' Molly's voice rang hard.

'Not even that. I'm a bumbler. I'm even uncertain about my own work, my writing I mean. There must be an element of surprise'

'You surprise me.' She laughed again. 'I expected you to approve of,' she waved her hands, conjuring reluctant words out of the air, 'works of art done with extreme skill in genres or styles that are widely accepted.'

'Old-fashioned, you mean?'

'If you like. It's very hard to distinguish the really original from the bogus. Both can shock.'

'In Camden Town,' he said, 'I saw a graffito that surprised me. It was done with an aerosol in big letters on the end of a house. In a literate way. Or artistic. The letters were beautifully formed: "My Karma has just run over your dogma." '

She laughed perfunctorily, then narrowed her eyes. She stroked the table.

'Give me a paraphrase of that.'

'Oh, dear. Well. My actions, the way I've lived, and their results have just destroyed the theory, the credo you hold.'

Molly considered.

'Is that worth saying?'

'It's witty, and surprising.'

'But why the "just"? It would make more sense if it were the other way about: My dogma has just run over your Karma. But that's no good. More wit than meaning.'

'I'm sorry.'

'Don't take me seriously.' She patted his arm. 'You look as if I've just stolen your last ha'penny. Let me buy you a drink.'

He indicated that his glass was not yet empty, but his obvious deflation had done for them both. He'd needed a laugh, some capping line from her, not this leaden dissatisfaction. She sat now, he glanced up, with her face quite unruffled, her mouth a thin, not unattractive, straight line, young and pretty and glum. She realized, he guessed, that she had put her foot in it, but had neither the energy nor the knowledge to set it right.

'Cheer up,' he said, making the effort, putting his hand on the bunched fist on the table. She smiled bleakly, from some other place, concerned by her unconcern.

'We shall soon be dead.' She capped his sentence this time, too late, too dully.

'Tell me,' he said desperately, 'if you had the chance to go anywhere you liked, for a holiday, money no object, where would you choose?'

'America,' she said, uncertainly. 'I think. It would be exciting. Or I imagine it would. Anything would be better than this.' Her voice resumed wooden incuriosity.

A voice broke in from behind Henry Fairfax.

'Excuse my interruption, but I couldn't help over-hearing your conversation.'

Gentlemanly, educated, not overbearing but expecting to be given audience. Fairfax did not immediately turn round. When he did so he saw a grey-haired man in a mackintosh.

'It is inexcusable, I know.' The thin hair was parted in the middle and thinly taken back in artificial waves. His face was narrow behind horn-rimmed spectacles, but healthily pink, and his hands clasped the pint pot on the table at which he sat. 'But it is such a tempting question.'

'Which you're going to answer for us?' Molly.

'Exactly. By way of preliminaries, I think I can boast that I have travelled the world widely. First of all in the army, and then, one might say, culturally. I worked abroad for the British Council. I have never made an exact calculation, but I guess I have lived *in partibus infidelium* longer than in this country. Where would you say I originated?'

They found no clues from his accent; he spoke standard southern. The BBC might still have employed him on Radio 3. Fairfax searched for other pointers, found none. The fingers were nicotine-stained, though the man was not smoking.

'London.' Socially.

'A foul way out, as Shakespeare has it.'

'Oxford.' Molly assuming brightness.

'I was educated there. Jesus College. Does that give you a pointer?'

'Wales?' Fairfax thought he noted the 'u' in 'educated' was iotated, English-fashion.

'Correct. South Wales. The valleys. Abersychan.'

The three stared round, temporarily at a loss. Fairfax called the meeting to order.

'But your answer,' he said. 'Where would you choose?'

'Ah, yes. It would be a toss-up,' he smiled mincingly at the colloquialism, 'between New Zealand and Japan. And do you know why?' Something of an old class-teacher appeared, fencing with the pupils, keeping them on the defensive so that the answer, the coup de grâce, would not be easily forgotten. 'These are two of the most beautiful countries in the world, and I have visited neither.'

'I thought the British Council did a great deal in Japan?'

'So they do, so they do. But they have so far managed without my valued assistance.'

'And is it possible that they will . . . ?' Molly began, but he was already shaking his head solemnly.

'I have retired.' His voice sank to the sepulchral.

'Here?' Molly.

'Here. For the present. And you may well be asking yourself with some justification why I have elected to alight in this philistine corner of the creation.' His eyes roamed the lounge, the green rexine-covered chairs, the varnished tables, the dull mirrors, the advertisements for soft drinks. He lifted a beer mat from his table, weighed it in the balance of his hand, found it wanting, but returned it exactly to its original position, taking time, estimating its coordinates. 'My sister and her husband live here; they own a house far too large for them. She invited me to stay until I made up my mind.'

'Have you done so yet?' Henry.

'No. I have been here only for four days. All I have decided is that wherever I settle it won't be in this place.'

The listeners neither bridled nor encouraged him

'The town has some slight advantages. But my brother-in-law is dullness personified. He has lived here all his life, but has no desire to go away even for a holiday. He potters in his garden, reads his books, very few, makes and mends and goggles at television. Never attends a concert, a theatre, a political meeting, a church service. He's dead to the world.'

'How old is he?' Molly.

'Two years older than I am. I shall be sixty-six in December.'

'Would you say,' Fairfax asked, 'that he's a contented man?'

'He's not alive. He's vegetating. My sister leaves him to it. She goes out, around, to meetings, to classes. She's a first-rate cook. Her brain is nimble as her ankles.' He frowned, combing the thin hair with his fingers. 'Would you allow me, as some sort of restitution for my unforgivable eavesdropping and interruption, to buy you a drink?'

Both refused, though Molly's glass was empty.

'Now please, please. You've treated me with such respect that I am deeply in your debt.' He stood up, laid a hand on Molly's glass. She yielded; Henry cleared his last inch, edged his jar forward.

'God,' Molly, eyes wide. 'We've found one here.' She swayed. The man returned.

When he placed Molly's glass in front of her he said, 'I asked the barman to add a drop or two of bitters to your gin and tonic. You will forgive me, I know, when you taste it. The improvement is inconceivable.' He settled comfortably to his pint which was barely touched.

'As I was saying,' he looked comfortable, having bought

118

his way in, 'if I were not considering ways of visiting Japan and New Zealand I should consider my life at an end. You, sir, if I understood you correctly, are a writer. Would you give me your name?' Henry did so. It meant, as he expected, nothing. 'What do you write, if I may be so bold?' Henry obliged. 'Radio plays. That explains my ignorance. Yes. An ephemeral but beautiful art,. As near poetry as could be in its higher reaches. And you, madam? A designer? Of jewellery? An endeavour I have never come to terms with. Diamonds sparkle; gold has value in itself, but . . . You must forgive my prejudices.'

He rattled on, glad of their company, lecturing them on the artistic, on foreign cities and customs, on education and the value of literature, on the pains and advantages of growing old. Fairfax enjoyed the fluency, but Molly's eyes were hooded, her face revealed nothing. She made the effort at last when asked what was worth seeing in the town. The man beamed; in spite of his loquacity, he had not yet told them his name.

'It does me good to come across a young couple like you.' He looked at Molly's wedding ring, and frowned, as if he suspected misdemeanour.

'We're not married,' Molly muttered. 'Not to each other. We are brother and sister-in-law.'

'Nor do we make a habit of pub-crawling together.'

'I'm sure. I'm sure.'

'Henry came round to see his brother, my husband. He was out, so we decided to take a walk.'

'And landed here to my delectation. My name, by the way, is Eric Owen.'

They gave him theirs in return, and he burst into a floodtide, this time about the state of Britain, economically, culturally, spiritually, intellectually. He bemoaned the loss of religion, though he was himself an atheist. The Authorized Version was dispensed with; great church music discarded. The classical languages went untaught; the treasures of the book were ignored; noise had replaced music, daubs painting. Owen seemed to speak without thought of audience, as if he lectured, in an intense whisper in the dark or to a microphone. He leaned

119

forward, disturbing his hair, eyes bulging wetly, lips as damp.

'You two understand me,' he insisted. 'You are artists. And I, wandering the streets because my brother-in-law's philistinism was driving me to distraction, came by chance on you. We decided all three, to patronize this rather unlovely place.' Owen laughed, adopted an actor's voice, an upright posture with outflung arms. ' "There's a divinity that shapes our ends/ Rough hew them how we will." '

He offered further drinks; they refused. Molly sat bemused, twitching , touching not emptying her glass.

'I will tell you,' Owen continued, 'how I see myself.' Back to the lowered voice and head. 'I sit here at this table in this room, surrounded , protected from the elements by Victorian brickwork. Walk outside, we come on houses by the dozen, hundred, thousand, each with its square of garden with multifarious plants, shrubs, trees, insects, creatures, leaves shaken by the wind. All this is part of a great stretching conurbation, little townships joined into a sprawl, a congeries, an aggregation of living-, working-, recreational-spaces, inhabited by such as I, and beyond that the fields, hills, mountains and fells, the rivers, the tracts of moor until we reach the next city with its factories and stir. And on again until we reach coast and spa and sea and ocean and new languages and climates.'

Owen paused. Fairfax would have thought the man drunk, except that his pint pot stood unhandled, mere ornament.

'And that's this earth. The dot over an "i" in a huge library. Beyond are immensities that stagger imagination. Icy silences crossed by light, untouched, huge nothings, limitless icebergs of emptiness.' He shook his head, either at the oddness of his last metaphor or the inadequacies of language. 'That places me. And yet it is my boast that the human mind, not mine, but that of the mathematical scientist, has imagined and measured and described these billions upon billions of acres of cold space. A few ounces of grey living matter have grasped conceptions fit only for gods.'

120

Owen looked his class over, estimating his success.

'There must be other earths, surely,' Henry Fairfax did his best, 'in a universe so immense, with their own living creatures?'

'I can speak only at second hand, but I believe there are scientists of great repute who hold it is not so. Earth, they say, is unique. Think of that.' Owen suddenly laughed, slapping his knee. 'Mark you, your point was often put in my boyhood in the better pulpits of chapels in Abersychan and Newport. "When we are able to travel and comb the universe we shall come upon other worlds and find out for ourselves how God's grace has manifested itself there as here in its immensity. I do not know whether Christ will have been crucified in some distant corner of the universe, or whether atonement was not found necessary with these alien races, but what my faith tells me is that God's love will be eternally established there, answering need, as with us." ' Owen's voice had, without raising itself unduly, taken on a new power, pulpit rant, Welsh. It attracted attention elsewhere; one or two looked round and the landlord, appearing, leaned on the bar. The speaker raised his glass to his lips, but when he returned it there was no noticeable alteration of the level.

He stretched his wrinkled neck.

'That is how I see man. And,' he now turned princely to Molly, spreading his shoulders, 'let us consider works of art. The small piece of exquisitely shaped jewellery on your work bench now takes its position inside the vast complexities that make up the vacuum of space. Does not this add to its value? It is as if all that is precious is confined, reduced, compressed into this beautiful small-ness, this tiny extravagance of art. Outside whirls the great unknowingness of dumb distance and uncompre-hended time scales, a universe expanding, each constituent part on the run from each other, and there under your eye, the work of your hands, a small attempt at perfection, drawing its power from its compact nature. You think that I exaggerate. Perhaps I do, but these are mysteries which have baffled me through my life.'

Owen wiped his mouth.

'I have no artistic talent myself, except perhaps a small gift for stitching words together. In another era I might have graced a pulpit, but I lack faith in the supernatural. I have preached art, after my fashion, about the world and it is my boast that I have not wasted my life. Books, exhibitions, lectures have flowered for students because I have instigated the first moves. These are matters of joy for me now sitting at the hearth of my uncultivated brother-in-law.'

Molly made signs that she had had enough; she did this openly since Owen's eyes were tight shut as he raked the air with his right hand. His nails were not altogether clean. The voice rolled on. The influence of death on great art occupied rising and falling sentences.

'I'm afraid,' Fairfax interrupted, loudly.

Owen opened his eyes. Henry tapped his watch, rudely.

'I'm afraid we shall have to be on our way.'

Owen looked offended, and sheepish.

'Ah, yes. Time is short, especially for me. It will not be long before the last mystery . . .' He was away again. They both stood, and that opened his eyes. 'Thank you for listening to me. I hope we meet again.'

It took a further six lengthy sentences before they wriggled into position to make for the door.

'My thanks, my thanks.' He shook their hands, eyes brimming. His last words sank to a penetrating whisper. 'May you find love together.'

Outside, Fairfax grinned as he fastened the last button.

'I thought we'd never escape.'

'I'm light-headed,' Molly admitted.

'On three gins? Or Cymric eloquence?'

They set off at a good pace, arm in arm, pleased to be moving and in silence.

'He's odd,' Fairfax began. 'And lonely. He hasn't come to terms with retirement.'

'A homosexual, don't you think?' Molly, primly.

'I've no idea.'

'I'm sure. Absolutely certain.'

'That means no home life?' he asked.

'Neither have I. Nor you, for that matter.' She spoke

cheerfully. 'There was something in what he said. About man's place in the universe. Don't you think so?'

'It's easy to give an impression of profundity when you spout on about the icy silences between the stars. I don't know whether it meant anything or not. Besides, he thought we were lovers.'

'I liked that.'

'There speaks the gin.'

Molly talked easily, exploring Owen's ideas all the way home.

'Just come in and see Jim if he's back. It's not ten yet.'

She let them in, examined the coat pegs in the hall, called loudly for her husband.

'No. He's not here.'

'Is he usually late?'

'Not really. You can't tell. I've no idea where they go. Let me make you a cup of coffee.' The house smelt damp, inhospitable.

'No thanks. I have to walk back.'

'I'll drive you.'

'No need, thanks. But I must be up with the lark.'

'Thanks, Henry. I really enjoyed myself with you.'

'I can take no credit for Brother Owen and his *hwyl*.'

Molly accompanied him to the door where she kissed him full on the mouth.

'You're so like Jim in so many ways, and yet so different.'

'Don't get us mixed up.'

She kissed him again, hugging him close.

123

XI

Jim phoned, as expected, and called in the next day.

He listened to his brother's report, grumbled that he understood Laura's reasons for delay, but wished she would exert herself. If she didn't get a move on, he wouldn't be able to start in the summer. He spoke reasonably, sitting back in his chair with legs crossed. His denim suit gave him the look of youth; he might easily be taken for one of his own sixth-formers. The visit did not last long; he asked pertinent questions, then leaped up. On the way to the door he said:

'Thanks for taking Moll out the other night. She enjoyed it.'

'We met this Welsh wizard in the Duke of Cambridge.'

'So she tells me. I don't treat her properly. I know that. But I can't seem to act otherwise. She can't do anything right for me these days.'

'Is that your fault, or hers?'

'Mine. Though she doesn't go out of her way to please me. But that's my fault too, I expect. Still, she enjoyed your company. It must be pretty lonely working away on her own, and only Martin Fowler and his cronies to interrupt. And a right bunch of homosexual creeps they are.'

'She thought Owen was a homosexual, the pub orator.'

'She should know. She has enough to do with them.' He stared from the path at a trimmed bush. 'What's that then?'

'A dwarf lilac.'

'Thanks, anyway, Hen. I'm not fair to either of them, Moll, or Christina.' He spoke as if he wished to go on, to confess. Henry waited. Jim touched the bush, tapping time and again, in expectation.

'Why don't you do something about it?' Henry asked in the end.

'I don't know what to do. I'm hog-tied. Inside myself. This London job might sort it out for me.' He pursed his lips comically, as if it were unimportant. 'So long.' He raised a stiff hand. 'Thanks for your efforts.'

Henry was surprised to receive a letter from Laura saying she was visiting Beechnall on Friday next, and asking if it was possible to stay with him until Sunday night. She was sorry about the shortness of the notice; he was to say frankly if the visit was inconvenient. Why she had not phoned he could not understand, but he sent off an immediate reply. 'Come, and welcome. With love.' He received a postcard, Wilson Steer's 'Walberswick, Children Paddling, 1894', Fitzwilliam Museum, Cambridge, on the Friday itself: 'Expect me about 10 p.m. Perhaps later. Oh, work!'

She arrived at 9.50 p.m., out of breath, fazed. She kissed him untidily.

'Are you hungry?' He had stocked his fridge.

'No. Give me a big scotch, please.'

Laura banged down in a chair, by her case. The whisky opened her lips. She had, it appeared, spent a good part of the afternoon and all the evening trying to persuade some local Scrooge that it paid to advertise. She had convinced him, in the end, and they had drawn up an agreement.

'And what's his trouble?'

'He's in computer programmes, and he's expecting to be taken over. The sooner the better, I guess. But if I can increase his trade, his pride and his status will rise. But that will take time. Is it worth it? Will he just shell money out on me and my fancy schemes, so that when the big boys buy him out he'll only get what he would have done without me in the first place because my stuff hasn't had time to work? This man, Gordon Boyfield, even suggested, rubbing his bald head, that I might make him too expensive for them to buy.'

'A shrewd operator?'

'A frightened little shopkeeper. He has some first-rate technical ideas, as far as I can judge, and hasn't done too badly, but he suffers from this puritan hang-up that if you have a good product you can of necessity sell it. You can't. People have to know about it. Then, even when it's taken off, you often need to give it another push. It seems wrong to poor old Boyfield. "Good wine needs no bush," he kept saying.'

'But you convinced him, in the end?'

'Yes. I shall have to go in again first thing in the morning. I'm sorry about that, but . . .'

She had a second large scotch, but sat fidgeting, unable to cover her weariness. That morning, she had started in her office at seven thirty, done five hours' work before she set off north, had found the motorway full of idiots, the meal uneatable, but had arrived at three on time for her appointment. They had talked until seven when they went out to an excellent Chinese restaurant in the next street and had then drawn up a contract in the office. Boyfield was 'going to sleep on this' and they'd met at nine thirty to come to agreement.

'The trouble with him is,' Laura said, 'that he's interested only in his bit of the field, where he is very good, I'll admit. But he's like you, he doesn't believe he needs my sort of help in selling his product.'

'So tomorrow morning, he's quite likely to back down.'

'That's it. Go on. Cheer me up.' Her voice wanted humour; he had never seen her as lacklustre. There had been at least two periods during their marriage when she had been under treatment for depression, but now she seemed physically shattered.

'Where did you come across this concern?'

'He was recommended to us, by a client of mine. That's why it was done in such a hurry. We've no end of work, but I can't afford to turn jobs away. Or that's how it seems to me.'

'So a hot bath and bed is what you need now.'

'That would be heaven.'

He looked into her room at eleven o'clock and she did not stir from sleep. At eight thirty she was up and about, in a different, impressive outfit and, he frowned, a new hairstyle. She spoke cheerfully over breakfast, both ate little, and said she had no idea when she'd be back, but

126

hoped it would be for lunch. Henry decided he'd do an hour's tidying in his own office to pass the time, though he'd cleared the way for a morning off. Outside the sun flashed in and out of clumps of white cloud. Wind livened blossom; people stepped brightly, swung shopping bags; cats slept on walls.

At twenty to twelve, he had been in only ten minutes, Laura arrived.

'Success?' he asked.

'Suc-bloody-cess,' she answered.

'What's that mean?'

'I've got my contract. Not quite as I wanted. Hardly worth the time I've spent on it, but it may lead to other things when he's been taken over.'

'You don't feel too bad about it?'

'Since you ask me, no. No, I don't.'

They drank leisurely sherry after he'd booked lunch at the Squire's. They travelled by taxi when she had indulged in another bath, a further change of clothes. Her case had not seemed very large. She complimented him on his appearance, comparing him with his unsmart, married self.

'Neat, but not gaudy.'

In the taxi she sat well away from him. Her perfume was over-strong, heady, he thought. She glued her eyes to her window, on the look-out. They enjoyed the meal, taking their time though the restaurant was crowded. The excellent service in the side annexe where they were placed pleased them. They drank sweet white wine with their beef and Yorkshire pudding; no one raised an eyebrow. The syllabub was delicious, the coffee passable.

'What's the drill?' he asked. One of his father's questions.

'Drill? Oh. We'll walk for about an hour.'

'Aren't you tired?'

'Oh, yes. But I'll come back to life. I make good use of my leisure. Sunday afternoon and evening's all I usually have.'

'You're not overdoing it?'

127

'Of course. What on earth do you expect? New businesses don't start themselves.'

They laughed; she held his arm as they stood among the shifting groups of people crowding at each pedestrian crossing. The world seemed a lively, multicoloured jostling place, full of talking heads, brilliant trunks, advancing limbs, fine hair. He drew Laura's attention to a young woman who was wearing a bachelor of arts gown partly covered by bright scarves and a scarlet cummerbund.

'What a mess,' Laura answered.

Down in the great square before the Council House, the pavements were packed, so that from time to time one came to a standstill. The fountains glistened white, rather ugly, without elegance in the sunshine, like lumps of misshapen peppermint. Pedestrians in a hurry carted carriers and large parcels; others lounged. Children watched the pigeons; winos occupied benches and offered a slow-motion, hairy entertainment, drinking, writhing, exchanging obscure obscenity. Flags fluttered from the high walls of shops; plate-glass windows offered rich fare.

'I love this place,' Laura told him, rather loudly over a din of humming voices and traffic. 'I was only too glad to leave it, but now it seems so peaceful and easygoing compared with London.'

Fairfax watched a father pick up and brush down his daughter who had fallen, a near impossibility in this press, and who now shrilly squealed her hurt.

'How's the Housman project?' Laura, after a five-yard burst of progress.

'I've dropped it.'

'Why's that?'

'It was like the Lenten lily. It died on Easter Day.'

'What do you mean?'

He did not repeat his answer. Once was enough. He explained in short, scattered gasps why he saw nothing in it for him. Laura did not appear to listen, breasting the crowd.

'I hadn't really the energy to take it up. Before you

128

begin you have to believe that the project has possibilities. I wasn't convinced.'

'What about real professionals? People whose living depends on it?'

'What about them?'

'They can't afford such delicate susceptibilities, can they?'

'Don't know. I regard myself as an amateur.'

'And is that wise?'

'My sort of writing depends on looking at life as it is.'

It was difficult to carry on such a conversation in this crowd. They stood by a children's roundabout, watching delighted and frightened pale faces wobble past. Laura seemed to be frowning after something hidden beyond or beneath these small, garish boats, cars, animals, steam engines. Perhaps juvenile Boyfields reproached her from their wooden seats.

'What's next?' he asked.

'Let's go down to the river.'

They crossed to the taxi rank. A Pakistani driver told them the football crowds were rampaging.

'Is there trouble?' Fairfax asked. The man shrugged.

'Not here. No. Not seriously. It is alcohol that is the pure cause.' the sing-song voice seemed unusual, somewhere at the back of the mouth, friendly but foreign, prophetic. He saluted brightly when they paid him off. 'You always find a breeze on the river.'

A cheer from the football ground split the air, followed by a second convulsion, this time a groan.

'It must be deafening inside the ground.' Laura.

'Years since I went.'

They walked in the sunshine, observed a racing four, a canopied pleasure boat, motor yachts, five grubby swans. Here the crowds were thinner, more sober, concentrating on children, dogs or pushchairs. The usual boys dashed in and out, shouting nuisances. There was little evidence of enjoyment.

They kept to the top of the embankment steps; the river flowed greyly in the sunshine, the surface divided into leaden shifting scallops.

129

'Is it fit to swim in?'

'I doubt it. Though they are beginning to clean up the waterways these days.'

After a few hundred yards, they turned back along the road to the main bridge, where they stood at a Punch and Judy show. The audience sitting on the grass shrieked; adults grinned broadly. Again Laura stood locked, mind obviously elsewhere. The football spectators reached vocal orgasm. Punch turned his head in mock alarm. Infants fell about.

'And now?' Fairfax asked. They had moved away from the entertainment, in silent reciprocity.

'We'll walk back into town.' Laura knew her mind. They crossed, with difficulty, the new wide roads brisk now with cars. She expressed her pleasure, as they stopped outside a church to read the foundation stones, or peered into shop windows. 'I feel relaxed altogether in this place. It's fit to breathe in.'

'As London isn't?'

'Don't get me wrong. I wouldn't live anywhere else than London from choice. That's where the action is. I don't want your Cotswold stone or your Lake District. But there's a stir here that I like which doesn't drive one mad. But . . .'

'It's second division?'

'Oh, yes, it's that all right. Did you never think of emigrating to London?'

'No. I'm a hole-and-corner provincial though I like London; it excites me.'

'But you can't do with too much excitement?'

They reached the city centre which was crowded, as multicoloured as before. Courting couples kept trysts on the Council House steps; young women, gorgeously dressed, waited, clasping their handbags by the stone lions. Laura decided against tea in town; they ran for a taxi.

Back in the house she threw herself into a chair, stretching with cat-like pleasure.

'Nice, nice, nice, nice. I can relax with you,' she called out and yawned.

130

Henry trundled in tea from the kitchen.

'New china?' she mocked. 'My, we're coming up in the world.'

'Bought specially for your visit.'

'This week?'

'No. After my trip, I bought these in readiness. This is their first outing.'

'Sometimes you surprise me.'

She had taken off her shoes and sat now with her legs tucked under her. He produced fancy biscuits which she refused.

'What would you like to do this evening?' he asked.

'Nothing. Lounge about. Why, what had you in mind?'

'Theatre. We'll get in. *Pravda*, I think. Or there's a baroque concert in St Mary's?' She frowned. 'No? We could slum it in a pub.' He told her about the Welshman in the Duke of Cambridge. She laughed, sipping his Earl Grey.

'We can't go there again. That would be asking too much of providence.'

'You make suggestions?'

'I can't. I'm too tired. I'd just as soon lie about here. I do like this house. It's not so interesting as ours was, but . . .'

'Would you care to go dancing?'

'No.' Slap, hard. 'Thank you.'

'You took me in London. And we both enjoyed it.'

'Yes. We should never try to repeat a pleasure. Or not too soon. Let the memory stand.' She beamed like a politician, holding out her cup. 'I was always surprised, when we were married, that you were fond of ballroom dancing.'

'My mother taught me. She and my father attended a club, and I went with them sometimes.'

'Did Jim?'

'Not that I remember.'

'We learnt at school. A ladylike accomplishment. We danced now and again, didn't we? You were a lot better than I was, so I thought I'd give you the opportunity to shine. Not difficult.'

131

'What about Beethoven?' He returned the full cup to her.

'What about him?'

'The all-Beethoven concert at the Barbican.'

'Just luck. Could have been "Gems from the Operas".'

'But it wasn't.'

'It wasn't. We'll stay here, Henry, and if we get so bored with each other then we'll go out to the pubs and the clubs.'

'Good.'

They ate, sparingly, careful of waistlines, but talked a great deal. He asked after the mugged Mr Rhodes, who had now reappeared, seemed unaffected, always made a point of exchanging a sentence or two with her. Laura had not patronized the dancing school again, had seen John de Courcy, but not the dentists. Henry arguing with himself thought he ought not to approve of the club. 'It's no more than bingo for the well-to-do. But then, isn't doing *The Times* crossword, never mind Portfolio, a way to waste your life?'

'You're a rotten little puritan,' she laughed. 'You can't improve every minute of the shining hour. No wonder you call your writing Scrabble.'

Laura, at his insistence, put her feet up on the settee. She spoke cheerfully, but seemed preoccupied.

'Is Boyfield still nagging at you?' he asked, preparing her first scotch on the rocks.

'No.'

'You're very subdued.'

'Can't I enjoy myself as I like?' She spread her arms, luxuriating. 'No. I was just thinking that we seem to suit each other so, oh, well admirably. Now. Don't you think so?'

'Yes. I enjoy your company.'

'That sounds grudging.'

'It's not meant to be. I can't think of anywhere else I'd rather be at this minute.'

'And yet we rowed and fought. At the end of our time together I could barely tolerate the sight of you. You were more interested in your work than in me; you were always holier-than-thou. And when I wanted you to sit down and talk, oh, about anything at all you'd slink off to your typewriter. I hated you, it, every damned thing. And yet here I perch, as my father would say, "like Lady Muck", the fat cat that has got at the cream, and I don't need to touch my whisky. I can take it or leave it.'

'Economical for me.'

'I can even put up with your feeble jokes.' Her voice hardened. 'Why is it? We can't have changed all that much.'

'We can put up with each other for a few hours on the occasional weekend, but not twenty-four hours a day.'

'Do you mean that?'

'I don't know.' Henry massaged his chin. 'I don't even know if it bears thinking about. Certainly at the end of our marriage I was,' he waited, 'lacerated. But now I feel contented. It's as though those quarrels and sessions with the lawyers never happened. I don't want to think about them; they were ugly and unpleasant, but now they seem unreal, happening to two quite different people. Perhaps they did.'

'Do you wish we were still married?' Laura pressed him, her glass still untouched, her hands still now, on her lap.

'In a sense we seem to be so.'

'Isn't that a miracle? Considering what we felt two or three years back?'

He shook his head, not certain of himself.

'You don't want to talk about it, do you?' she asked. 'It's embarrassing.'

'That's the wrong word. Three years ago it was killing me. I despaired. I was angry and bitter. I couldn't put it into words. These frustrations burnt, scalded my whole life. I hated coming home.'

'Go on,' she spoke flatly. 'Get it out of your system.'

'Spit it up in poppa's hand?' He cringed, recovered. 'No. You served meals in a grudging way so I didn't want to eat them. You vetoed any suggestions I made, about going out, holidays, decorating the house. I couldn't do right. Or so it seemed. Sex was more like a battle. You wouldn't look at me. I was ruined, emotionally. And it all started so quickly out of the blue. With a row over a bill for your car.'

'I've forgotten. Really. What . . . ?'

'You thought they hadn't done the job properly. I was in no position to judge. And you said I didn't support you. We had a hell of a set-to. My line was how could you expect me to go down there and accuse the garage of inefficiency or overcharging when I knew nothing about it. You said that was typical. Any difficulty I left to you. It all came up out of the clear sky one breakfast time. knocked me flat. You were so furious. And unreasonable. You stormed.'

'Do you know I can barely remember anything about it?'

'You ran upstairs shouting and crying, banging every door you could.'

'And you?

'I was taken aback. I didn't expect this. I ought to have gone after you, but I didn't. I was busy that day. I just gobbled my cornflakes and went off.'

'And?'

'Things seemed much as ever when I came home. You'd cooked the meal. I came back on time though I could have done with an extra hour. You didn't seem too bad. You'd settled your difficulties with the garage, it appeared. But from that time on nothing was the same. You'd fly off the handle at the slightest difference of opinion.'

'Whose fault was it?' Without stress.

'Now that's what baffles me when I think about it. I wonder whether most of it was in my mind. That I misinterpreted everything? That I was too suspicious?'

'Do you think about it often? Now, I mean?'

'Not so much as I did while it was going on and then immediately after the divorce. But, yes, I do. Sometimes. A bit more recently since we've been so friendly. Do you never . . . ?'

'Not really.' She offered no further gloss.

They sat quietly. She patted the sofa by her side; he

moved to her. Laura put her arms round him, laid her head on his shoulder.

'Three years ago that would have been a burst-up,' she said, soothing him. They made love, went out about ten to the nearest pub, watched dominoes till closing time, staggered home.

XII

They did not wake early on Sunday, but by nine-thirty were drinking tea together in bed.

'How do you manage to look so, so composed after a night's sleep?' he asked.

'Your company.'

Henry insisted that he brought breakfast upstairs, and she excelled herself, recalling that this was how they had acted in the first months of their marriage. She spent at least an hour in the bathroom before they took a turn in the park. Lilac blooms hung thickly in the sunshine; ducks queued and squabbled for the children's bread.

'I've never been here before.'

'The corporation has spent time and money on it these last two years.'

'How often do you come?'

'Never. But I haven't somebody like you to parade in my spare time.'

'You're giving the neighbours a treat?' She stroked his arm.

On their return they ate potatoes baked in their skins, cheeses, salad, mayonnaise knocked up by him, pickles; they broached hock. He washed the dishes; she took to languour on the settee.

'I'm enjoying this,' she shouted. 'I don't want to go back.' He opened another bottle.

'Do you ever consider,' she asked, 'giving up your job with Le Jeune's, and concentrating on your plays?'

'No.'

'Come on, now. It needs more than a one-word answer. Let's suppose Conrad gave you the chance of a big redundancy pay-off. Would you welcome it?'

He dropped his chin on to his chest, weirdly wounded. Was that the reason for her visit? Had Conrad sent her down to break it to him gently that his time with Le

Jeune's was up? Suspicion choked him. He could barely speak, coughed drily. Laura lay smiling, clean and at ease, on top of the world. Before he tried to answer, he cleared his throat.

'Is that what you've come to tell me?' he managed.

'Is what?' She spoke as if the conversation were only half serious and her mind elsewhere.

'That Le Jeune's is going to lay me off?'

Her face jerked with fright, eyes widened. There followed the pretty frown, and the smoothing of the face, the half smile, the bland eyes.

'Why do you say that?'

'I wondered,' Henry began slowly, a fool already in his own eyes, 'if Conrad had said something to you. About the firm here. We had the assessors down.' His voice trailed away.

'Weren't they satisfied?'

'As far as I know. And since then we've got this Quentin-Leach contract . . . But you know all about that. It wasn't satisfaction they were concerned with, but reorganization. Has Conrad, or have his advisers, decided that there's no place for me in an enlarged E. Midlands Le Jeune's?'

'Why should they decide that?'

Question and tone hurt. She had no notion, toying with her wine, of the damage she had done. She smiled encouragingly, schoolma'am to struggling pupil.

'I've no idea how or why these people come to these decisions. Nor why they are placed in the position to make recommendations. Their experience is limited, or at least their experience of responsibility. There was one young woman, not as old as you. What were her qualifications to lay down the law?'

'Don't tell me you're anti-feminist?' Laura looked pleased.

'She was a young woman, who on that account, could not have worked at any level at our sort of business. So how could she . . . ?'

'Were her ideas sensible?'

'Insofar as she discussed them with me. God knows what she put down in her written report.'

'She was a hypocrite, you think?'

'I don't say that. How can I? All I'm telling you is that these people come in, spend a few days asking questions, and then make a report. And I've no idea what they'll propose.'

'They talked to you, did they?'

'Yes. And to everybody else. I'm not saying they were aggressive. Or unpleasant. Or suggested that I was inefficient. And away they go. I'm suspicious, Laura.'

'You are that.'

The three words fell like stones in still water. She shrugged herself upright, making the effort. Now she smoothed her frock over her thighs before she began.

'Henry,' she said, and stopped. 'You can take my word for it that I know of no plans whatsoever to sack you, downgrade you or anything else. As far as I know, Conrad is very satisfied with your work, as he should be. Knowing him, if he'd any ideas of getting rid of you, he'd tell you himself, not send his little sister, one, because he knows his mind, and can fight his corner, against you or anybody else, and two, because he likes you, admires you. I see I've got you into such a state that you're wondering if I'm lying.' She half closed her eyes. 'I asked my question, because I want to know how you consider yourself as a writer, not because I've inside information about the demise of your job.' Laura looked uncomfortable now, disturbed. 'I'm sorry I asked. It's spoiled your afternoon. I can see that. You're angry.'

Outside the brightness had increased; sun caught the wind-shaken leaves; shadows lay black, substantial; windows flaunted their gold.

She was right, but he had not expected her to see it. She pulled his head to her breasts, stroked him, murmured over him. He found no comfort; he no longer trusted Laura. They drank another cup of tea. Both sat or moved quietly; conversation was difficult.

'Is Jim in on a Sunday afternoon?' she asked, suddenly.

'I've no idea.'

'Would you ring to see if it's possible to go round?'

Henry telephoned. Jim and Molly were both at home. They could be visited.

Laura next asked permission to use his phone and spent half an hour on four separate calls. He tried not to listen, and, failing, found her conversation indistinct and, though quick-fire, uninteresting.

'That's that,' she said, dusting her hands. 'Now for Brother James.'

He had to wait again while she repaired her appearance. They went in her car. Jim and Molly were in Sunday best, indoors in spite of sunshine. They made small talk; Laura, very lively, quite unlike the woman of an hour earlier, hit it off with Molly. They refused offered drink, walked round the sunlit garden. Molly, good on flowers, explained that she drew inspiration for her work from blossom and foliage. 'Of course, I need to translate it.' The women walked in front, intent on words, laughing out loud, touching each other. Jim hung back with his brother, tense-lipped, laconic.

'What does she want?' Jim asked. The women had turned a corner, made for the house.

'A weekend visit. And business trip.'

'Has she said anything about this job?'

'No.' Henry felt his own soreness.

'I'll bloody ask her.'

'Do.'

Back in the lounge which seemed plain and dark after the brightness of the garden, they arranged themselves in front of a humming gas fire. Again the ritual of offering and refusing drinks.

'Are you still keen to join me?' Laura, turning on Jim, after a tense three or four minutes on the planting of spring bulbs. She spoke sharply, cutting through social niceties, making certain that all knew the importance of the question.

'Yes.' Jim answered, and his smile was charming. Henry remembered the boy's receiving school prizes from the hands of the distinguished visitor's lady wife with the same modest delight. 'If you still want me.'

139

'That was never in question. If you hand in your resignation now when can you start?'

'End of July, beginning of August.'

'Do that, then.'

Jim thanked her; Molly looked at the carpet; Laura sat queenly; Henry wondered whether the decision had just been made here in this room. If not, why had Laura not told him? Jim leaped up, opened the drinks cupboard. They formally toasted the agreement, still seated. Laura briefly outlined their initial tasks together. Molly invited them to tea, but Laura refused, saying she had a bushel of work waiting for her in London, and that she'd like another hour or two with her ex-husband before she started next week's work later this evening.

'That's made someone's day,' Henry said, out in the car.

'Not yours?'

'I'm glad you've taken Jim on. Did you just make your mind up today?'

'No. I've known all along. But I'd put back the announcement from week to week, in case some snag emerged. None did. I can use him. Now, really.'

'Molly seemed delighted.'

'Yes. She's a simple sort, isn't she? No frills. No airs and graces. The sort of wife he needs. She doesn't give the appearance of being artistic? Temperamental?'

'She'd scrubbed her fingers up today, I noticed.'

If Laura had made her announcement to comfort Henry she succeeded. He felt energetic; the burden of proposed redundancy slipped away. They kissed and touched like young lovers, blatantly enjoying their openness, all freedom from restraint. He drew the curtains, Laura stripped in seconds, but neatly; they groaned together, thrashed, bit, dug with the nails, shouted wild pleasure, lay sated. After quiet she sent him out to make tea.

'You've not lost your touch,' she said when he returned. He comically wore the striped shirt he had pulled over his head, God knows why, when he went out. Naked still she had resumed her ease on the settee.

'I don't want to be too late,' she murmured, stroking his hair.

'How long will it take you?'

'All of three hours. But if I'm home by midnight that'll do.'

'You won't start work then?'

'I shan't work then. Goodness, I feel relaxed.'

Later, on her third cup of tea, she said, darting obliquely at the subject for they had been discussing without heat, anecdotally, whether serious theatre existed in London:

'Would it be a good idea if we married again?'

Henry started, taken aback. Briefly he wondered whether she had actually posed the question.

'Well,' he began, slowly. 'Well, now . . .'

'You're a stick in the mud.' She laughed, massaging her firm whiteness of thigh. 'You needn't say any more. You've given me your answer.'

'I have . . .'

'Have what?'

'Never been proposed to by a naked woman.' She punched him jovially. 'Do you mean it, Laura?'

'If I do, what then?'

'I'll think seriously about it.' He held up his hand. 'Hush, now, you. Give me a minute and I'll tell you what I think. After I've found out. You've shaken me. You really have.'

'That's twice, then.'

They sat in silence, she examining the perfection of her right knee, he with his back to her.

'I couldn't answer that today,' he said, finally.

'Why not?'

'It's too serious and surprising.'

'Do you mean it had never crossed your mind? Either in London or here?'

'No. I can say that.' Each word dropped slow and soft and separate. 'I didn't think you'd want it.'

Laura folded her arms across her breasts. She gnawed at her lower lip. Now she began to stroke her upper arms.

'I see.'

141

'Hold on,' Henry warned, in exhilaration. 'Hang about. Just give me a minute. Let me find out what it is I want to say.' He rubbed his cheek hard, knowing that until he began to speak he would not know what that was. 'Here, and when I was with you in London, I felt towards you as I never thought I would. You excited me. I don't mean the sex, though that was marvellous, and must be, be connected. I am in love with you. Yes. Again. No, let me try to get it straight. I felt so drawn to you, and so benignant, if that's the word, that I wanted to do something for you, work some miracle, make you happy. I couldn't believe it.'

She nodded, gently.

'I couldn't believe it. I still can't. We'd been married for nine years, and parted in a blood-bath. Do you understand me?'

'Henry,' she said, voice limpid. 'Why didn't you write and tell me? You were always better at putting it on paper than saying it.'

'I didn't believe it. It didn't seem possible.'

'Why not?'

'The way we fought. The bitterness. That happened. I can remember it. I shan't ever be able to forget it. And now this. Human beings are prone to self-deception. You excited me. And . . . And . . . But marriage. I had to tell myself that we can love for a few days and that's the limit.'

'Perhaps that's the sort of marriage we need. One hundred and twenty miles apart, and meeting twice a month.'

Now he nodded, not in agreement, merely acknowledging that he had understood the intention.

'Let me ask you a question,' he said.

'Go on.'

'What would be the point of our marrying again?'

Laura dropped her eyes. Even the bright body seemed mournful.

'What I mean is,' he continued, 'if we're not going to live together. It can't be financial. Is it the legality of it? The relationship between us is there. We can intensify it, or the opposite, if we so wish. You haven't told me what it is you want.'

'I'll give it you in one word.'

'What's that?'

'Commitment.' Laura examined his troubled expression. 'If we remarry we make a public statement of our commitment.'

'And that's important?' he queried, for she had surprised him again.

'To me. If I married you I'd take bloody good care that I made it stick the second time round. You're not the only one to remember how we finished up. I can barely believe now that we acted so rottenly to each other. But we did. I was probably worse than you. So it would be a public act of reparation. Done in a hair shirt.' She looked down on her nakedness and giggled. 'Is there any more tea in the pot?'

He served her.

'I'm going to get dressed. I don't think so well like this.' Laura bent, picked up and straightened her brassière, slipped it on with speed, fastened it. When she had resumed her clothes, she walked over, barefoot still, to scrutinize her face in a mirror, presenting him with her back. She pushed and patted her hair, dabbed her cheeks with the ends of her fingers. The silence oppressed him; he accused himself of falling short. She breathed in, heavily, returned to the settee and her position, smilingly picked up her tea cup.

'Will you think about, it, Henry? Please.' Winsome.

'Yes. You caught me on the hop. But I love you.'

'Thank you. You're a marvellous man in your way. A bit of an old fogey. And suspicious of change. But unutterably, ineffably nice.'

' "Eff and ineffable," ' he quoted.

'I'm not sure I know what it means. There's just one more thing, Henry, and then we'll discuss it no more. Or at least not today.' He waited for her now. 'There's no question of children at present, if that's what you're thinking is behind all this. In the hectic state of my affairs there's absolutely no chance of starting a family. You

143

must realize that. I'm not so sure that I ever shall want children. Even if I'm capable. But if anything comes of this, you'll have to do it for my beaux yeux. Don't look so glum now. The world's not coming to an end. You've just received a further proposition, proposal to consider, when the lorries and coaches and your plays and the pretty ladies in your office have palled. Don't be bored. Reconsider marriage. Now come and give me a kiss, and then pass me my handbag so I can make myself fit to be seen. There's no need to say anything.' She took his kiss, coolly, on the lips. 'Not a word.'

She extracted a small looking glass, and again examined her features. Laura put her feet gingerly to the floor, reshod herself and standing by his mirror dragged the comb through her hair as if she had a grudge against it. Henry removed the tea things to the kitchen, where he washed up.

'It's been a marvellous weekend,' he said, returning. Laura sat by the window, looking out on yard and garden.

'Not long enough.'

'It made up in quality what it lacked in quantity.'

'Oh, Henry Fairfax.'

They laughed together at his awkwardness.

'And don't forget to think about my proposition, will you?'

'I can give you the answer now.'

'I don't want it, thank you. I need to work on it myself. To mull it over.' She laughed again. 'To find out what I think when I'm away from you.'

'Does that make a difference?'

'You're angling for compliments, young man. But, yes. It does. I shan't tell you how much.' She faced him exactly. 'This has surprised me as much as it has you. I thought it wasn't too sensible when I invited you over. I enjoyed the visit, at the time, ballroom dance and all, but no more than that. Since then . . .' She flung her hands forward. 'In between all the rush and hustle and scares and long hours I kept thinking to myself, "I'm happy. Because of Henry Fairfax." It seemed utterly unlikely, but there it was. Now we'll leave it. I don't want it to go

144

any further just at present. You know how I feel. Like a schoolgirl. But we'll leave it. It might change. We don't know. Anything.'

They sat together for an hour before she packed her bag and left him. She would be home soon after midnight. He imagined the house, the letters in her box, cars parked, the street leaves in artificial light, the stillness behind closed doors. He could barely sit down; walked with violence about his rooms, unable to contain his excitement, a man above himself, ready for the Monday which had already come.

XIII

Laura and Henry exchanged letters, hers short, factual, loving, his excitable, at four or five times the length, each everyday occurrence an occasion for extravagances, hyperbole, word play. His work at Le Jeune's occupied long hours which he enjoyed while his second-in-command was taking an annual holiday. Henry outstripped himself in every way. He spent the whole of the Sunday a week after Laura's departure starting on a play about murder: in it two prim, well-brought-up girls killed their father because of his treatment of their dead mother. He'd read the story somewhere, in a newspaper, had made a note, months back, and deliberated over it, without conclusion, and had started dialogue without a plan of the whole, an unusual procedure for him.

He began to write at nine in the morning, with none of the procrastination, research, hestitation, self-deception, lethargy, inertia that accompanied by custom the beginning of a new work. Down went the first words; his typewriter did not hinder him. At eleven he took ten minutes off for coffee, stopped at twelve fifteen to warm up the casserole, was back at his desk by one o'clock. Neither radio nor television hindered his progress. Excitement mounted. He cut himself a sandwich at four, made a huge pot of tea. Soon after six he dashed out for a short walk, but was back for seven, and drove on until nine, a man lifted out of himself.

When he had collected the pile of typescript he straightened it, but made no attempt to read what he had written. Now he was fagged out, so that his arms seemed to have shrunk inside the sleeves of his pullover. He stumbled downstairs, lassitude combining with an unusual sense of achievement. None of his bits and pieces this time. He'd written, composed, created something out of nothing for ten hours on end. It had not happened before. Two hours left him exhausted in the ordinary way. He stood at the bottom of the stairs, one hand on the wall, in a histrionic pose, Cincinnatus called from the plough, King Charles at the scaffold. 'Hurt not the axe.'

He made for the kitchen, brewed coffee, poured a large whisky. He tried to recall what he had written, but his mind reeled, excitable, untamed. The quality of his work remained an enigma; he was in no position to judge. He'd gone at it like a giant, hacked down a forest, flattened a town. Groaning he sank to a chair, scalded his lips on the coffee. He did not understand himself. He'd been granted a boon. 'All that was a trust,' the poet had said. He'd been tumbled into an acceleration of industry that had left him dazzled. Inspiration? He laughed at the word, level with it, its master, its purveyor, its handler. Fairfax stood, staggering.

He would ring Laura.

Abandoning whisky and coffee he dialled Laura's number. No one at home. Disappointed he listened to the signal disturbing the air in her flat. Mr Rhodes, library book open, could hear it faintly, but Laura was not there. He was surprised she had no answerphone. Letting it ring on, he stood breathing deeply. If only he could have told her how changed he had been. He replaced the instrument, straightening it in its lightweight cradle. It did not do to boast; perhaps he had not done well. He could barely believe that.

When on Monday he'd re-read the typescript he was not discouraged, and spent an hour or two each evening writing at speed. No letters or calls from Laura pleased and distracted; he received a card on Saturday from Paris. She had not mentioned the trip when she visited him or in her notes; sudden swoops of extra-curricular activity seemed part and parcel of her life. He felt both envious and over-awed at her style. Laura, the person, he could manage; Laura Le Jeune, the executive, outsoared, scared him.

Henry rang his brother who was out. Molly said that her husband had received a formal written offer from Laura and had submitted his resignation at school. She did not seem pleased, though she expressed satisfaction. Yes, she was extremely busy with a large order that would occupy her wholly for a month, if not two. It would be boring before it was over, but had a certain technical interest now, if he understood her, and would make her some money, give her time, if she weren't too tired, to sketch out some new ideas. The snag was that, if she did it properly, as she would, the order would be immediately repeated.

'You could do with a technician to help you?' he asked.

'I could not. How would you like a hack to knock out bits of your plays for you? I'm not into factory intensive methods yet.'

'But couldn't you come up with designs that a modified assembly line could produce?'

'Modified.' She scoffed, then stopped, gulping. 'I have, in fact, submitted just such designs to a West German firm. They're considering them.'

'And you'd receive a small payment, I take it, on everything they sold?'

'We haven't got as far as that, but yes, I suppose I should.'

Molly sounded sullen, indifferent, confessing to disheartenment. She would tell Jim, get him to ring when he returned. He never did. A week later Henry saw him walking the street with a fair girl, both in green track suits, striding out, elbows proud. He stopped his car to allow them to pass him again, but they recognized neither him nor his vehicle.

Henry made good but not extraordinary progress with his play. If he'd had nothing else to do, he considered, he'd have completed the first draft inside a week. He worked hard to differentiate between the girls, making one dominant, then the other. There was a year's difference only between them, and from what he remembered, or had imagined in the meantime, neither was the leader. Parts together were greater than the whole. Two girls, both affronted by the bullying treatment of an obsequious mother, would separately have come to terms with the trauma, kept quiet about it. Together they had become

148

lethal, and the father had ended his respectable and worthless life at the bottom of the cellar steps, head stove in. Henry wrote in anger, beside himself, amazed at his own capacity to understand or underwrite evil. The girls had become monsters, but he fought to make them credible and sympathetic. The father had little time for women, but his wife had been subservient, encouraging his attitude, perhaps even drawing satisfaction from her own pain, instructing her daughters in humility. Fairfax sketched an adolescent quarrel between Fiona and Carol after their father had forbidden them to visit the theatre on a school trip to see *The Merchant of Venice*. The girls had shouted, even taken to violence not so much at the decision, they had expected that as well as resented it, but at their mother's weak role as bearer of the decree. Their father thought that the play was immoral; their mother knew that it was not, had seen it in her own youth, but had come tripping along with 'Your father and I discussed this . . . We do not want to impede your progress in literature classes . . .' Language revealed embarrassment. 'But we could not allow . . .' They had argued with their mother, who assumed the obdurate harshness of her husband, rejecting all reason, even threatening reprisals, stoppage of pocket money, so that the two had flung out to the bottom of the garden to take their ill temper out on each other with red faces and daring swear words and blows, wrestling, tears.

Fairfax hated the heat within himself, but knew he must convince. Two well-brought-up middle-class girls, successful in grammar school and secretarial college, holding down positions with prospects, had murdered a pious, teetotal, well-regarded quantity surveyor. Henry must not mislead his audience, nor himself; the one wild but long-planned action must seem credible, inevitable. But should he approve? Ambivalences boiled and seethed. One moment he sang Sankey and Moody with the father, or refused to countenance a pet with the mother, the next he scuttled along the street with Carol to listen to pop records she was not allowed at home.

The writing darkened his day. Crotchety in the office,

149

he bawled out a subordinate in the car park, was uncharacteristically rude in a shop, ticked off a boy cycling at speed on the pavement, rebuffed a neighbour's attempt to detain him in conversation. Only in his note to Laura could he find sweetness. He did not like what he was doing, but knew it must be done. He drove himself, woke tired, wrote with fervour, thrashed himself, dredged his conscience and turned out pages of dialogue.

One evening at about ten he left his typewriter and the fifty lines that represented two hours' exertion. Too fagged to fetch the whisky bottle he filled the kettle. The phone rang. He swore, twisted the lid back on the instant-coffee jar.

'Hello.'

'Oh, Henry. It's Molly.'

He said nothing, looked at the calendar of events for May on the phone table, bit at his free thumbnail, took up the Biro by the writing pad.

'Jim told me today that he's not taking me to London with him.' Grim silence.

'Go on.'

'We'd just settled down to the evening meal, and he said, before we'd even started to eat, "Let's get this clear. You're not coming up to London to live." Just like that. Brusque and cruel. And then he began his dinner.'

'I'm sorry. Had you no hint that this was going to happen?'

'No. He was pleased when Laura's letter came. Handed it over, asked me what I thought. But then he became very quiet. In the next few days.'

'About that? Or about everything?'

'Oh, everything. Back to his usual self. He's not been very communicative for months. But I wasn't surprised. He's unsure of himself, and I thought the move might be preying on his mind.'

'Has he been out much?'

'No more than usual. He locks himself away in his room when he's at home. I don't see much of him.'

'And you? Are you busy?'

'Yes. But I've tried to be home at a reasonable hour

each night.' She drew in breath. 'I've had to work Saturday morning and Sunday.'

Fairfax thought; tired by his writing, his struggles amongst extremes of emotion and motive, he lacked sensibility. The wall, the table looked solid; he stood, swayed reed-thin in will, propping himself by thighs and fingertips. His shoulders ached.

'When he announced this, Molly, were you surprised?'

'I don't know what to say to that. I suppose that once he'd come out with it I wasn't. But I don't know. I'd been expecting to go with him, trying to get myself ready for the event. He'd go up first, and look about. That seemed sensible. I think he said Laura would fit him up with somewhere to live temporarily. And then I'd join him. I was silly perhaps even to imagine it would work out. But I did.'

'There was no mention of putting your house up for sale?'

'No. I'd continue to live here and get on with my stuff until I could look about and find somewhere to work in London. That was the story. Martin, Martin Fowler, y'know is, has some friend who's quite interested in my bits and pieces and might be able to find me a corner somewhere to dabble. I think Martin would be glad to get rid of me now. I'm a liability to everybody.'

'And Christina Brown?'

'Nothing. Just that I'm not to have any part of his life in London.'

'Where is he now?'

'He went out about ten minutes ago. Didn't say anything. Just slipped his anorak on, and off. He'll walk round the streets.'

'Go pubbing?'

'Not usually. Just wanders about. But he might. He knows he's acting like a shit.'

Molly talked on. Jim was not without conscience, would realize the effect of his behaviour on his wife, might even feel bad about it. She rehearsed all this in a low voice without energy or conviction, dully, passing time. She recalled other crises her husband had undergone: whether

151

to report a colleague who was fiddling funds but who had three dependent children, whether to doctor evidence he was due to give about a car accident he had witnessed, whether to buy a set of Hardy novels at a low price from an old acquaintance ignorant of their value.

'He's a puritan, Henry, in some ways. Your father and mother were strict, weren't they?'

'I suppose so. Yes, they were. Sticklers for the letter of the law. But why is he acting as he is, Moll?'

'Because he can't see any other way, or can't bring himself to act otherwise. Anything between us is dead, done, over as far as he's concerned. I don't know why it is. I can't believe that I've acted badly or unsympathetically, or that I've missed something I ought to have spotted.'

'I see.'

'It's bad, Henry. He's a man of so much potential, but he'll throw it all away. He'll start off on this job like a bullet, but in a year's time it'll be rotten, with everybody cheating him.'

'Unless they make a great deal of money.'

'That'll only put it back. Or make it worse. There's no pleasing him. Ever.'

Both were silent.

'You'll have to have it out with him, Moll.'

'Have what out?'

'Finance, for a start. If he starts laying the law down, you'll have to answer in kind. Your house, now. Will you continue to live in it? He'll have a half share if you sell up. And this wrangling can make it all worse. It did in my case. I hated Laura; she'd not only left me, but wanted to get out of me all she could. I think now it was her solicitor. Oh, I don't know. But you'll have to make it clear to him that he can't just walk out on you and take what he likes when he likes.'

'I don't want to make it worse for him.'

Fairfax was surprised at the humility in her voice.

'You still love him?'

'I don't know how I could say that. After all we've been through these last months. It's been hell for me. And as

152

bad for him, I guess. It's the edge of a volcano.' He could tell now that she was crying though her voice did not break. 'I've tried to go easy with him, my God, I've tried. To put up with things. Tantrums, sulks, depressions, violence. My God, Henry.'

'Molly, let me ask you something. Suppose by some miracle he came back from his walk tonight and told you he saw how unfair he'd been, that he wanted you to go to London with him, and asked you to forgive him, what would you say? Or do?'

'He won't.'

'I know. But it's you I'm thinking about. What would you do? Would you be prepared to start again?'

'It isn't likely. When you've been through all I have, you know damn well what's possible and what isn't.'

'Answer my question, Molly.'

'I can't.' A dull, muttered misery.

'Why not? Please try to think.'

'I've been down on the floor too often, now, to get up. I'd do my best for him, if I could. I can remember Jim when I first met him. So young and pleasant and funny and marvellous. Now he's locked away from me. I can't help him. If I tried I'd only make things worse. I realize that if I went to London with him, we'd be just as bad as we are now in a few months' time, even if he made a success of his job. We've failed. Our marriage is over.'

'You've only just, this evening, realized this?'

'Yes.'

'Since you've been talking to me?'

'Oh, I don't know. What the hell does it matter when it was?'

Fairfax waited a moment.

'What I'm trying to say, Molly, insofar as I know what I'm trying to say, is that you are suffering from shock. I don't want you to do anything desperate. Lie low. Keep your counsel until you've both had the chance to see what it is you're doing.'

She did not answer.

'Is there anything I can do?' he whispered.

'Such as?'

153

'Come round and see me in a day or two. Things may have changed. Let's fix a date.' He reached for his calendar.

'What do you think you can do, Henry?'

'Nothing. It's not me, Molly, it's you. You're the one who'll have to move, make your mind up. I'll just listen. Come on, now. When will suit you? Not Tuesday, please.'

Thursday, seven thirty at his house. Both made a note.

XIV

Henry Fairfax's play made progress.

Each time he sat down he typed half a dozen pages, not easily, but working through difficulties. Determined to finish his first draft at speed, he realized that the second would then be crucial. His everyday slog at Le Jeune's became mere routine, plenty of it for they were busy, but demanding little beyond time or care, clerk's work. This gave him opportunity to consider his writing, but he found that unproductive among his files and computers and charts. He could not determine the next development until he squared up to the typewriter. He rarely finished before eleven, and then took a relaxing turn round the streets.

On the night before Molly's visit, he did not set out for his stroll until well after eleven. In the warm air he walked satisfied, untired. At lunch-time he had written at length to Laura, outlining his latest efforts on his play, but nowhere mentioning either Jim or Molly. Their quarrel and imminent break-up played some part in his creating; the sorrow, the unease enacted by them emotionally fuelled the mad but vigilant plans of his murderous sisters. He wrote nowadays in terms of love to Laura and looked out expectantly each morning for the postman with her reply. Life seemed profitable.

He turned out of his own avenue into the main road. The doors of the Horseshoe were shut, though lights blazed behind drawn curtains. Cleaning up, he supposed. Cars hurried on the deserted roads. Some houses stood completely darkened now. In the far distance a burglar alarm sounded, falsely, he guessed. The Council House clock, two miles away, struck a quarter to twelve. The wind, not that he felt it, must be blowing from the south. Since his encounter in January Henry walked away from the walls and entries, somewhere near the middle of the pavement.

155

A figure he recognized emerged from a side street, athletically, twenty yards ahead.

'Jim,' Henry called.

The brother stopped, turned, waited for him.

'You're a long way from home ground.' Henry.

'Cooling the fevered brow. And you?'

Henry offered a brief explanation of his presence. Jim, much at ease, smiled, gently flattening his curls with his right hand.

'Bed offers fewer inducements these warm nights.'

'Aren't you tired?'

'Nothing to shout about. It's ironical, but since I put my resignation in, things have gone like a dream at school. I suppose it's because I know that in another six weeks it'll all be over.'

'And you won't miss it?'

Jim shook his head very slowly, with a wry confidence.

'No. I shan't. One or two things, of course. It's not been all bad.'

'Do you hear from Laura?'

'Yes. Her secretary sends me projects to think about, and some details of contracts they're engaged on.'

'Interesting?'

Jim bit his lower lip, breathed out aloud.

'Yes. But they don't concern me. Not yet.' He put a minatory finger out towards his brother's heart. 'You know, Henry, this is going to be a completely different life for me. I either make my way, or I go bust. In school, I chug on, and as long as I don't allow the kids to wreck the joint or kill anybody and they make some sort of showing at exams then nobody bothers. You're one in a hundred, all ambling towards mediocrity. Up there, I'll have to get my head down.'

'Is that good?' Henry asked.

'I'd say so. I think I'm competitive. Schools don't bring the best out of either teachers or pupils. Reaching the standard is all they bother about. And pretty low standards, many of them.'

'That's all some of us can manage.'

Jim shrugged, good-humouredly enough.

156

'I hope you don't rub that in too often with Conrad Le Jeune, or you'll soon be on the way out.'

'We don't often discuss principles.' With sarcasm.

'It's what's wrong with this country these days. Too easy for everybody. Nobody allowed to starve, work or not. It doesn't do. "In the sweat of thy face shalt thou eat bread." Too many people don't understand that.'

'I see.' Henry refused to argue. 'When do you move?'

'It's not fixed yet. Around August the first.'

'And Molly?'

'What about her?'

'Is she ready?' He wondered if he did right to mention this. Perhaps she had talked to her husband about their phone call. Jim seemed in no hurry. Night air lapped them warmly. Jim had folded his arms, squeezing himself.

'She won't come up with me. Then.'

'You mean she'll follow you when you're settled.'

'Something of the sort.'

'What's that mean?' Henry snapped.

'Nothing. Nothing.' Jim seemed about to utter but thought better of it and scratched his cheek.

'I rang you the other night. Did Molly tell you?' He lied easily, almost believing the untruth.

'I think she did. What was it about? I can't remember.'

'I'd rung up before to find out how things were. You were supposed to call back.'

'Was I? What about?'

'Laura came up, oh, over a week ago now. Nearly a fortnight. You know that.'

'And what has she to say for herself?'

'About your job? Very little. She is chasing some contract. She certainly works for her money. Moll's coming round to see me tomorrow evening.' The Council House clock signalled midnight with distant soft clarity. 'This evening. Are you coming with her?'

'No. I can't.' No hesitation. Jim shifted his feet like a boxer. 'Things aren't as they should be between her and me.' He snatched breath in. 'Not by a long chalk. But I expect she'll tell you. She'll spill it all out.'

'Christina Brown again?'

157

'Oh, fuck Christina Brown.' James swayed on the balls of his feet as if he intended to aim a punch. Henry tucked chin into cheek in readiness. 'I don't want Moll round my neck in London. Nor Christina, if that's any satisfaction to you. Nor any other woman.'

'But you're married to her.'

'We all make mistakes. You did. It came to divorce in your case. You and Laura.' Jim spoke the names as if he had heard them for the first time, with surprise, suspecting numinousness or feckless weight. 'I've ballsed it up, and I'm not blaming anyone more than myself. But that's that.'

'What's Molly say?'

'You can find that out for yourself when she visits you. Ask her. She likes you.'

'You owe her something.'

Jim thought that over, breathing heavily in and out.

'Ye'. In a way. Yes. She's not perfect, though. Anyhow you'll hear what she says when you see her.'

'It's not what she tells me. It's between you and her.'

'Nothing will set matters right between us. I wish it was otherwise. It isn't, it just bloody isn't.'

'Yes, but can you say where you went wrong?'

'No. We just don't suit, that's all. We've found it out, at last, as you did. We can't put up with each other when the going's rough, when I'm depressed or she's short-tempered, when there are snags about our work. We haven't the necessary cooperative . . .' He thrust his arms downwards and stood silent.

'Does it ever cross your mind what it was like when you first met Moll? And what you thought of her then?'

'Occasionally. I'm not inhuman. Molly's a decent, attractive woman. But we're two different people from what we were when we married. We've grown out of each other. There's no need to tell you. You and Laura . . .'

'We're very friendly. Marvellously so.'

'You hardly ever see her. If I had a few days with Moll every three months we'd get on all right. It's day after bloody day.'

158

'So when you go away from her, things might straighten themselves out?'

'I doubt it. That's not what it feels like.' Jim spread his hands. 'I may be wrong, but see what she has to say for herself. I think that relationship's over and done with. There it is. Bad luck.' He waved his arms about. 'Must run, or I shan't want to get up. 'Bye, brother.'

And he strode off at a pace while Henry listened to the clattering, swift footsteps.

Molly appeared at eight o'clock that evening, neat in dark skirt, spotless blouse with scarlet cravat, blue tights and shoes.

'You look nice,' he said.

'I don't feel it.'

She sat down.

'Whatever you're having,' she said to his question.

'I fancy a cup of tea.'

'Fine.'

On his return from the kitchen she was leaning back in her armchair, awkwardly, spine arched, eyes closed, arms loose.

'I could go to sleep here,' she said.

As he poured the tea, she straightened herself, took the edge of her chair.

'I saw Jim last night,' he began. 'This morning.'

'Yes. He told me.'

'You're still on speaking terms?'

'Just about. We even washed up together.' She fiddled with her tea cup, waving away his offer of scones and biscuits. At length, when they were both settled opposite each other, she asked, rather indistinctly, 'Had he anything interesting to say for himself?'

'Well,' voice and sigh telegraphed his bad news.

'He told me,' she interrupted, 'to come here and spill it all out to you. "At least Henry'll listen," he said. "And he's been through it all once." That's what he said. "Once. Laura threw him over." Is that right?'

'Yes.'

'You wouldn't have divorced her?'

'No.'

'You tell me,' Molly urged, 'how it was with you. You'd have hung on, presumably?'

'That's what I thought. At least for a start, when she first, first began to wreck the marriage. I was for keeping quiet, patching it up.'

'But she wouldn't have it?'

'Ye', I think that's about the truth.'

'Why?'

'That's interesting. At the time I thought it was mainly concerned with me, and my inadequacies. I was busy at work, late home, tired, not keen on going out. Usual thing. If you asked me now, though, my answer would probably be different.' He paused, proud of the adverbial cliché, administered for her need, keeping the discussion logical, reasonable. 'The life didn't suit. I didn't realize it at the time. It's amazing that I could miss anything so obvious, but miss it I did. She'd been a teacher, pretty successfully until she became pregnant. We lost the baby. She didn't go back to work at once. I think now it might have been better if she had, but she was run-down and depressed and there was no need financially. It didn't suit her, skulking at home, polishing the furniture.'

'Hadn't she friends?'

'Yes. And they came to see her. But they seemed more like acquaintances. Not close. She didn't confide in them.'

'Did she confide in you?'

'We talked. A great deal. At the time I'd have said she spoke openly to me. Now I'm not sure. She didn't know what she wanted, herself, that was half the trouble. We both thought the miscarriage and its aftermath made her feel as she did. We allowed it to become worse.'

'Could you have prevented it?'

'If I'd had more sense. Or Laura. If she'd gone back to teaching and a career right away it might just have turned the scales. But she didn't.' Molly watched him, eyes mournful. 'Now, when she's found her feet in London and is making money and occupied all hours of the day she's a different woman altogether. She thinks she's like her brother, ambitious, out to make a name, a pile. And there was no chance to do that cooped up in our house and dull schools back here.'

'You wouldn't have stood in her way?'

'No. Not if I'd known that was the difficulty. But I didn't. It's amazing that people can be married, live in and out of one another's pockets for so long, and know so little about each other. But that was the case. With us.'

'Do you think,' Molly started tentatively, holding speech back, 'that there's something between Jim and me that's causing a split? And, and we don't see it?'

'I'm in no position to judge.'

'I think,' now she spoke firmly, 'that it's Jim and his temperament. He's thoroughly disillusioned with education, isn't sure how to replace it because he's so uncertain about himself and takes it out on me.'

'Then if he makes a go of it with Laura up in London it may set you right.'

'I don't know. You find yourself on a certain course, and you can't turn back. We're into the habit of hating each other. Oh, it sounds cynical to put it like that, but it's right. If he won the pools tomorrow, it wouldn't save us. I can't help thinking that there is some defect in Jim. Is that possible? When we did A Level we used to write essays on the "vicious mole" in Hamlet's nature. What was your mother like?'

The suddenness of the question unnerved him.

'What do you mean?'

'I was talking the other day to old Mrs Sanderson, Irene Sanderson, who used to live next door to you when you were children, and she says Jim never recovered from his mother's death. I wasn't talking about our marriage, or complaining. As far as I know Irene has no idea that there's anything amiss between us, but she came out with that. She said he was sunny and lively until your mother died. She also said he was her favourite. Was he?'

'I suppose so.'

'And you didn't resent it?'

'Not really. He was seven years younger than I was,

161

an afterthought. I think I expected her to make a big fuss of him, seemed right, proper. I don't think I minded.'

'Are you sure?'

'I've told you I can make bad misjudgements, but no.' He laughed, pointed at the teapot. She ignored the gesture.

'What was your mother like?'

'Strict. Limited. A bit distant with me. She did her duty, but there weren't too many overt signs of affection. No cuddles. By the time Jim arrived I think she'd softened up a little. Or perhaps Jim was more immediately attractive than I was.'

'Was she religious?'

'No. Neither she nor my father. What she wanted was for us to do well. Use our lives, not waste them. Kept us at our school work. Nagged us. She wasn't very good at congratulating us, now I come to think of it. Dad was much better.'

'She'd been a teacher?'

'Yes. And the daughter of teachers. Her grandfather had been a miner. Salt of the earth.'

'Did she bully you?'

'For our good. And if we let her.'

'She didn't press you too hard. That's what I'm getting at. Or tie you to her apron strings.'

'Don't all mothers?' he asked. 'Or try to. She was pleased we both won university places, but she was put out, I guess, when I trained as an accountant, and joined Le Jeune's. Organizing fleets of lorries or buses wasn't in her eyes altogether suitable work for a university graduate. I would have been more properly employed passing something of my knowledge on to others. She'd have been better pleased with Jim, going into teaching, but she died while he was still at Cambridge.'

'Is that why he chose it?'

'I've no idea. He never liked the look of my scruffy office at Le Jeune's.'

Molly handed her cup over. He filled it, ruminatively.

'Was Jim subject to depression, bad moods when he was small?'

'Not particularly. Not as far as I can remember, but you mustn't forget that seven years is a hell of a separation between boys of that age. I was at the high school before he'd started in the infants. He could sulk, and play up, but he could be marvellously charming.'

'Just as at present.' Molly sipped. 'What can I do, Henry?'

'I can't answer that for you. You'd probably be wisest to play it quietly, and hope the change of circumstance will have a good effect in time. That is, if you want to keep him. I mean, we fall into habits there. I am married to James Dale Fairfax and that is an inflexible law of the universe which nothing will alter. It's not so. If the marriage breaks up, we feel desperate, our pride's damaged, we've failed somehow, we've disgraced ourselves in the eyes of the world, but then so have thousands of others these days. Marriage as an institution is rapidly changing now. The likes of us brought up by strict parents with old-fashioned ideas of "till death us do part" – and I think I was, in spite of my parents' lack of religious belief – can't understand that marriage to one other only can be given up like tobacco or spirits or golf or foreign travel if there are good reasons for so doing.'

'Isn't it better like that?' Molly's voice was strong and clear, that of one disinterestedly seeking enlightenment.

'Well, now.' Henry stopped. 'I suppose I'd agree. But I'd have to admit that such belief would undermine commitment to an unbreakable contract in the the middle ranges. And they must hold the largest numbers.'

'What do you mean?'

'If escape by divorce is not easy, then people under the rules of a stricter society will have to hang on and might even make a success of their marriage eventually. We have to weigh one against the other. Couples living together, hating each other, poisoning their lives and that of their children have to be set against a free-and-easy wish to give up as soon as the going gets rough.'

' "The going gets rough" hardly describes what's happening to us, Henry.'

'I'm trying to put it as lightly as I can, as far from

exaggerated statement as possible. I'm baffled just now, Molly, because Laura and I fought like cats. By the time we'd parted I hated her every fibre. And yet now we're friendly as we ever were.'

'You're not thinking of remarrying, are you?'

'It's not quite reached that point yet. But I'll admit I've considered it.'

'If Laura said she wanted it, would you . . . ?'

'I'm a cautious man. I don't rush into anything easily. But I'd be tempted. And that would have been unthinkable a year or two ago.'

'I'm glad for you, Henry.'

They sat very still for a time, with solemn faces, until she brightened.

'We sit here discussing marriage so seriously, so that I forget for a moment what mine's like. All the tears and hurt and apprehension. I hate the house we live in. This place of yours seems peaceful and ordered, but ours is an emotional slum. Just to walk into it makes me want to throw things about, smash them.'

'Because of its associations?'

'Because of your bloody brother, Jim.'

'From what he said,' Henry calmed her, 'Christina Brown's out of it now.'

'What did he mean?'

'He led me to believe that she'd have no part in his life in London.'

'Typically selfish. Anyhow, I'll wait until I see it.'

She sniffed, stifling weeping, sitting unnaturally still.

'How will it all turn out?' she asked, and her eyes filled, flooded with tears which she did not wipe off.

'I don't know, Molly. I can't promise you anything. If you want to keep him, just play it cool until he goes, and hope that'll solve it.'

'He taunts me.'

'I'm sure he does. Laura and I insulted each other like fury. And we could do it properly because we knew each other so well. We knew the weaknesses, where it hurt most.'

'And that's all changed?'

164

'It has.'

'Don't you ever think back? To some of the things she said?'

'Yes. I can and I do. I can remember the circumstances and the exact, killing words. They're branded into my memory. And this is the oddest bit of the whole business. When I recall these quarrels and gibes they don't seem to matter much now. I ask myself why I grew so distraught, as I did. And I can only conclude that more than half the fault was mine, that I was, no, that I made myself vulnerable to her attacks.'

'Deliberately?'

'Perhaps not that exactly. But I took no precautions.'

'You were as I am now. You couldn't help yourself.'

'Married couples are under one another's feet. It takes considerable skill, or compromise, or . . .'

'Don't say any more, Henry. I know all this. I'm sure what you're suggesting makes sense, but I can't bear it. It doesn't apply to me as I am. It's like asking somebody with two broken legs to stand up and walk. He can't. I can't.'

Now she cried openly, letting the tears swill down her cheeks. Henry sat opposite, looking away from her, making no effort to speak, to comfort. Her eyes reddened, her cheeks were blotched, though her hair kept its beauty.

'Shall I make another pot?' he asked, in the end.

She shook her head, tears still dropping.

Finally, he stood, took out a newly ironed handkerchief from his pocket, flapped it open, and offered it.

'Have a good blow,' he said. 'That's what my mother used to tell me.' Molly took the handkerchief from him, screwed it in her fist, making no use of it. Henry sat on the arm of her chair and pulled her to him. She rested her head on his side as he caressed her cheek. Now her sobbing grew louder, more insistent, croup-like. He gently touched her with his fingertips, repeating her name. It was awkward, uncomfortable to perch as he did, but he did not move until she seemed calmer, or more silent. Only then did he slip his hand loose, prised himself

165

upward, and stood comically massaging his hips. Molly mopped at her face.

'That's better,' he murmured. She hid behind the handkerchief. 'We'll manage.'

It was twenty minutes before she was sufficiently in control of herself and satisfied enough with her appearance to leave him. She sounded tremulous, but refused his offer to accompany her. She thanked him, almost formally, but in the voice of one recovering from a cold, very quietly, without force.

He accompanied her to the front door, holding her hand, but she walked straight and without faltering down the path.

XV

In the next few weeks Henry Fairfax made sporadic attempts to keep in touch with his brother and with Molly. Both said little on the phone, claiming they were 'all right'. Neither visited him; their silence seemed conspiratorial.

Still busy by day in his office, Henry completed the second draft of *Two Sisters* on the fifteenth of July. Pleased with it, for it seemed both convincing and striking, he put it out to a professional typist and determined on a month's rest from it. From the one or two emotional loose ends he constructed poems, odd, unshapely, unrhymed *pensées* which rewarded his scrutiny with a rawness that frightened and surprised him. He had no idea what to do with these verses, not even how to revise them. He made fair copies on his word-processor of all the stages and encaged these in a stiff, metal-bound folder.

Laura was in Canada, on some concern of her brother's. He had heard nothing from her, but she had warned him that her fortnight there was so jam-packed that he'd be lucky to receive a postcard of Niagara Falls. He had no address for the new world, so stored his bits and pieces in a notebook to be consulted once she'd returned and he could write letters to her again.

Her existence and their relationship brightened his days. He was young again, enamoured. What he could not come to terms with was that his love for Laura had strengthened him to such an extent that he was able to complete his play with surefire quick competence. His emotional fulfilment had made it possible for him to portray the desperation and murderous connivances of these sisters, Fiona and Carol, to sketch believably the decent respectability that cloaked the family but which could not prevent the hammer-blow, the knife-thrusts. His exultation had lifted him to their depths of despair. His life-scenario lacked morality, or obvious justice, spelt out his own ambivalences; from his measured delight arose this study of death and wild darkness.

In the last week of July James moved to London. Henry heard the news from two quarters, Laura and Molly.

Laura wrote two long letters on her return from Canada, mostly concerned with the work she was doing for her brother. Long hours and lavish entertainment had been the order of day after day, and she'd returned exhausted. She had, moreover, to fly back almost at once, though during the brief interlude here she hoped to see that her own affairs were progressing favourably. In the second letter she mentioned that Jim had arrived, and that he had 'put him under instruction' with one Tony Beasley, a new name to Henry. It was a pity that she had to be away, but there were plenty of humdrum tasks Jim could be set to, and which, she hoped, would give him some idea of the 'nuts and bolts' of the organization.

The letters were long, lively, interesting and slapdash; she had not re-read what she had written. Each carried at the end a paragraph expressing her love, her regret that they would not see each other during this period of upheaval. The tone was warm enough, but these references seemed perfunctory, not insincere, but lacking the dash and drive of her descriptions of business transactions. Henry read the letters three times a day, and replied with the help of his notebook daily and at length. He settled to his desk as if he was writing a play to describe the trivia of Beechnall with brilliance, to warn Laura against overwork, and to demonstrate his love for her. On her receipt of his eighth, she telephoned him to tell him to write no more for the present, as she was off to Toronto, Montreal, Ottawa, possibly New York and Washington, in the morning. She congratulated him on his letters, said she had packed them all into her case so she could read about the real world in his handwriting, and so keep sane. 'Better than any novel,' she pronounced. 'Or play?' he riposted. She loved him. She'd drop everything once she was back to visit him or have him with her in London. Le Jeune's and Associates were going big in Canada, and possibly the States, and this trip also concerned, he did not question her, some opening up in South America. Very exciting, cut-throat, male-chauvinistic and wearing, but she reckoned she was on course for victory. He was to keep his fingers crossed for her. He need not write; trans-Atlantic mail seemed dodgy and, in any case, she'd be constantly on the move, she expected. He could do what he had done before, keep a notebook, and let her have the lot in a series of epistles when she returned. Yes, she had seen Jim, shortly. He seemed to have settled, was cheerful. 'Tony Beasley'll look after him. And work him to death. He won't have time to be homesick.' She loved him, but she must go now and pack her personal case, have a bath and get to bed. She'd be up at six in the morning. Laura left Henry breathless, slightly disturbed with six written pages he could not send and his occupation gone.

When he telephoned Molly she had spoken warily. Jim had spent the first week of his holiday making preparation for his departure. He had not said much, but had never faltered from politeness. He had answered questions; on three days he had even prepared an evening meal for her; he rang London during the day. On Henry's last call she gave news of Jim's unexpected exit. She had returned from work on a Wednesday evening to find a note from him telling her the firm had been in touch, that they were unexpectedly busy on account of Laura's absence, that they wanted him up at once and so he had packed his traps and gone. He knew no private address, so she should write c/o the firm. He'd twice tried to ring Martin Fowler's to let her know but on both occasions the number had been engaged. In due course he'd inform her how things were working out. Since that time almost a fortnight ago, she had heard nothing.

'I don't know whether I expected to or not,' she said glumly.

Henry gave her the snippets of information from Laura.

'Did she give you his private address?'

'No, and I never thought of asking. You can always find him at his office.'

Molly did not want to see him; she was extremely busy at work. The order she had expected had been repeated, doubled. She was 'knocking up' some samples for European buyers. She felt very fit, but tired. She had not time to think about Jim yet. Perhaps that was as well. She promised, without enthusiasm, to keep in touch.

Christina Brown rang his office one morning, introducing herself, apologizing with decorum. She spoke with more energy than he had expected, crisply, having no difficulty with her sentences, as she asked for an appointment 'to talk about Jim'.

When she called by arrangement at his house, on a Saturday afternoon, he recognized her as the fair-haired girl he had seen out with his brother. Taller than he remembered, she was less than pretty, with flopping hair, a pale skin, faded blue eyes. There was something Swedish, athletic about her; her hands were large, her steps long. He had expected a fluffy, retiring miss.

He invited her to sit, listened to her apologies, did nothing to smooth her way. She asked if he had heard of her.

'Yes. Someone, a colleague I guess, wrote to Molly complaining about your association with Jim.'

'What did they say?'

'As far as I remember, that you spent all your spare time at school in Jim's company.'

'I can guess who that was.'

'That's what he said.'

Christina settled herself again, she sat very upright, and dropped her eyes.

'Of course,' she began. 'I know quite well that I've no right to question you, but you must believe me when I say I'm deeply concerned about Jim.' She waited for an answer she did not receive. 'We were attracted together, I don't deny. Your sympathies are properly with his wife, but I'd like you to hear my side.' Again the pause.

'Go on.'

'Jim was unhappy at his job. He was good at it, if impatient. But the ethos of the place was totally wrong for him.'

170

'And for you?'

'Yes, for anybody with any standards, but I could put up with it better than he could. We used to grouse together. About his head of department, and mine,' she smiled, with excellent feral teeth, 'and the headmaster. But I soon began to see that there was something more seriously wrong with him than mere dissatisfaction with his work. There was a deeper, underlying melancholy or depression, give it what name you will.'

Henry gave it, and her, nothing.

'Jim,' she continued, 'can be extremely charming. Open and witty and imaginative. He also knew a great deal. That's what he was like when I first knew him. We laughed very often. About little things. Yes, at the foolishness and blinkered ignorance of our superiors. But we could laugh. But not in this past year. He seemed to sink. He became sullen, and aggressive. Then there'd be a period of apathy. He'd attack colleagues in staff meetings quite ferociously. He could do it. And then wouldn't talk, or would snap somebody's head off.'

'Was his relationship with you affected by these moods?'

'Less than most, but, yes, to some extent. But he would always talk to me. Sometimes in a way that was frightening. I don't mean he threatened me, he didn't; he could sound suicidal. Or so bleak as to be almost mad. But I suppose you know all this.'

'No, Miss Brown. Jim could be rude to me when he thought I was interfering. I knew he suffered from depression, but I saw very much less of him than you did.'

'He admired you, Mr Fairfax. He said once, "I wish I had my brother's steadiness." '

'But did he mean it?'

For the first time Christina Brown seemed taken aback, nervous. She refrained from answering his question directly.

'I'm trying to explain all this so I can ask about your brother. I owe it to you. Since he went off to London I've heard absolutely nothing from him. And that makes me wonder if there isn't something seriously wrong. But even if something has happened, I can't expect you to spill out private family affairs to a stranger. At least, not without some establishment of credentials on my part.'

Henry pondered the phrase.

'I see. Let me say for a start that I have heard nothing from Jim himself since he's been in London. He's working, as you probably realize, for my ex-wife, who has been away a good part of the time Jim's been up there. From the one or two things she's said, and it's not much, he's settled in and making a go of it. That's the extent of my knowledge.'

'I haven't his address, even.'

'No more have I.'·

'You can write c/o his firm. I expect you know that. He led me to believe that as soon as he'd found somewhere to stay he'd let me have the address. He hasn't.'

'Does this surprise you?'

Christina jerked her head again.

'Yes. He promised.' Her eyes were bleak, prominent. 'Would you give me the firm's address?'

Henry did not hurry himself.

'I think I could do that.' He reached for a notepad, scribbled, passed the paper over. 'This doesn't mean that he'll write back.'

'I know. But at least I can make contact with him. After that, it's up to him. I'm genuinely worried.'

She began to spill sentences about Jim's moodiness. They were not enlightening, dull more often than not. Jim's refusal to speak to the head of his department; his reduction of the second mistress to tears by public sarcasm at her pretension; an attempt to interview the director of education and the chairman of the education committee about their proposed reduction of the numbers of peripatetic music teachers, not really his concern. The evening they had sat on a seat in the Abbey Park and he had spoken not a word; in the end, after an hour, an hour and a half's trying, she had left him. He had made no attempt either to detain or follow her. She spoke of Jim's complaints about Molly's lack of sexual interest, her concentration on the jewellery, 'her bloody trinkets'. Chri-

172

stina's account bored the anxious Henry. She did not try to affect or dramatize events. A policewoman reading out officialese from her notebook could not have lost sympathy sooner.

'Did you not have any, any, good, pleasurable exchanges with him?' he asked, in exasperation.

'No, not recently.'

'Then why to God did you spend so much of your time on him?'

'I felt a responsibility. He was going to pieces. Somebody had to try.' The tone was accusatory.

'It must have been depressing for you.'

'What do you think?'

She stared with undisguised dislike. Henry tried again, in conciliatory vein.

'Did he show some improvement after he had sent in his resignation?'

'Yes. I suppose so. He seemed excited. But it was so much up and down. And when he heard nothing for such a long period he was suicidal. Well, unbearable. He varied. Sometimes in his classrooms he was bursting with high spirits, but the next day he'd punish anybody who stepped the slightest inch out of line. Savagely. The children didn't know where they were with him. Nor did anyone else.'

'But you stuck by him?'

'How could I do anything else? I had to sit and hear his complaints. It was awful sometimes. There was no pleasure and no companionship in it for me. I'm not a masochist. I used to dread school. I'd stay behind in my room at lunch-time, but he'd search me out.'

'So it was something of a relief when term ended, and he went off? For you?'

'Yes. But I expected change. That he'd be put right. That the new job . . .' Her hands flopped.

'Miss Brown, I don't want to pry.' He waited. The cold blue eyes met his, hopelessly. 'Did you expect the relationship between you to continue in some way?'

'Yes, I did.'

'And you wanted that?'

173

'Yes. I suppose you want to know how things stood between us, whether I expected a break-up between him and his wife. That's the way he talked.'

'And did he make promises to you? Of marriage? Some permanent relationship?'

'Yes, but only on his high days. So I couldn't take them altogether seriously. If he'd cured himself sufficiently, he'd have gone back to his wife. If he hadn't, he wouldn't have married me, or I wouldn't have wanted him to. I'll be honest with you, Mr Fairfax, I don't know why, or how, I put up with it so long. There was nothing in it for me in these last few months. But I suppose I'm stubborn, I don't like to be beaten. And I felt desperately sorry for him.'

'I understand. There's something attractive about Jim even when he's rude.'

'It's easy to forgive him. He's hurt me, time after time. I didn't really want to be entangled with him. I knew he was married. What's his wife like? Is she really selfish and unsympathetic?'

'No more than you are, or I am.' He put his fingers together. 'I don't know whether I should be telling you this, but I offer it as a token of good will, um, on my part.' Henry stopped. That sounded off like a bogus sentence from one of his plays, but Miss Brown showed no sign of either recognition or aversion. 'Molly, Jim's wife, has not had a word from him since he left for London. Or she hadn't when I last heard from her. I don't know what that means, one way or another.'

He gave a succinct account of Jim's sudden departure. 'What will she do, Mr Fairfax?'

'I don't follow you.' Brusque again, Jim-like.

'Will she go up to London to try to find out what he's about? I mean, I can't, can I? I've no right.'

'I don't know. I shall report our conversation to Molly, because I think that is only proper. But what she intends I cannot say. She may be relieved. She may have found out that she's doing better without him. She's not said as much, but it's some days since I saw her. He may have written and given some explanation.'

'Do you think so?'

'What I think is not very important. I seem to know Jim, so, so badly, so inadequately these days, that my views are guesswork. There's something radically wrong with him, but I don't know what it is.'

'You're not suggesting that his association with me has had an adverse effect.'

'I can't say that. It's a possibility, I suppose. It doesn't convince me, no. It all might have been worse without you. You'll write to him?'

'Yes.'

'And offer to go up to see him?'

'I'm going to Egypt next week for a fortnight. With a friend. I'll make my letter as conventional as I can. That's best, isn't it? Tell him what Marie and I want to see on our holiday.'

'I shall be away for two weeks in August.'

'Can I get in touch with you? Again? Whether I hear anything or not?'

He gave gracious permission and she refused his offer of drinks. For some time after she had left he sat in his chair, thinking of those washed blue eyes, the steadfast figure. She had seemed inhibited, clinical, like a nurse hiding concern under indifference or professional calm. He could not imagine her raving, beating the table with her fists. She had been clean, too starchy.

XVI

On the second Saturday in August Henry Fairfax went on holiday to mid-Wales. He booked into a hotel in Dolgellau taking with him walking boots and waterproofs, and the fair copy of *Two Sisters*. He was not sure how he would spend his time. At the last moment he had, on inspiration, offered Molly the opportunity to go with him, but she had refused. She had far too much work on hand.

She grumbled that she had heard no word from Jim, but when Henry gave her a detailed account of Christina's visit, she listened quietly, asking surprisingly few questions, as though visit, account, woman were all marginal to her interests. She seemed preoccupied, but not distressed. He sent her his Welsh address on the back of a postcard view of Cader Idris, but had nothing in return.

The weather turned favourable, as he sampled beaches, tramped the woods, rode the miniature railways, inspected castles, slate mines, museums, Port Meirion. He did not once take out the typescript of his play, though he considered it sporadically as he walked the sun-dappled mountain roads and tracks. He had written interestingly; of that he was sure. How convincingly he had observed the psychology, how exact or powerful the language he had employed he was not prepared to check. The change in his life due to Laura had livened his reactions. He had thought, planned, written, revised with unusual speed, and this made him suspicious, if delighted. Hurry spelt a botched job, he cautiously warned. He'd chance it; as soon as he reached home he'd dispatch a copy to the BBC, uncorrected. At this decision he felt slightly pleased with himself, cocky, sinful; he imagined his father on his annual seaside jaunt would have felt the same about blueing a handful of coppers on a one-armed bandit. No, the old man would not have risked any such endeavour. I am not better than my father.

176

Henry Fairfax ate well, lost weight, acquired a tan, drank whisky in the evening, grew to be a new man, thus far undiscovered to himself; the new, spry, energetic being was as strange as the Welsh signs: *Canol y dref, arafwch*; *llwybr cynhoeddus*, but they had appended translations. He had no real means of interpreting himself; he did not fret, enjoyed the new man, instructed himself that was what holidays were about, recreation, re-creation. He did not even regret the lack of news from Laura; she would have enjoyed these hills, stony walls, the drama of clouds, but she was otherwise engaged, in achievement, making a new woman of herself in the new world.

One bright evening he stood after dinner in a hill village. The church rising above him was small, locked, on a mound, approached by a steep climb too bucolic to be called steps, strips of shallow stone with earth and pebbles between, precluding use by all but the hale and athletic; either side of the lych-gates were tablets of stone, commemorating the life and demise of George III, English on the left, Welsh to the right, placed there, large as death, in 1820, by the squire, a double-barrelled, unhyphenated baronet, whose family tomb, inscription in English with Roman figures, stood grimly but grandly grey among the tottering memorials to plebeian Joneses and Davieses, all in the vernacular worn to illegibility in any case by winter and rough weather. A little further on the school seemed large, urban, too high for so small a place, but catering, and that before the days of school buses, for the outlying farmsteads, the keepers' cottages, for chapel-goers, as well as adherents of the parish church. Now, with a car or two in the lane and a Bedford van, the building emitted the small sounds of education pursued, though in what language it was impossible to say, or why during the summer break. Henry Fairfax looked at the dark windows and turned back to walk through the village.

He stopped on the edge of the place by the war memorial, a stone cross railed off from the side of the road, with a dozen, twenty names and regiments and farms, 1914–18. Suddenly he felt jolted into a kind of anger. These young men, farmers' sons and labourers, had been snatched by bellicose bureaucracy out of their quiet lives to hell-holes of shell-fire and shrapnel in France. Perhaps they were glad to leave, to be transported to training camps where they were bawled out and threatened, and then huddled on to ferries, marched singing into base camps, into trenches and blasted into French graveyards, their little lives over. Fairfax read the names, forgot them immediately, pawed the tarmac with his toecap.

Jim in London.

Henry could write a play about that, a man lost in a new, demanding place, amongst the strange faces.

There were no mentions of military honours on the memorial, no ranks, names only, place of origin, regiment. That was all. No battles, defeats, victories; no dates of death, no army numbers. He remembered the passage the headmaster periodically read out at school. 'But these were merciful men, whose righteousness hath not been forgotten . . . Their seed standeth fast and their children for their sake.'

Jim?

He kicked the road. On the wall of his own school hung a memorial tablet, with an inscription he had never understood as a boy:

There is
One great society alone on earth:
The noble living and the noble dead.

Henry Fairfax could not grasp why in this place of late evening sunshine, just beyond two smart bungalows, in front of a small piece of monumental piety he felt changed as he hunched there, saddened but strengthened, as if humanity meant the more by this gauche cliché of a public gesture. The mountains, the dark forest trees, the absence of men, he had seen one householder swilling down his car, the mildness of the air, his own pleasure stopped him in his tracks for a moment, chastened, before he stepped off smartly downhill to his vehicle, hotel, festive nightcap. Their seed standeth fast.

For two days he vaguely concerned himself with the

Jim-figure; Laura, now, he told himself, also tested herself out in strange environments but would soon return the better, the richer for it. The Jim of his imagination, however, could not win, must suffer, die even. His brother was a personable, clever young man; there was no reason why he should not do well in London, in a new career. Henry would write his play as a kind of ju-ju, a fetish against defeat. The fabled Jim would protect the real man. Henry smiled at his superstitions but could not laugh them off.

A day or two later he walked on a morning of sunshine and huge clouds along a sheep-path near the summit of a nameless mountain. Below, the river and the road were reduced to narrow ribbon width; cars and lorries the size of match-boxes crept in silence, though from the other side of the valley he could hear and recognize the screech of peacocks.

The Molly of his play knew that she must rescue her husband; only an intervention on her part could save him from himself. Against her wishes, fearful of her own comfort, she would drag Jim back, from London, from suicide.

Henry Fairfax weighed this melodramatic scrap of plot as he stood looking down the length of the valley into a misty distance. The bare outline did not please; it lacked complexity, but he knew there and then with emphatic certainty that he must write it, must add to detail to make it credible, to convince. He feared that he came short. 'Ibsen lacked steel,' pronounced the playwright's mousy wife the day after the great man had died. Henry Fairfax must provide his own metallic strength.

He stared down, over the rough, fiercely sloping ground. What names should be given to the fictional Jim and Molly? He must take these simple decisions, make up his mind about the shape of his play, force himself to choose words. In the bright beauty of the morning a sense of desperation overtook him so that the real world was blotted out, his perceptions enclosed and limited in a cold greyness. It seemed that every decision he had made in his life had been mistaken: subjects at school and university;

holidays at home and abroad; the choice of companions, girlfriends, wife, home, job, leisure had all been misguided. 'Indirect, crooked ways', the phrase from Shakespeare sounded echoing in the hollow box of his head. Common sense reasserted itself; he held a responsible job, had made something of a name for himself as a writer, was rebuilding the broken relationship with his wife; he was on holiday, he had just finished a serious piece of work and was about to begin another. At thirty-six years of age, well turned out, strong, he ought to expand in confidence. He could not. Looking at his shoes, he breathed deeply, unable to rid himself of his dejection. His was a life of missed opportunities, of huddling in wrong corners; yet he was about to embark on a further ill-contrived enterprise. He punched his thigh with a painful downward blow, and again. A noise disturbed him to his right.

A couple were approaching, middle-aged, in shorts and walking boots, led by two spaniels. Fairfax stood back from the path, then bent to stroke the dogs. 'Morning,' the man called. 'Isn't it gorgeous?' said the woman. 'Makes you feel good to be alive.' They stopped, talked, not forcefully, delighted. They hailed from Bedford and after their picnic lunch they would drive back there. They had spent three heavenly days. Of course, the weather made all the difference. The man rubbed his hand through thick hair, adjusted his spectacles. They had to get back, but they made no complaints. Now the dogs were lying down, exploration temporarily abandoned, panting. The man asked when Fairfax was returning home. Saturday, he told them. 'Lucky you,' answered the woman. 'The forecast's still good.' Calm and sane, all three stared down the valley where a small caravan of miniature cars fretted behind a tractor they were unable to overtake. 'A god's eye view,' said the woman. The man hitched his rucksack, summoned the dogs. 'Enjoy it,' said the woman. The husband grinned, raised a hand in a comical half salute and set off. Wind played tricks with cloud shadows along the ground. Dogs and wife followed strong, retreating legs.

Henry's mind emptied itself.

180

When he recovered he had learnt sense. The couple were striding away now, higher on the edge of the mountain, dogs furiously in the lead, short caterpillars. Fairfax breathed deeply, able to put his problems aside. He would begin his play on his first free night at home. He wished he had asked the walkers their names. He would then have used them. He guessed. Francis and Helen. At this he laughed out loud, freed from constraint, temporarily a holidaymaker full of the freshness of the morning. Breathing deeply, he stepped away.

XVII

Henry drove back on Saturday afternoon, shopping on the way.

A pile of mail littered his hall, but nothing from Molly or Jim. He read the rest, advertisements, appeals, holiday cards, a long letter from a school friend now in Sierra Leone, a diatribe from a lonely man complaining about the content of his last radio play, two joyless invitations. He settled to an evening of boredom. Tomorrow morning he would pack up a copy of *Two Sisters* for the Beeb, unread. He wondered if he should call it *Death and The Two Sisters*; he'd suggest it in his short covering letter. On Monday evening he would begin *Francis and Helen*; he laid an unopened pack of typing paper by his machine, inserted a new tape so there would be no excuse for dilatoriness tomorrow. Some snag at the office might prevent the start. At seven thirty, he determined, p.m. the first working day, he would make a beginning if Le Jeune, (E. Midlands) had burnt down, Harry Dexter had disappeared with the petty cash, he himself had been reorganized into redundancy, he'd caught summer flu, broken his collar-bone, received a telephone call from Laura with good news or tragic, the world had turned itself upside down. He checked his fantasy with prospective opening words: Francis shouting from the top of the garden to Helen in her kitchen the day before he left for London. He had made a discovery. Dead cat? Pot? Clay pipe? Something larger, a statue or garden ornament, buried for obscure reasons? A cache of coins? A re-sited plant thought unsuitable and thus neglected found thriving? That was more like it. 'Helen. Are you busy? Helen.' With exasperation. 'Come up here a minute.' Henry tried it over, out loud. It carried no conviction. Obvious symbolism.

On Sunday morning at ten o'clock he telephoned Molly

without result. No one at home. He felt slightly annoyed, as if his sister-in-law should have held herself in readiness for his inquiries. Disgruntled he replied to three letters, made a light lunch of two poached eggs on toast, and set out to walk. As he stood by the pillar box at the end of the road he knew where to go, and why. He'd walk to the other side of the town, to his father's old house. Francis, he decided in the empty street, would live there, would call from the top of that long, narrow, overgrown dark garden. He walked at speed, glad to have made up his mind, to embark on something potentially useful. 'In my father's house,' he told himself at four miles an hour, 'are many mansions.'

Fifty minutes later he was climbing the hill between mature lime trees and elaborate brick houses behind Bulwell-stone walls towards his father's home. The street was short, consisting on one side of ten semi-detached villas each with squat wall, iron gates, privet hedges; on the other a great barracks of a residence showed its ugly areas of almost blank wall behind pollarded trees. Most of the houses, with bow-fronted windows, were now broken into flats, with variations of not very clean curtains, some still drawn at this hour of the afternoon. Front gardens and paths were neglected; bushes ramped; clumps of grass splayed between paving stones.

Henry reached his objective, the end house, No. 2 Linden Grove. Curtains matched here, brown, faded, unappetizing. A panel of eight white cards and bell buttons indicated the type of occupation. His father, on his departure for Penarth, had sold the place to a Mr Hodgson, a wholesale greengrocer, but that must have been five years ago, six.

Henry stood outside the front gate; privet struggled behind a low wall, capping regularly scarred with the stumps of sawn-off iron railings. The grass of the front lawn was rank; nothing had been pruned or shaped. A climbing rose sagged and dipped. He looked upwards. The windows were uncleanly; the curtains in the downstairs drawing room were those he remembered, a faded salmon. Soil was untilled. Stillness occupied the house, the street; nobody breathed, moved, peered out. He could not see into the front room; one of the pieces of stained glass in the door had been uncouthly replaced by cardboard. The flagged path was unbrushed; grass sprouted; earth spilled. Twenty-odd years ago the grove had been smart, though Mrs Leopold's house, No. 8, had already been divided into flats for young professionals with briefcases and new cars. Sunshine did nothing to camouflage present decay.

Henry edged through the gate which was ajar. When he tried to open it wider he found it jammed. He advanced halfway along the path, and paused, waiting for someone to ask his business. No one bothered. He looked over into the next garden where an equal neglect spread. The number of his house was screwed to a wooden black block on the wall by the door. He remembered his father replacing an older fixture and asking him to paint it, the block in black, the figure in white. He and the old man had admired their handiwork; his father had liked nothing better than to do jobs about the house. Henry felt the wood; firm as a rock still, but unpainted since. Wind agitated the lime trees as he sidled round the back.

Unemptied dustbins spilled over. The concrete of the yard was contoured with cracks. Paint peeled and blebbed on the doors. A bicycle rusted by the coal house. No noise of habitation came from this side of the house.

The garden was in size exactly as he remembered it, but rankly overgrown. Bushes tumbled; flowers hinted at colour but hesitantly among a jungle of green. A bucket was almost buried in the uncut grass of the lawn. His father's trelliswork was down, and the greenhouse lacked glass. Henry stared at the spot from where Francis would acknowledge Helen's call. They had grown vegetables there, but now it appeared a wilderness of bramble. He turned to Helen's kitchen window; an unmended crack crossed the unwashed surface. A carton of Vim occupied the sill with a handle-less cup. He looked inside, recognizing nothing. Wishing someone would challenge his credentials, he stamped round the yard, opened the door of the outside lavatory, thick with dust and spiders' webs, straightened a pile of bricks with his foot, picked up a crisp packet, screwed it, thrust it angrily into a stinking bin. He looked again to Francis's place, imagining him, in shirt-sleeves frantically grubbing in a neatness that bespoke anxiety and energy. A nervous man fulfilled his wife's wishes.

Fairfax, disappointed, aggrieved but reassured about the accuracy of his memory, returned to the front, treading quietly, determined not to disturb. In the streets a studious West Indian with white shirt, orange tie, striped suit, black shoes brushed past smiling. Henry wondered what his father would say about the state of the house which he had bought, a young married man, as a suitable domicile for an established solicitor and his family.

Henry walked away, at speed.

Thirty yards along the street he stopped suddenly by a huge buddleia which had been allowed to spread. Still, perhaps on account of the summer's rain, purplish blossoms flourished. As Henry admired, a man turned the corner, made towards him. Henry knew him at once. The Welshman in the pub, Owen. Henry smiled and the man frowned.

'Good afternoon.'

'Good afternoon.' Owen's progress was slightly hindered in that he took a step to the side. He screwed his eyes.

'You don't recognize me,' Henry said. Clearly not. 'We met one evening in a pub. The Duke of Cambridge, a month or so ago.' Still Owen cringed, expecting the worst. He seemed less well in the daylight, his narrow face grey, his hair thinner. 'You said you wanted to visit New Zealand and Japan.'

'Oh, eh, yes.' Suspicious, watching for the catch.

'We talked about art, and its place in the universe.' Nothing. 'I write radio plays. Fairfax.'

'Yes.' Without enthusiasm, but light dawned. 'Oh, yes. You were with a young woman. I remember now.' He shifted his glasses about his face. 'I don't see so well. Especially out of doors. I remember. You're out of your way, aren't you?'

185

'I came to look at the house where I lived as a boy. Number two. I intend to set, or at least start, my next play in it.

'Has it changed much?' Owen asked. He seemed ill at ease still, anxious to slip away.

'The street's gone downhill, I'm afraid. In a short time. It's only six years since my father sold it. Now all the houses are turned into flats.'

'Yes,' Owen answered. 'These houses are just the wrong size for the modern family. They're not quite grand enough for the rich, and they have too many rooms for four or five people. It's a pity that they are not better cared for. What are they, now? Speculative building of the eighteen-nineties, but materials were good then, timber properly seasoned, bricks hand-made, and labour cheap. So you've an excellent product in spite of age. The years take their toll; they must. As they do with me.' He smiled broadly, with yellow teeth, much at his ease. 'Which way are you going?' Nodding, he took in the details. 'I'll accompany you if I may for a few hundred yards, if you can put up with my limping pace and grandiloquent expressions.'

They set off together.

'I'm sorry I didn't recognize you. My eyesight is failing. Especially in sunlight. But even worse is my inability to retain names. Onomastic aphasia. I comfort myself with the phrase. Once, not long ago, I had an admirable verbal memory. But now. I've forgotten your name again, you see.'

'Fairfax. Henry Fairfax.'

'Like George Herbert's friend. See, that name came straight to my lips. Amazing. Ageing is a peculiar process. One does not feel old. Not inside the person. Painful joints, fatigue, failing powers are more and more noticeable, but the real self is young still, indefatigable, blest, illimited. I don't expect you to understand that; you think a moment's perusal of my face in a looking glass should disabuse my mind of such mistaken ideas. It is not so.'

Age or breathlessness had compelled Owen to halt to complete this. He shook his stick, caressed his hair, leaned

186

forward. He needed no stimulation to further verbal acrobatics.

'There is,' he began, 'in this county a family which has lived in the same place since before the Norman Conquest.'

'There must be dozens.'

'Traceably, I mean, traceably. My brother-in-law is interested in such things. Now what have I to match that? You may think it is nothing, obtained without merit, but it distinguishes. What equivalent do we boast, Mr Fairfax? Old age demands an answer. What have I managed in my sixty-five years of life to set me apart from my neighbour? It is a question I increasingly put to myself.'

He began a disquisition on old age, and this led to lugubrious considerations of the number of houses being turned into nursing homes for the elderly, then on to premature senility, Alzheimer's Disease, all delivered with flourishes of the stick and a display of considerable energy. He concluded these resonant paragraphs with a serious sentence. 'The saddest consideration, Mr er Mr, is the thought of opportunities missed.'

'Exactly what had you in mind?' Fairfax kept his voice level.

Owen shuffled about, as if to find a suitable stance for confession.

'I think of the numerous opportunities I have thrown away, the money, the time I have wasted. It seems that I was geared to non-achievement. I was born with social disadvantages, I know, but at least I had my brains and was coached by learned and dedicated teachers, but all to no end. I might have been a poet with more ambition, or even risen higher, and thus become more influential in the service I chose to follow. But I took the easy road, never exerted myself, was pleasant, useful, mediocre.'

'Were you never married?'

'I was.' So much for Molly's guess that the man was homosexual. 'But we separated. Another miscalculation. My wife did not wish to gad, that would be her word, about the world. We had no children. The poor woman is dead now. Do you know, she bequeathed to me what

187

little money and property she had. It amazed me. We had not corresponded or seen each other for years.'

'But it doesn't sound like failure, if she . . .'

Owen raised his stick for silence.

'If feeling was there, still, genuine affection, not mere sloth, then the sense of failure is the greater. We were young people in love. If we had committed ourselves to marriage, to family life, she might still be alive. Oh, I know what you're going to say. The children might not have succeeded as I wanted or emerged as drug-takers, Gonerils and Regans, spongers, drop-outs. All that, all that, but I should have felt that I had made the attempt.'

'Family life is difficult. One rarely gets one's own way.'

'My own way has proved wrong. I was, I am a foolish hedonist, and what have I achieved? No secure place in the world, a pittance of a pension, a sense of grievance.' Owen glared down the road, stick lifted, narrow face intense. Suddenly, like an actor, he relaxed, brushed back his sleeve to consult his chunky, gold wrist-watch. 'I shall be late for lunch, earning my sister's remonstrances. I have enjoyed our time together. Would it be possible to exchange telephone numbers so that we could meet again?' They did so: Owen moved ponderously up the hill.

In the afternoon Henry telephoned Molly again, and found no one at home. He wondered if she was on holiday. Staring at the phone he remembered Owen who had called out as he left, with courtly exaggeration, 'Give my regards to your lady wife.' He tried Molly in the evening. She was in.

'I've been down at my bench today until five.'

'Do you work seven days a week, then?'

'I've had to. I eat out.'

She had heard nothing from Jim, and did not expect to, now. 'I don't know what he's doing, and I don't think I care very much.' She delivered the sentence firmly, without dejection of voice, an expression of common sense. 'What are you on with?' When he'd given some account of himself, she said, 'Would you like to come over for a drink? I could do with company. Give me an hour to have a bath and straighten my mop.'

When Henry arrived, Molly was already taking her ease with a library book and a glass of gin. She poured whisky for him, and resumed her chair, legs straight out.

'You'll have to forgive me,' she said, smiling, 'if I drop off to sleep.'

She looked lively, to him, lounging but alert; he was reminded of what Laura said about her half day a week to herself. He mentioned this, but Molly said, 'Oh, she'll take time off for her hair, or a sauna, or a manicure. She needs to look good. I'm just tap-tapping away with no long breaks.'

'Is it boring?'

'No, oddly enough. I've got to the stage in the process where I can do the things without concentrating too hard, and that gives me idea-time. Especially as I'm actually using the materials. I'm full of designs. In fact I'm going to take two days off this week, whatever happens, just to sketch.'

'Is that tiring?'

'Oh, yes. And time skids past.'

He described his holiday; she agreed it might suit her, that she could use a working week in such a place with her sketchbook. Henry asked again about his brother. She narrowed her eyes.

'When I think about it now, I'm not surprised I've heard nothing. It's the end.'

'And how do you feel about that?'

'Hard to say. It's getting on for four years since our wedding. I don't miss the quarrels, I can tell you that for nothing. Or the times he'd hide himself away, only to come out shouting. Or the lies about his Christina. The place is peaceful. I don't dread what will explode next.'

'What happens to the house?'

'It's in both our names. He'll want his share in due course, I expect. I don't mind that. I shall invest in one of these new little town houses. There are plenty about in all sorts of convenient places. Not very big. Double glazing and F.G.C.H. Quick sale if I do decide on

189

London. I've no attachment to this dump. But I dread the first solicitor's letter.'

'Why?'

'The onset of trouble. I'm settled, and free, and busy now. Then I shall have to talk to lawyers, listen in courts, pay money out, hang around, waste good working hours. I want, to tell you the truth, to be left alone. That's me. Desert island castaway.'

'I'd better go.'

'You're the gentle wind, Henry, in the palm trees. You add to the pleasure of solitude.' She lifted her glass. 'Jim didn't think so. "Henry's a bit of a thug," he'd say. He reckoned you were a good boxer at school, and very strong at the shot and weight-lifting. "Don't be misled by that humble expression." ' Molly laughed out loud. 'Did he dislike you?'

'No. We were too far apart. All hearsay, my prowess in the ring. He was captain of the school; I wasn't. He went to Cambridge; I didn't. No, there was no firm reason why he should dislike me. I was a provincial nondescript. And ever shall be.'

'But you did better financially, didn't you?'

'Luck. He'd put it down to mere luck.'

'You don't dislike him, do you, Henry?'

'No, I don't. First of all I remember him when he was a youngster. He was attractive, and quick, and to some extent he depended on me. I think we all had great expectations of Jim. I've never quite lost them.'

'You don't,' Molly spoke quietly, 'blame me for his failure, do you?'

'No. Why should I? He seemed to change with my mother's death. But he . . . No. I hoped you could pull him out of whatever it was.'

'Will he do well in London?'

'He could. But I don't know enough about him these days. What do you think?'

'I'm in no position to judge. We've had such a rough ride recently and I'm glad he's off my back. Our marriage is finished and over. I don't want him in any shape or form.'

'But suppose he failed, and came running to you, tail between his legs?'

'No. It would make no difference. I wouldn't touch him.'

She asked him, calmly enough, to refill the glasses. Henry thought about his play, pondering whether to say anything to Molly. In the end, he decided against it.

'Tell me something interesting,' she demanded, at length.

'I saw Brother Owen this afternoon. The Welshman.'

'What had he to say for himself?'

'The whole of his life had been a failure. In seventy-seven long paragraphs.'

'Do you ever feel like that?' she asked, straightening up.

Briefly, soberly he recounted his feelings on the mountain path in Wales.

'Every decision you'd taken had been wrong?' she pursued, having heard him out.

'So it seemed. Up there, on a fresh morning I ought to have been bursting with life, but I wasn't.'

'At our age,' she sounded solemn, 'we can always comfort ourselves that there'll be plenty of other opportunities. Owen realizes that there aren't for him.'

'That's so only if you can think logically. I couldn't. And a close series of defeats could have a catastrophic effect.'

Now he changed his mind, outlined his new play. She listened, quite still, fingers clasped.

'I suppose you got the idea from Jim's jaunt to London?'

'Yes, and Laura's to Canada. Embarking on the unknown. Both.'

She seemed interested, but uninvolved, sat unspeaking.

'I have to decide what the play is about exactly. So I have to work out the relationship between Francis and Helen, and decide whether Francis's failures are to be dealt with at first hand, or through her eyes, or probably both, switching from one to the other. She can save him

191

from himself, and his suicidal tendencies, but I shall have to establish that with the audience. It's not easy.'

'I'd say it wasn't likely.'

'Why?'

'I suppose you'll think it's my guilt, about Jim, speaking up here. If a man is in that amount of dire trouble, and I imagine that Francis has threatened or tried suicide before, I don't think anything except long nursing care or exactly the right drugs will save him. Mark you, it might make an interesting play, the dragging him back from the pit.' She considered this. 'I tell you something. If Jim went to pot in London, I'd be in no position to sort him out, physically, financially, psychologically, any way. He'd have to do it on the National Health Service, or by himself.'

'You don't think it could be done?'

'I'm not saying that. It depends on how bad you make him.' He realized with a start that she was not speaking about Jim. 'Yes, I suppose it could. I take it your Helen would drag him back and then gradually prise out of him the cause of his trauma. She, and you, especially you, would have to know what was wrong with him.' She rubbed her face with the back of her hand in puzzlement, sipped her gin and said, almost mournfully, 'It sounds fair enough for a play, but not for life.'

'Why not?'

'Too slick. Too easy. Not complicated enough.'

They argued with spirit for perhaps ten minutes before taking to drink and thought. The intervals of silence were comfortable, companionable. He told her that he had written two postcards to Jim, and how he had chosen the names of his characters from the couple from Bedford.

'I wish I'd asked them their names. I always slip up on these crucial issues.'

'There you go again. For all you know their names might have been absolutely ridiculous and unsuitable. Stanley and Lalage. Cuthbert and Kate. You'd have been forced back on your imagination.'

Soon after ten he stood, said he must leave.

'No hurry,' she countered.

'I'm at work again after a holiday. I've a parcel to post. And tomorrow evening, wet or fine, I start on Francis and Helen.'

'Jim and Molly.'

He made a playful swipe at her; she staggered as she dodged, fell into his arms, leaned heavily on him. She kissed him full on the mouth, earnestly.

'Thanks for everything.'

Henry held her body, heavy and yielding. He let her loose, gently.

'We'll have another session,' he said, 'to stop you working too hard.'

'When? This week?'

'What about Thursday? I shall have had, D.V. as my grandma used to say, three full evenings on my play. I finish early that night, and so I'll get half an hour in. As long as I write a line or two I feel comforted. So you come round.'

'Nothing to eat. I'm slimming.'

'You've not lost weight in these bad few weeks?'

'Unfortunately not.'

She kissed him again, heartily this time, and rushed him out of the house. At the front door he asked:

'Shall I ring Owen up, ask him to appear?'

'Do you want to?'

'Not particularly. We shouldn't be short of topics of conversation.'

'No, Henry, don't ask him. It sounds a good idea, but he'll be round your neck for the rest of your life. I know his sort. Besides I need a rest, and you're just the man. You say the right amount of interesting things.'

'Not many.'

'Exactly.' She slapped him across the right buttock, stingingly. 'You do me good.'

He felt grateful to know women who knew their minds, even if one never wrote.

XVIII

Henry Fairfax made an adequate start on his play.

Once he had a few sentences, then pages complete, the burden tilted slightly away. He'd have difficulties, self-doubts, re-writings, arguments, heart-searchings but at least he was off the mark, not prancing around, shadow-boxing.

On Tuesday evening he arrived home to find two letters from Laura and a postcard from Jim.

To say that he read Laura's letters, one from Ottawa, the second from New York, with disappointment was not exactly just. Written within a few days of each other, the first from Canada on the eve of her departure for the States, the letters were not short, both occupied four sides of smallish writing, but they were concerned with places, people and incidents, with her business. She apologized in her first letter for her long silence, pleading desperately occupied days and nights, chess-like roguery or pusilla-nimity on the part of hard-faced businessmen, who lacked flair, imagination, vision and yet appeared extraordinarily successful.

Laura wrote without spark, so that he wondered if she had failed in her mission. The letters lacked all personal delight, reminding him of the cyclostyled bulletins sent round with Christmas cards by people too busy to scribble an informative line or two. Except that Laura declined to boast. She had not shaken hands with the President of the USA or the Prime Minister of Canada; her visits to places of interest were listed but without mention of being breathless with adoration or soaked with spray or sweat. She had been, and presumably had looked. Even the second letter written because of the Ottawa promise on her first day in New York, fell short and unenthusiastic. The flight had been dull, the food unappetizing, everyone talked too loud or buried heads in files from new briefcases. In New York it was sunny, fearfully hot, but she had not been out yet, and the air conditioning, though noisy, was effective. She was to have lunch with a man she'd thrice met in Canada, and whom she disliked. She did not expect to be there for more than a few days. She would be glad to be home, when she'd lie in a warm bath for a week. She loved him.

He read and re-read the letters, chiding himself. Laura was working herself to death, and had still found time, if belatedly, to write to him. Twice in three days. And here was he, Mr Literature, looking down his nose because of all the talk of contracts, negotiations, meetings, taxi rides and martinis. Laura lacked verve; these were schoolgirl essays, forced labour. He read for missed clues to satisfaction and failed again and again to find them.

Jim announced from his card that he was fulfilling his life's ambition to enjoy a few days in Southend. 'Wish you were here. J.' On the other side were a couple of dark brown, shaggy donkeys photgraphed before the First World War.

Deciding that news of such importance could not be held over until Thursday he twice tried to ring Molly, but both times she was out. He grimly ate high tea, read the small tragedies from the front page of the evening paper, tried to make sense of them, to empathize, create imaginative sympathy inside himself, without success. He trudged upstairs to his study, glad to lose the day for an hour or two in a quarrel between Helen and Francis about a cat the husband had run over. Fraying his nerves thus, Henry took the rough edge off his life. By ten fifteen he was downstairs again feeling satisfied. He prepared to walk the town.

Henry stepped out,, glad to be on the pavement, and shot of the house. The sky, slightly luminous, soothed him and a wind from the north touched him with chill. Making great pace, he'd been out for half an hour hardly meeting a soul, he saw a figure turn out of a street in front of him. As he began to catch up, he thought he recognized the man, and quickened his step. When he was almost up to the shape's shoulder, he spoke, rather roughly.

195

'Good evening.'

The man half stopped, leaned forward to look round, made no answer. Henry was almost convinced of the identification.

'Don't I know you?' Henry asked.

'No.' Neither here nor there.

'I think I do.'

They had started to walk alongside each other, but without haste, suspiciously but easily. The man had so far said no more than his one word.

'What d'you mean?' Unwillingly, in fear.

'Have we seen each other before?'

'What you on about?'

The dark figure seemed to hunch away. Perhaps he suspected some kind of sexual approach. They walked together, accelerating, neither yielding.

'You tried to rob me?' Henry croaked.

'When?' It seemed an inept question, as if admitting guilt.

'January.' His pulses raced as he established superiority. He could punch this man into submission. No answer, but now their pace was ridiculously fast. 'I hit you.'

'Ugh.' A rough grunt of acknowledgement.

'Do you remember? At the top of Logan Street? Just past the playing field?'

They were almost running now, both breathing heavily, shoulder to shoulder, unspeaking in combat. The man made up his mind suddenly, darted away, swooping at speed. Fairfax watched, trying to match the retreating figure to that of the fleeing thief, but he failed. He stopped abruptly. The young man could run. Coughing, he wondered whether he had made a mistake, and frightened the life out of some hapless youth going about his lawful business. In a shop window near a street lamp he could make out his dark outline, hatless, in anorak, broad, formidable. He swaggered on. Jim had called him a thug, and now he had acted like one. He'd heard of hooligans picking on passers-by, threatening to lay one on them, beating them up; but they were wild with drink or drugs, mad with disappointment, crazy to get their own back on a world which provided neither job nor satisfaction except violence against someone incapable of defending himself, snatching a pound or two for further spurious comfort.

He, Henry Fairfax, had nothing against society, the environment, God; on a night admittedly cooler than one expected in August, he had tried to impose himself on another human being. No, that was unfair. He was now walking with great energy, taking himself away from temptation. Exhilaration had gone; he felt ashamed, would be pleased to creep in home. He must first get there.

He had been convinced that the figure he had accosted had been the robber. Now it seemed unlikely; they were in another part of the town and faces are not recognizable in the dark. But, but; the man had taken to his heels. Not surprisingly at eleven at night in deserted streets with an accuser dogging every step. If the young man stepped out now, confessed, begged mercy, Henry would have forgiven him, slipped him a tenner to buy a drink and forget the whole affair. No, he had done right to challenge the man. It did not do to let the world trample on you, kick your teeth in while you whimpered and cowered. Somebody had beaten up that poor sod, what was his name? Rhodes, in Laura's place. Somebody had to lay down the law, issue a warning. Even to the wrong party.

He remembered a story with which Harry Dexter had returned from holiday in Spain. Dexter was a dull man, in his fifties, the ideal second-in-command, hard-working, not unintelligent, but uncertain, frightened to initiate. In the past ten years he and his wife had taken to package holidays abroad, flew like veterans to Marbella and now talked, if vaguely, of retiring to a villa on the Costa del Sol. The husband would be quite content, himself, to sit on the beach with a cold drink, splash in the sea, admire the topless beauties, eat English meals and drink moderately in the evening, but his wife organized outings, coach trips. 'What's the good of going abroad if you're going to sit on the sands all day,' Harry reported her as saying.

'You go on your own,' he'd reply. 'Don't be so idle.' And her word prevailed.

This year they'd become friendly with a couple from London, the Wests, who had told the Dexters a curious anecdote.

'It would just be right for one of your plays,' Harry announced.

Fairfax showed only a moderate interest; always enthusiastic to share his reminiscences, Dexter was no raconteur. His offerings usually took the form of garbled accounts of the previous evening's television watching, and were nearly unintelligible to anyone who had not seen the programmes he attempted to describe. The mention of Henry's plays was unique. Almost certainly, Harry had never listened to one, even by chance.

The couple Harry described were decent and middle-aged, living in Fulham. Their neighbour, an architect, was a homosexual. Here Dexter became slightly flustered; he used the terms 'homo' and 'gay' painlessly, but went to great lengths to explain that the neighbour was, in spite of this, thoroughly respectable, a quiet young man in his thirties called Hilary. For some years he had lived with another man, well turned out and professional, also, who had six months before broken off the relationship and gone to live in California. This had greatly upset the architect, his neighbours said. 'He walked about like a ghost; he looked really haggard.' He began to confide in Mrs West next door. He had regarded the arrangement with his lover as permanent, as a marriage, though they had made no formal vows at a ceremony, and the partner's decision, taken at speed, had left Hilary desolate. He had hoped fervently, he told Mrs West, for a contrite return, but this had not happened.

Dexter's tale needed reinterpreting by the listener, and was made more opaque by attempts to suggest character or gender by variations of voice. Harry unfortunately had neither skill nor practice.

Hilary, the Wests reported, recovering slightly had gone out occasionally in the evening to gay bars or clubs and had, it appeared, brought back on a casual basis suitable young men. He hoped for the beginning of another durable relationship, he said. Promiscuity he claimed to hate.

One night he brought back a young actor, not beautiful, but charming, lively, well educated, at present out of work. They drank a good deal, or at least Hilary did, and then retired to bed 'to do', as Dexter put it, 'whatever it is they do'. On the next morning, a Sunday, Hilary awoke, still slightly fuddled as he was not usually a heavy drinker, to find his partner of the night gone from the bedroom. Neither was he anywhere about the house. Nothing was missing but on the bathroom mirror a message was scrawled. 'You have now joined us. You have AIDS.'

Mrs West had received this confession from Hilary who had concluded that the young actor having caught the disease was now spreading it in revenge. She had in the end prevailed on Hilary to visit his doctor who had been sensible and unshocked, not always the case Dexter reported, and sent him for tests. So far it was too early to say, apparently, whether anything had happened. Hilary lived like a zombie.

'What do you think of that, then?' Dexter proud of his narrative skill.

'Um.'

'It's a bastard, in't it?'

'If you believe it.'

'What do you mean?' Dexter sounded affronted.

'It's the sort of myth that always begins to go the rounds.'

'Such as what?'

'Jamaicans eating Kit-E-Cat sandwiches.'

'I've not heard that so much lately.' Dexter frowned. 'You don't think it's true, then?'

'I'd be a bit loth to accept it.'

'They said it happened to them.'

'It's possible. But the number of AIDS cases is fairly small. And it's amazing what people will tell you to make themselves interesting.'

'The Wests didn't seem like that. Not liars.'

Dexter backed away, chastened. He had never

presumed to doubt the story, and now here was his boss showing him up as credulous or naïve. Henry felt sorry for the man whose pleasure he had spoilt. The story stuck with him. Later in the afternoon he asked Dexter if the message on the mirror had been properly punctuated.

'How the bloody hell would I know that?' Dexter obviously thought the gaffer was again making fun of him, and went off in a huff.

For Fairfax the tale had a kind of truth. It was the equivalent of those acecdotes his headmaster had told them at morning assembly. The old man, an unhistrionic nonconformist hypocrite, could send his pupils away impressed and silent. 'You are one of us' matched Father Damien's 'We lepers' with which he opened his address on the day he realized he too was a victim of the disease. You are one of us.

The next morning Dexter faced him.

'I told Annie' (his wife) 'that you didn't believe that story, and do you know what she said?'

'Go on.'

'She didn't believe it, either. She thinks she'd read it in some magazine.' He grinned, cheerful again. 'And do you know what I said to her? I said, "And there you sat nodding, taking it all in as if butter wouldn't melt in your mouth." And she said, "You could tell they were romancers." '

'I see.'

'But they made the name up and the profession of the man. And they must have agreed to spin the same yarn. Now, why?'

'Don't ask me,' Fairfax answered. 'That's more interesting than the original story.'

Dexter moved away as if the scenario had been played out or his interest exhausted. He'd worry it again, raise it once more. He did.

'It's not as if those Wests would get anything out of it.'

'What?'

'Making up that story like that. Conspiring. To cheat us.'

'They caught your interest. They gave you something to think about.'

'They did that. Folks act odd.'

Fairfax, somewhat reluctantly, told Dexter of his passage with the man in the street. His subordinate had heard the original story.

'And were you sure it was the right one?' he asked.

'By no means. And the more I think about it the less certain I am. But what bothers me is the bold way I went up and challenged him. Would you say I was aggressive?'

'Er, er, yes. I think I would.'

'I don't see myself like that, as a man always throwing his weight about. And yet I didn't seem to feel any hesitation. I don't understand it myself. It's proper to issue warnings, I suppose.'

'Not the same as the Wests, though.' Dexter stroked his chin. 'You did right. You let it be known there are those who are not going to be knocked around and say nothing.'

Fairfax remembered walking home that night, on the look-out for the assailant, ready for lightning striking twice, feeling a fool. His play, *Francis and Helen*, was like that, an unease, a combination of shards, nothing coherent, without shape, inchoate with powerful emotion. *Two Sisters* had at least been shaped, but this was wildness, wilderness, suspicion ruining all with its anarchy.

He had crept in, locked his doors and stared out into the deserted streets, not understanding what he was about.

201

XIX

The next week Laura rang, much in command of herself.

She had been home, she announced blandly, since Saturday but had not had the opportunity to call him. She would, she said, like to visit him on Sunday for a few hours.

'I'll come down to you, if that's more convenient,' he offered.

'No. I'll arrive in time for lunch. Yes, you can take me out. That'll be the eating over for the day. I'm bloated with food and drink. Healthy living from now on.'

'Tell you what you can do for me,' he said, once arrangements had been agreed. 'Just find out how Jim's shaping, will you? He doesn't write to his wife, to girl-friend, and all he's managed for me is a postcard of donkeys. Make a few inquiries.'

Laura arrived earlier than expected, soon after eleven. Certainly she seemed plumper, but was elegant still, perfumed, settled, ready to enjoy herself. She kicked off her shoes over coffee and began to talk. The American venture had, it appeared, been supremely successful, so much so that it had put back the floating of Laura's own company. That was still on, but she was so engrossed in her brother's affairs that her scheme would be handled by others, was 'small beer'. She had been voted on to the board of Le Jeune.

'Did you expect that?'

'Yes and no. I knew that if I did well enough they'd take me on sooner or later. The only snag was that if I concentrated on my own affairs then I wouldn't do enough for them, and they wouldn't consider me. But this trip has changed all that. As soon as I was back, Con told me. And off I go again next week.'

'I take it there are advantages in it for you rather than working on your own?'

'I'll say. Money, for starters.'

Laura laughed out as if her vulgar phrase disguised the gigantic size of financial advantage.

Her easy attitude did nothing for Fairfax. Laura could have been a royal, condescending but affable over a cup of tea on a photo-call. She spoke about a print he had recently bought and had framed and which she dismissed as 'beautiful but useless'. He queried the expression.

'Being beautiful is what a picture is meant to be, isn't it?'

'Yes, but that does nothing else. I don't want a moral story, as you might guess, but I need to be puzzled, or caught up artistically, made to think and feel with, and this is the wrong word, a kind of violence.'

Laura seemed a different woman as she made her pronouncement. Success impregnated every part of her life so that she would, he expected, demonstrate her expertise everywhere, on painting, politics, oh, religion, philosophy, computers, aerobics, architecture, cookery, the mathematics of tides. That was unfair, but she was borne up by a new valuation of herself.

At lunch she ate a plate of salad, piled high, and drank water. She spent most of the meal describing a two-day jaunt to Florida, a reward for hard work. Again she expounded her theory that one did not need a long holiday, that one could learn to relax sufficiently to recuperate inside a few hours. When they left the restaurant she demanded to be driven round the town, and then to the suburb where they had spent their married life.

The road was pleasant, the long front gardens on each side had ornamental trees, now large, masking the mock-Tudor gables. The pair sat in silence before No. 38, Laura pondering.

'It all looks very prosperous,' he said.

A Muslim lady, beautifully trousered, ushered three small children into the back seat of a Volvo estate and drove off.

'Who lives there now?' Laura asked.

203

'I've no idea. A man called Longley bought it, but I don't know whether he's . . .'

'What was the name of the old fellow next door? The one with dahlias and roses.'

'Daniel Collins.'

'Is he still alive? He used to come round with bunches of flowers for me. I wonder if he's still there?'

'Shall we go and ask?' Henry in suspicion, and enthusiasm.

Laura shook her head, thoughtfully.

'He'd be older, and vaguer. He wouldn't remember us. Anyhow, he's probably dead.'

'He used to sing "Silver threads amongst the gold". And talk about rabbit pie.'

Laura said nothing. Henry felt he was being examined, without being allowed to read the questions. In the end, with a gesture of impatience, Laura instructed him to drive on.

'Where?'

'Oh, home. Your house.'

Back on the settee, shoes off, she recovered her spirits, cheerfully refusing alcohol, explaining again why she must lose weight. She accepted black coffee.

'You never said anything about Jim.' Henry spoke early, as he sat down, determined. She looked him coolly over.

'You never asked.' Again finger play on saucer. 'I made inquiries. They say he's doing very well indeed. He's fitted in to the satisfaction of everyone. I had a few words with him on the one occasion I saw him. He looked fit, sounded cheerful. They're pleased with him. He works hard, doesn't mind staying on, and isn't short of ideas. He has his own place now. To live, I mean. A little flat.'

'I'm glad.'

'Yes,' she said. 'Good move on his part.'

Henry considered that.

'He hasn't contacted his wife at all. Not a word.'

'Isn't that for the best?' She beckoned towards him. 'I didn't make inquiries about his private life. Why should

204

I? But isn't it possible that that's the best thing? The marriage may be over.'

'Why doesn't he say so, then?'

'I imagine, and this is only guesswork, that he doesn't want to rock his boat. He's content to get on with the new job, make a success of that, and then see how things work out.'

'It's bad for Molly.'

'I'm sure it is. Has she written to him?'

'I think so. And Christina Brown, the lady friend.'

She paused, uncertainly quiet.

'He's taken one of the girls in the office out a time or two. Of course, it may mean nothing.'

'Why do you tell me that, Laura?'

'Somebody mentioned it. Just to show that Jim's not leading a life of monkish celibacy, that he's a human being.'

'He's not doing right by Molly.'

'No. I can see that.'

Constraint grew between them. He had expected at the beginning that Laura would renew her proposal, but it was not mentioned. Very gently she repulsed sexual over-tures on his part. They took a turn in his little garden, which was replete with green leaves, but here flowers were not plentiful.

'There's been so much rain,' he explained. 'Growth galore.' He pointed at a red shoot from Mermaid.

'That's how I am. Expanding, but unfloriferous.'

'Crescive in your faculty.'

'And then some.'

Back in the house, Laura once more talked about her American trip. He could understand her excitement; Le Jeune's seemed to have taken over a series of petrol stations as well as introducing a new system of cartage. 'The distances are enormous. No, firms can't always buy what they want locally. Odd, isn't it? Nor have they worked out sensible schemes. It seems incredible but it is so. Con's bright boys have had a field day. No, in some ways they're years behind us.'

'It'll be Russia next,' he mocked.

'If they've the money to pay, we'll do it.'

He quite enjoyed this forceful, preaching Laura with her low voice, her head tilted forward, her eyes bright with modest confidence. She knew. She was not to be shaken, at least in public. They were the experts, the empiricists; they would make profits for you. The tone was hypnotic; the mouth generous but intelligent, the skin palely beautiful. About six she drank a cup of tea with lemon, said she must not be too long here.

Henry made up his mind, as he listened to a story about Lord Bridger, ex-civil servant, now on the board. He was the restraining influence on Con. 'Not that he needs it just now. We're huge and we're growing bigger by the hour. Nothing can stop us.' Bridger was sharp, didn't mind cutting corners, but did not take easily to what he called 'extemporization'. Con argued that one always played it 'off the cuff', so that no time was wasted, or allowed to rivals. It was an intellectual pleasure, apparently, to hear these two fighting their corners; they remained, she said, the best of friends, each full of admiration for the other man's powers.

When this chapter was complete, Henry spoke, quietly, firmly.

'Did you think any more of what you proposed last time you were here?' he said.

The words were clearly articulated; Lord Bridger could have done no better.

'About what?' The voice did not shake, but her head jerked nervously back.

'About remarrying.'

She consulted the fingernails on both spread hands, as if they held the answer. The room crumbled to silence, after the brilliant precision of her talk. When she began to speak again she did not lift her eyes.

'Yes, Henry,' she said. 'I have thought about it a very great deal. In the interstices.' She glanced up to judge the effect of her word. To him it rang false, but his expression did not change. 'I don't think you can realize just how busy I have been. I've rushed about on planes and trains. I've attended conferences. I've never been in bed before the small hours. It's a man's world, and I've kept up with them, beaten them sometimes. But it hasn't allowed time for serious thought about personal matters. Time and again, I've considered our life, but always I've had to put it to one side.'

'I see.'

She pursed her lips.

'You don't, do you? In this last month or two I've stretched myself. More than is sensible perhaps. Look at me. I've grown fat, because I've taken no exercise and eaten between meals; I was so edgy. It doesn't mean that I've forgotton you, or what I said. But I was so exhilarated and exhausted. It is like one's first free-fall parachute jump.'

Henry made no answer, poured more cool coffee, sipped.

'You do understand, don't you?' she pressed him, not hard, sweetly. It was as though she was considering something else. 'Tell me what you think.'

'You've found your real métier.'

'I guess that's so.' A trans-Atlantic touch.

'And it doesn't include me.'

'No. That's not true. I can see why you think it is. For the first time in my life I've achieved something above my expectations. You've got to believe that, Henry, and make allowances for it. I showed them the way home. And one doesn't do that without bruising or loss. Your life has been comparatively sheltered. I know that sounds condescending, but I don't mean it so. But you've never been dashed off your feet. You've always had time and elbow room. And you've made a success of yourself, as a writer and as a business man, perhaps because you've had the capability of standing back. I'm different. And for the first time in my life I've been fully extended, with every minute caught up and used, and I have seen results. It's only now in these last two months that I realized what I'm capable of. I didn't know before, honestly. I thought I was doing well, and in a sense I suppose I was. But I've learned in these past weeks something I never

207

knew, something I'd heard but dismissed as a saying, that the best is the enemy of the good.'

'That's me condemned,' he said, bitterly light.

'It has nothing to do with you as a man, or husband, or anything else. I've just learnt something about myself, something important. And you'll have to understand it and accept it if we are to come to any sort of terms.'

He did not answer, so that they sat in an uncomfortable silence, staring down at the floor or cold half-cups of black liquid. Henry fumbled in his mind to know exactly what he thought outside the darkness of disappointment. He imagined that Laura, certain that he would question her about remarriage, had concocted this reasonable answer. It wasn't improbable that she had been so fully engaged and excited by her success that she had had no time for his affairs. He saw that as acceptable. There was a case. But in presenting it Laura had stepped over the bounds, shown such self-regard, self-aggrandisement that he felt banished and, worse, disgusted. That was unfair. He had not prepared himself carefully enough, had left himself wide open to wounds. The absence of regular letters should have given the clue, the delayed phone call days after her arrival back.

Yet she had insisted on coming to see him.

That made no sense, unless she had determined to drop him for good. Then why did she not keep quiet, like Jim, let him know her decision by default? He had expected her to come back, in success or disaster, with an offer of resumed relationship, eager as he knew she could be, a woman, generously womanly, queenly submissive. His cheeks burnt and he closed his eyes.

'I don't think you understand any of this, do you, Henry?'

'Only too well.' She made to speak but he interrupted her. 'No, just one minute. You excelled all your expectations. You found out things about yourself that you didn't know before. And I can't help being pleased for you. You've surprised and dazzled me. You're in your brother's class.' He came out with these remarks in a kind of sycophancy, not knowing whether what he said was true or even why he said what he did. Mortified he tried to give an impression of reason, stoic capacity to suffer; he did little to convince himself. 'But it means you're going to live a different sort of life from now on. And in this rarefied atmosphere I shan't be able to breathe.'

'You underestimate yourself.'

'I don't think so.' He answered glumly but at once. 'You'll meet important and influential people; your money will be increased by a factor of ten if not a hundred. And here I shall sit in my provincial corner. No, Laura, you do well to keep away.'

'What are you saying, Henry? Telling me you're not interested?'

'No. That's the last . . .'

'You sit there in your provincial corner, with a sulky face, telling me that you're not good enough for me. What am I to conclude? I'll tell you. That you're politely trying to get rid of me. Now just let me add something else while I'm about it. I've met a good number of these – what did you call them? – important and influential people with millions invested or at their command, who make crucial decisions on which the quality of life of hundreds if not thousands depends and as human beings, or companions, or husbands they're no more interesting than the men managing one of their small concerns or even sweeping their factory floors. They're often driven, have compulsions strong enough to flatten a city, but that doesn't make them any more attractive to sit next to at dinner, or in the theatre. Let alone marry. Not that I want a doormat for a husband, either.'

'All I'm trying to say is that at present you don't know what you'll want in twelve months' time. Your life-style is about to change. Radically. You've admitted it.'

'So what do you suggest?'

'When you were away, Laura, you hardly wrote to me.'

'You didn't write to me at all.'

'On instruction. I'm not blaming you. I guess you were doing the right thing, concentrating exactly on what you were there for. But it suggests I am not going to have much of a part in your new life. Let's be honest . . .'

'You mean "Let's quarrel".'

'No. You are going to be occupied as you have never been before. It would therefore be unwise to commit yourself to me for the present. Or to anyone else, for that matter.'

'Don't you think that at a time like this, when I'm changing, being changed, I might need some steadying mark, somebody who'll remind me that one of these days I'm going to have to die?'

'That's a long way ahead,' he muttered, caught out, taken aback by the swerve of her conversation.

'We don't even know that. But I shall need some criteria and you could, if you wanted, provide them.'

'You please me when you say that, but I'm no better for your purpose than a dozen or a hundred people you'll meet in the next few months. And you must remember, Laura, we tried once and failed. I don't want to be shown the door again.'

'That's just what you're suggesting now.' Her voice shrilled; she frowned; slapped the settee. 'Isn't it?'

'Before we involve ourselves deeply,' Henry stroked his face, uncertain where to look, 'I'm afraid, Laura.'

'You don't trust me.'

'Say that if you like. But the temptations will be overwhelming. We might not see each other for weeks on end. What sort of commitment will that be?'

She composed herself, swung down her legs and sat straight, giving herself time.

'I'm glad we've talked like this, Henry. At least it's cleared the air. I'm still too excited for sense.'

'Why did you talk about dying?' he asked.

'Oh, I don't know. To sound impressive. Shouldn't I have done?'

'You've not been ill?'

'Fitter than I've ever been. And fatter.' She giggled. 'But now let's say no more. We've not made our minds up. Agreed?'

'If you wish.'

'That doesn't sound very forthcoming. What's wrong, Henry?'

'Nothing. I think . . .'

'Well?'

'You've already made your mind up. You might not know it, or admit it, but the decision's taken.'

'And you're not prepared to wait until I find out what I've decided?'

'It just makes it more difficult for me. I'm convinced now . . .'

'. . . That I'll show you the door?' Her tone was bantering. 'Don't be such a fool to yourself. We've by no means done with each other.' She stood, patted his arm, smiling. Henry stiffened, determined to yield nothing to her; he lacked all strength, froze within to defend himself. She clutched his arm warmly, went out and upstairs to the bathroom. Miserably he cleared cups and coffee pot, swilled, dried them, tidied sink and draining boards.

Above, all was quiet; Laura's preparations for departure took long enough.

Henry picked up a book, read a paragraph, retained nothing. For another ten minutes he occupied his chair. Relief flooded him as he heard the opening of doors, the flush of the cistern, footsteps.

'Clean and decent,' Laura said, spreading her arms.

'There's just one thing . . .'

'Yes?' Much at ease, not to be baffled.

'What am I to tell Molly about Jim? She's bound to ask.'

'He's doing well. About her hearing nothing I've no comment, really. That's up to her. I'll ask if you like, though I don't think it's wise. It's up to her. If she wants to get at him she knows where he works and how to . . . No. She may think it's better as it is. But he's not ill, and he's making a good impression.' She swivelled to examine her head in a mirror. 'Thanks for lunch. Not an ounce on. Tried it on your scales. We're winning, Henry, aren't we?'

'I'm glad you think so.'

She took him into her arms, but warned him not to spoil her face. Their parting was swiftly accomplished, and he on his own stared round the empty house, at the

211

cushion she had dented. Weariness rather than disappointment overcame him; he felt as if he had performed a taxing physical feat but without a corresponding sense of achievement. He sat about, moving from chair to chair, room to room. He tried the Sunday newspapers, books, the radio, television, sorties into the garden, round the block, up and down stairs. Twice he rang Molly; she was not at home. In bed by ten he fell, against expectation, asleep at once.

On his return from work the next day he found a letter from the BBC. Tom O'Riordan, a script editor, had read *Two Sisters* and had discussed it thoroughly with Anthony Friend who wished to produce it in proper time. Friend, however, agreed with him that considerable changes would be necessary before it approached a standard for broadcasting. They had admired the precise idiom of his dialogue, but felt that the pace was too often wrong and so robbed the play of dramatic impact. Tony had a long list of suggestions that he would communicate in due course, and he, O'Riordan, with reservations was certain that with revision they had a script of distinction. He was etc. etc.

Henry Fairfax re-read the fluent, emollient phrases, and yet a third time out loud. Blood banged about his head. He thumped the open letter on the table-top, hurting his fist. All day he had been contained, congratulating himself on sorting out snags in the schedule, imbecilities on the part of work-people, with grace, considerable grace the bloody BBC would call it, without ill temper, in spite of Sunday, Laura, his own shortcomings.

And now here were this pair of prize pricks with their ifs and buts. He made an extravagant effort to control himself. O'Riordan he had never heard of, but Tony Friend, who had handled his other plays satisfactorily, was experienced, on radio and in the theatre, by no means stupid, a man for all seasons. But that was his shortcoming. He could recognize, foster, present talent, but only inside limits. What he knew, he knew thoroughly, but he would be in immediate difficulties with any experiment, especially something different but still inside an old

212

convention. Blatant modernism he would recognize, and even welcome, but make alterations inside a well-accepted form and he was baffled. Fairfax's anger did not diminish. He warned, chided himself, but grew more agitated.

Henry stormed upstairs to write a reply.

He thanked them for their letter. He could tell them that he had spent considerable (ah, ha) sweat on the shape of the play, that it depended on this format for its effect. In his view, he had made a notable advance on anything he had done before. This was a difficult subject on which . . . He broke off. He was not willing to argue with them. If they felt that the play was unsatisfactory as it stood, he did not, and he was not prepared to make 'considerable changes'. In view of this they had better return his script without delay. He would waste no more of their time. He was theirs sincerely.

Cutting and polishing his scorn to a mere four lines he decided against a final copy. He knew they would not care about sending his script back; they'd their salaries to earn by hints and suggestions and niggling alterations and improvements, and if Henry Fairfax did not toe their line, he was welcome to do the other thing. That would be the end of this particular venture; as it was written it was suitable only for radio, not for television or the theatre. It would lie on his shelves along with other unsatisfactory or half-finished projects. So be it. Thug Henry had drawn, not toed, the line.

He walked downstairs easier in his mind.

Of course he had not yet committed himself. It would be more sensible to wait for Tony Friend's long list of suggestions and make up his mind when he considered that. His temper rose, he kicked the skirting board on the stairs, and hammered the wall on either side of his head in the approved cell-block manner. Henry the compromiser. Grinning, he reached the whisky bottle without mishap, helped himself.

He carried the letter to work in the morning, thought about it once or twice in the rush, and retyped it on his secretary's machine during the lunch hour. His attempt was poor, badly set out with alterations so that he had to ask Sally to make a copy on her return. She rearranged it easily, made no comment on the content; a clever girl, she seemed always unconcerned about what he dictated. Yeats's typist refused to handle his Leda sonnet. Henry could have written to the Queen, threatening to murder the royal family, and Sally's workmanlike job would be completed and brought in for signature in silence. Henry provided his own first-class stamp, he was meticulously honest about these matters, and laid the letter in the posting tray. There were doubts in his mind; he had acted foolishly, but he felt a modest satisfaction. Someone had spoken up for the writer, had put the administrators and sideline critics into their subordinate place. His play would be lost, for the present, but in a good cause. He whistled through the afternoon.

On Wednesday he heard from Molly.

'Was it this Sunday you were seeing What's-her-name?' The vagueness was uncharacteristic.

'Yes.' Awkward silence at both telephones.

'Did she say anything about Jim?'

'I asked her.'

'Well?'

'Just what I expected. He's settled, is doing nicely at work, has pleased everybody and found himself a little flat. I don't know the address. I also told Laura he had not been in touch with you since he left. She said she knew nothing about that. When I pressed her she answered that she would be prepared to question him about this, though she didn't think it either wise or her own business. So we left it. She said you could always get hold of him at her office.'

'Well, yes. Thanks, anyhow. How did you and Laura make out? Are you joining forces,' she injected humour into her phrase, 'again?'

'No.'

'Are you disappointed? I am. I thought . . . Oh, never mind what I thought. The woman's a fool.'

He began to explain Laura's success, surprising himself with the enthusiasm he lavished on the account.

'Is she a millionaire yet?' Molly interrupted.

'It's a bit early for that.'

'But will she be?'

'I shouldn't be surprised.'

'And she's given you up on the strength of this affluence?'

'No. She was dazzled with her own success. It was unexpected. She's shocked herself, and didn't know what was what. They've made her a director of Le Jeune's.'

'Yes, you said so.' Molly hummed. 'And will Jim be dragged up in the ascent, do you think? Or forgotten in the excitement?'

'I don't know. Laura was bemused.'

'I'll bet.'

'But at least she took the trouble to come down and explain.'

'I should think she did.'

On Friday Molly rang him as he was on his way upstairs to grapple with *Francis and Helen*.

'I've heard from Jim,' she announced. 'I thought you'd better know.' Crosspatch.

'What does he say?'

'Inconclusive. Leave everything. Laura apparently told him you'd complained to her about his non-communication. He goes on to justify himself. As always. He thought it better that we leave one another alone for the present. He's taken no legal steps. He'll continue with the mortgage payments for the time being, though money's rather tight in London.'

'He gave you his new address?'

'He did. "Tell Henry to keep his nose out of it" was another of his gems. Not very long.'

'Are you going to reply?'

'No. I don't think so. It shook me up to see his handwriting on the letter. But when I'd read it, I ought not to say as much to you, I felt relieved. He wasn't going to do anything. There'd be no lawyers to cope with. I'm a coward, Henry.'

'You'll leave it?'

'I could manage the mortgage. Marty Fowler's just put

me into contact with some Japanese agent. I could do seven days a week for the next two years.'

'I hope to God you don't.'

'No fear of that. But it's comforting to know the work's there. Marty thinks I ought to employ an assistant, but I'm too cautious yet.'

'Are you still hanging on to your bit of teaching?'

'Yes. I've signed up to start in September. I don't go overboard just because I'm doing well now. Everything could change. I'm no Laura sweeping the world before me.'

'I was just thinking how well you ladies were doing for yourselves.'

'Thank you, thank you. And you Fairfax men aren't exactly dragging your feet.'

'Did Jim say so in his letter?'

'No. Very short. Not very sweet.' She growled comically. 'What are you doing?' He explained, and she apologized for the interruption. 'Tell you what. I'll make you a meal on Sunday evening. Will you come?'

They fixed the time, gruffly.

Molly had taken great care with her appearance. She wore a rather long dress, of multicoloured patches and black lines, which swirled wide at the hem as she moved. Her hair shone, tight-curled and formal; she wore make-up. Her hands were scrubbed, with the nails beautifully level. She seemed unlike herself, he thought; a formal drawing as opposed to the rough sketch. No sooner had he seated himself than she poured him a whisky. He commented on its size.

'I could have a bath in this.'

'Not in here you couldn't.'

'I hope you're not thinking of giving me wine.'

'It will be on the table, but you can refuse to mix grain and grape.'

She sounded pleased with herself today.

'Now, tell me about yourself. Have you heard any more from the egregious Laura?'

'No.'

'Good. Excellent.' She laughed. 'And your play?'

216

'I'm struggling. As usual.'

He began an account of his dealings with the BBC over *Two Sisters*. To his surprise he spoke more cheerfully than he expected. He described a minor setback, not a world-shattering tragedy.

'You were annoyed with them, were you?' she inquired. 'Jim always said you were a bit of a lout, once somebody had crossed you.'

'I've ditched the chances of a good play. I know that.'

'They've not replied?'

'They're in no hurry. They never are. Their view is that it will do me good to cool my heels before they kick my arse.'

'Oh dear, oh dear.'

'What about you, then?'

She produced her sketchbooks, spoke with energy and enthusiasm, explaining that now she made drawings for the joy of it. When she began as a student she had always scribbled down what was translatable into metal or stone, but now she made 'pictures'.

'What's the advantage?'

'Financially none. But it's relaxation, taking my mind into corners where it's never been before.' She showed him a drawing which began as a bracelet but which she had developed into a series of round towers, and by the third page was beginning to square itself into a ziggurat.

'When you're famous, these will be saleable?'

'Possible, possible. But my work depends, first, on shapes, so I can do myself no harm practising.'

'Do you stick to the original design, or do you modify that at your work-bench?'

'Depends. If it's a mass-produced job, I just try to repeat myself. But no two are exactly alike. That's the beauty of hand-made objects. Or so they say. But at other times I get ideas in my hands, so to speak. That sounds pretentious. But it's right. I try this and that out. Depends on the material. That has to be tractable for sudden changes.'

Molly spoke with brisk cheerfulness, as he imagined

217

she would speak to her students, making no great claims, a craftsman.

'Did you ever talk to Jim about what you were doing?'

'Very often when we were first married. He used to look through my sketches, say which he preferred. And he'd set off on some verbal track suggested by my lines. He was imaginative. Had all sorts of fancy ideas.'

'And were these verbal arabesques any good to you? Practically?'

She thought that over, touching, pressing the end of her nose.

'No. Not really. Though it's always an advantage when somebody shows an interest. And Jim's verbalising was his way of doing that.'

'So you'll miss that now?'

'I haven't had it for long enough. One puts up with what one's got. You must know that from your writing. If I take an assistant it will, one way or another, alter my working methods. But that won't matter, if I'm any good. A good workman would just use the altered circumstances to his advantage.'

'Luck doesn't play any part, then?'

'Of course it does. Being in the right place at the right time. Catching the eye of somebody influential. Yes, all that. But if you're really good, all that doesn't matter ultimately.'

'Ultimately?'

'If you're outstanding you'll translate all your errors into advantages. That's what being a genius means.'

'And that's what you are?'

She aimed a slap at him. He guessed she'd already been drinking.

'I'd like to think so. Martin Fowler brought some Victorian rings in to show me. Wants me to copy them. We were both excited.'

'Were they unusual?'

'No. That's the oddity. Run of the mill, but once one began to look hard at them, all sorts of ideas crowded in. It's set me off, I can tell you. And yet they were nothing special. Nice. Well made.' Molly held her breath. 'Mine will be variations on the ordinary. If anything comes of them.'

All through the meal, his favourite beef casserole then meringue circles with fruit and thick cream, without wine, with whisky, he encouraged her to talk further. She was intelligent, ambitious, prepared to push herself, but, he guessed, tired by her unrelenting slavery, if not by loneliness at home. She rarely visited friends; conversation with Fowler and associates, with her students when she had them, was all the social life she needed, or so she claimed.

While they were drinking coffee, with more whisky, she produced Jim's letter. It was exactly as she had reported it.

'And have you heard any more from that Laura of yours?' The demonstrative adjective struck ironically.

'No. Nor have I written.'

'Where is she now? Still in London?'

'To the best of my knowledge. She is going back to the States, but I don't know when.'

'Why haven't you written to her, Henry?'

He stroked his chin, gaining time he did not need.

'I could give you plenty of sensible answers to that.'

'Go on, then.'

'I don't want to harry her. She must decide for herself whether or not I'm dispensable.' He tossed his head. 'I don't know whether that's the truth. I don't want to write. That's the length and breadth of it.'

'Because you've too much to do? Your play and so on?'

'Play? This BBC business has knocked the wind out of me as far as that's concerned. Oh, I go up, add my mite every day, but I might as well be writing jingles on a lavatory wall. No, I think I don't want to write to her. Full stop. We had these few months of reunion, rejuvenation, regeneration, call it what you will. It filled the little bit of spare time we both had for private feelings pretty adequately, and that was all. We, or at least I, misconstrued it, made more of it than was there. Then suddenly it's put into its petty place by her success. She doesn't need a husband, let alone a provincial nobody earning not a fifth of what she does. She sees me for what I am.'

Molly rose to refill his cup, and when this was done, she stood in front of him, arms extended. He clasped her hands, and she heaved him upright to kiss him, deeply, passionately. Dazed, tipsy, he responded, and they swayed together. She returned him to his seat, slopped more whisky into their glasses, and sat beside him.

'What was that in aid of?' he asked, out of breath.

'You poor, poor man.'

'I'm not sorry for myself. Don't go thinking that. I've asked for all I've got. It could never have come to anything. I must have known that, however I deceived myself at the time. And now it's nothing. That's why I don't write, because it would be a waste of time. Just as writing these bloody plays is a waste of time.'

'Critics praise them.'

'I felt happy dancing, or making love or walking the streets with Laura. But it was all irrelevant. Cloud-cuckoo land.'

Molly laid her head on his shoulder.

'We're a poor pair,' she announced. 'But what if Laura wrote and asked you to remarry her?'

'She won't.'

'But if she did. Would you be prepared to accept her?'

'I don't think so.'

Tears coursed down Molly's cheeks; she buried her face into the cloth of his jacket. They sat together. The girl pushed herself upright, dabbed at her eyes with a tissue.

'I look a mess.'

'Beautiful.'

'You're drunk,' she said. 'Finish your coffee.' She sprang up roughly to fetch hers and drank it still on her feet, before making her way to a mirror where she frowned at herself, doing nothing to repair damage. After a pause she sat down again, rather slowly, into her armchair. 'Not much to be said in our favour, is there?'

'We've had an excellent meal . . .'

'That didn't take up much of my time.'

'But it gave me pleasure. And we can sit here complaining, explaining. We're not cutting our throats or being strapped into straitjackets.'

Molly smiled distantly, as if at some other conversation. He stood up, not too steadily, walked over to her, pulled her head into his belly and stroked her face.

'That's nice,' she said. 'Don't stop.' He obeyed.

Finally, dizzily he perched on the arm of her chair, staring glumly forward. Molly reached over him, and murmuring took his right hand which she squeezed, kissed then placed blatantly on her left breast. The nipple hardened under his touch. She held him to her.

'I don't know whether this is . . .'

'You don't know anything.'

She struggled up, took his face between her hands and kissed him violently on the mouth. The position was awkward for both, but their mouths at once matched and competed in a lush affinity. Under the wide skirts of her dress he stroked her legs, gently, hardly allowing his fingertips to learn the rough surface of her tights.

'Stand up,' she ordered, laughing, jerking on his upper arms. He obeyed. She kicked off her shoes, dragged down tights and panties, screwed them comically, threw them at the floor.

'You'll spoil your frock.'

Again Molly moved with athletic speed, reaching behind her back to unzip herself, to lift and flick the dress over her head. So swiftly did she move that her hair was barely disturbed. She folded and laid the dress in one sweeping operation over the chair they had vacated. Her mouth pouted. Now she wore only a small, white brassière. She kissed him again, bearing him backwards on to the settee.

'Molly,' he protested.

'Shut up,' she commanded. 'Love me. Henry. Love me.'

She scrabbled at the fastenings of his trousers.

They made love, skilfully in the end, without hurry, both noisily, and then sprawled naked, his head on the settee, hers comfortably on a cushion.

'That was something,' he said. Molly did not answer, stirred companionably, perfectly at ease; her body had strength about it, and great beauty, unprovocative now, white except for face, arms and legs.

221

'Would you like a cup of tea?' she asked, at length.

'I wouldn't say no.'

She sat up, smiling, went out as she was. He hauled himself upstairs to the bathroom, washed and dressed. Dazed, still, he sat back, waiting, trying to make up his mind. When Molly returned she wore a faded house-coat.

'The cup that cheers,' she said.

'I don't need cheering.'

'You don't know what you want.' She pointed towards the tray. 'Let it stew for a minute.' She picked up her dress and underclothes, marched out with them and upstairs. She returned spick and span, hair in perfection, to pour out tea.

'I need this,' he said.

'There's no need to talk.' Her rebuke was kind enough.

They sat in a sleepy comfort. Molly turned down the lights, put on a record of Boyce symphonies, cheerful and serene. The tea tasted delicious. Adultery did not trouble, carried no stigma, opened no wounds. As yet, he decided, not thinking.

XX

At twenty-five minutes past ten the telephone brayed.

'At this time of night,' Molly said, stirring herself. 'Who's that, I wonder?'

She waved cheekily back as she left the room.

Henry picked up a magazine, failed to read the table of contents, allowed his eye to play on a fashion advertisement, a thin model with a clownish, beautiful face, short skirt, schoolgirl hat, standing in a position of reckless abandon or high spirits. Too comfortable or drunk, he studied the sober colours, the nacreous background, the spread fingers.

Molly stood in the doorway.

'It's for you.'

'Who is it?'

'It's about your father. A Mrs Anderson.'

'Is he ill?'

She hesitated, not shifting.

'He died this evening.'

'Is she still on the phone?'

'Yes.'

Molly moved aside to let him pass. He had not heard anything while she was out. The phone lay on the hall table, crudely upwards.

'Henry Fairfax.'

'Oh, Mr Fairfax. I'm so glad I found you. I've been trying all evening on your number, but there was nobody in. Then I looked through some papers; I couldn't find your fath . . . , Mr Fairfax's address book; I've found it now. I got your brother's . . .'

The woman's breathless voice flushed his head clear. Quietly, soberly he helped her with questions. His father had gone out for a stroll after tea, after six o'clock, had called round on his way back at Mrs Anderson's house next door, had seemed rather quieter than usual, but had not complained of pains or illness, had walked out with her and into his front garden and had collapsed there while she was still standing on her path. He'd staggered and toppled over. She'd seen it. She thought he must have tripped. When he didn't get up, she'd run round, dialled 999, gone with him in the ambulance. He'd died soon after they reached hospital with a massive heart attack.

The woman sounded sensible, if flustered; not old, north-country, wits about her. She came back at eight o'clock and had been trying to find him ever since. She had had his number and address in case of any emergency, she said. She knew there was another brother, but she couldn't find Mr Fairfax's address book. She had only just come across it. It was tucked inside some papers.

Steadily he explained that his brother was in London, and that he would let him know. He thanked her, said he'd come down to Penarth tomorrow to make arrangements. Perhaps he could call in on her first. Efficiently he took her number to announce his expected time of arrival. Mrs Anderson began again about the suddenness. Yes, Mr Fairfax had been off colour a fair part of the summer, but nothing to be alarmed about, as far as she knew. Oh, yes, he had been to the doctor's, she gave name and address, several times, and had been taking some pills, she'd no idea what for. He'd laughed about them. He used to say, 'What good are these things now I've passed my three score years and ten?' He never complained, though; he was a quiet gentleman. He always went for a walk at that time in the evening on Saturday, and called in with his evening newspaper so that her husband could check his football pools when he came back from work. This was his late turn.

Henry Fairfax realized that the woman was crying. Her sentences broke, syntax and intonation buckling. Sniffs, a hiccough of sobbing, her apologies seemed direct but subdued inside the small earpiece. 'I was as quick as I could be. He'd been very good to us. About some trouble . . . legal advice . . . you don't want to hear all this rigmarole, do you now?'

Calmly he thanked and soothed her.

224

'How old would he be, Mr Fairfax?' she asked.

'He was seventy-one in February.'

'That's not old these days, is it?'

He assured her he would be down soon after lunch on the next day, and that he would let other relatives know.

Back with Molly he gave her a brief résumé. She had not sat down, but stood behind the settee, very pale. She listened, face stricken, hands wandering.

'I'll try now to ring Laura to see if she has Jim's number,' he said.

He allowed Laura's phone to ring on beyond reason; it steadied him to hear the double burr; he listened to it, occluded from thought. When finally he gave up he found Molly in the doorway.

'No go. I'll ring her again in the morning. If she's not in I don't know what we can do before Monday.'

Molly took his arm.

'I'm so sorry, Henry.' He nodded thanks. 'Had he been ill?'

'Yes. Seems so. Must have been. Consulted the doctor. So he must have felt off.'

'It's terrible. To die like that.'

'It's quick. If your time's up, it's as good a way to go as any.' He realized that he was not fit to drive and said so.

'You can stay the night here, and welcome.'

'No, thanks, Moll.'

'We. I don't mean, you . . . There's a spare bed all ready.'

'No.'

'Shall I get you a taxi?'

'I'll walk, thanks. Half an hour, three quarters will do it. It will sober me up. And I'll get up early in the morning and collect my car.'

'The streets aren't safe. The pubs and clubs . . .'

'Oh, all right. Go on, then.'

While they waited for the taxi, they stood arm in arm, embarrassed, silently afraid.

'I liked your father. He was a really nice man. Very quiet. Did you know he had been ill?'

225

'No. We sent each other cards when we were on holiday. Wrote a page inside our Christmas greetings. We never phoned unless something out of the way had happened. It seems poor now, but it's what he wanted, I think.'

'He didn't ever get in touch with Jim.'

'No? I'm not surprised. He knew we'd squeal loud enough if we wanted him.'

'Was he happy?'

The question angered him, not least because he could not answer it.

'I don't know. I don't even know if he was capable of happiness. Or if he'd thought that a proper end of life.'

Recognizing the sorrow in him, she edged closer. Henry breathed deeply, trying to find himself. This woman clinging to his arm, asking for a word of reassurance, seemed a stranger, their earlier intimacy dismissed.

'I'll keep you in touch,' he said, doing his best. 'I'll be round here soon after eight.'

They heard the taxi in the street. He kissed her briefly; she watched him down the path.

On Sunday afternoon he stood in the Andersons' front room in Penarth peering out over his father's garden. The lawn was cut and deeply green: lines of dahlias massed behind flashy tagetes; phlox, Japanese anemones, rudbeckia, roses, tall mallows and hollyhocks spread large, gorgeously. All glowed bright in the afternoon sunshine, organized, planned, luxuriant, colourful as a municipal park, cared for.

'He was always out there, clipping and small-pruning and hoeing,' Mrs Anderson flowed. 'He had a man to do the heavy work. Hedges, lawns and so on. Once or twice a week in accordance with the seasons.'

She had a West Riding accent which spoke both sincerity and sense, but he found it difficult to listen to her. He had visited the hospital and the undertaker; tomorrow he would register the death. Sunday was a day of rest here. Bath chairs and sandals.

In his father's study before he had come round for tea, he had taken calls from Laura, then Jim. Molly, following

226

final instructions, had telephoned Laura who had routed Jim out. Laura had another week, she said, or thereabouts at home before she set off for New York; she would attend the funeral if she could. She sounded unmoved, expressing sympathy by rote, her mind elsewhere. She hardly knew her father-in-law; he had been subdued compared with his wife, and yet feared at the poly. 'I liked him, but he made a vague impression.'

Jim grumbled, recovering from a hangover. He blamed, or so it appeared, his brother for their father's death, or for foisting the news of it on him at an inconvenient time. Grudgingly he said he would allow Henry to 'wind up the estate'. Jim would leave it to him; he knew his way round.

'There'll be no need for me to come down, will there?' Jim whined.

'No. I don't think so.'

'I thought as much. Dad will have it all sorted out. He was that sort of man.' He coughed. 'Ring me if there is anything.'

'Give me your number.'

'Sorry.' He appeared more dashed by the implied rebuke than by his father's death. Henry put down the phone.

Mrs Anderson now made it clear that she and her husband would walk along to the pub at seven thirty or eight and invited him to accompany them. She did not stop talking. They liked to hear the hymn-singing on television, and then they dressed themselves up and made their way out, winter or summer. Of course in the season the saloon bar could be crowded, but always with a nice sort of people. No, Mr Fairfax senior never went with them. He wasn't a pub man, if he knew what she meant. The voice rolled on; the husband kept his silence, except once when he interrupted, and his wife at once was silenced, to tell how Mr Fairfax had been of great assistance when their son had fallen foul of the police about some stolen property. 'I don't know what we should have done without him,' said Mrs Anderson, recovering.

Henry was tired.

227

He'd slept badly the night before, been woken early by the alarm clock, driven down, eaten on the motorway, scurried about. Now he sat in his father's lounge. The furniture was newish, and comfortable, the carpets thick; he recognized the picture over the mantelpiece, two horses in a late-winter field, one bridled. That had hung over the living-room fireplace at home in his boyhood at No. 2 Linden Grove. He stretched his legs, sure that he had done all that was possible.

It hadn't taken him long to find the will. Jim had been quite right; Thomas Broad Fairfax had neatly arranged it all. A codicil had been added less than three months ago, making small bequests to Oxfam, The Heart Foundation, Cancer Research, a CAT Scan Appeal. Henry had no idea that the old man took any interest in charities. For the rest it was equally divided between the two sons, except that the ornately framed photographs of his wife, Louise, hanging in the main bedroom, were to be given to his younger son James Dale Fairfax. That touched Henry. The old man had somehow felt that Jim would be the right curator of his mother's photographs. The title *On the Receipt of My Mother's Picture out of Norfolk* came into his head. Cowper? He'd read him for A level. 'Oh, that those lips had language.' Well done, Father Fairfax. The old solicitor had been a human being, made right judgements, one, anyway, about his sons. Correct.

Not thirty hours before in afternoon sunshine Thomas Broad Fairfax had sat in this room enjoying the colours of his garden, not knowing that he had two or three hours to live. He could not have felt too ill or he would not have set out on his evening stroll. Henry dared not even say that. His father, the nondescript man, would not have been put off by aches and pains. Saturday evening is walk-about time; George Anderson would want his football results; lock the door and out into the street. He knew his duty.

Henry felt no real sorrow, only the shock that life, with its multiple perceptions, anticipations, memories, light and dark, could be so suddenly baulked, cut off, obliterated. The father would stroke his chin, he always did to indicate thought, as he walked to the window to admire his orderly riot of colour. The son did likewise. Those ephemeral flowers had been marked for change or retention, by the dead eye. The shadows, the pergola and paths; the brick wall with its small, capped pillars had not altered. The sky with pink-tipped clouds had forecast the fine day that would never come. What had the old man been doing? There were no open reading books; he hated litter of any sort. The morning's *Telegraph* and *Financial Times* had been read, noted, folded and put away. No crumbs; every knife and fork was back in its drawer. The pyjamas upstairs were clean; on Saturday night he'd take a bath, prepare for the godless and decent Sunday he'd never see.

An image cluttered Henry's mind.

His father died and had entered to his surprise, but not delight, consciousness in the next world. Henry did not visualize his father in white robes, or winged, not at Golden Gates having impeccable agnostic credentials checked, not meeting his wife again, the pair of them young lovers, but frowning rather as he did on earth at some slightly puzzling problem he had to sort out, briefcase open, concentrating, not altogether sorry to be challenged.

And when he looked back to mortality, able now in this new superconsciousness to scrutinize everything, what did his transcendent vision light on? The elder son committing adultery with his sister-in-law while the younger drank himself into sleep. He'd stroke his chin at that, bite his lip, but what would he understand? Or take responsibility for? A poor start to eternal life, but the father would not complain, nor have it otherwise. That was how it was. People piled up difficulties for themselves; that's why they needed solicitors. Farewell, house, and farewell, home. Eternity might well be martyrdom.

Henry Fairfax back at the table drew up a list of his duties for the morrow. Efficiently he put them in an order of action, racked his brain for omissions, found himself satisfied. He rang Henry Dexter to warn that Le Jeune's would have to do without him, and as he listened to

Dexter's stumbling commiserations he felt moved. 'I met him once or twice,' Harry rumbled. 'Thorough gentlemen. Quiet. Very sure of himself.'

Henry wondered, trying to piece together his thousands of memories without success. Their mother dominated front stage; father congratulated, tipped, accompanied, occasionally advised or mended for his sons, but that was about all. He provided money, but choice of furniture, décor, holidays, outings, education, social gatherings was made by Louise. When she consulted her husband, Thomas, never minding, left the decisions to her. Henry remembered the few occasions when his mother had ventured an inquiry about legal matters: the deeds of a friend's house, a dispute over a boundary, a case concerning a motoring accident reported in the local newspaper. Then Thomas, voice normal, unemphatic, had clearly outlined the law, the steps to be taken, the possibilities of success, the costs involved. The worm had turned, and Henry recalled the exact details because it had so shaken him that his undemanding father had known so much and had laid down rules or procedure with such clarity and firmness. 'Very sure of himself,' Harry Dexter said. Odd, but perhaps true.

At the funeral in Beechnall on Friday, no inquest had delayed the ceremony, Henry troubled his thoughts again. Laura, who had been driven up with Jim, said again that she had never really got anywhere near Thomas Broad Fairfax. 'He was always charming, but he never had what you might call firm opinions.' 'Except where his work was concerned.' 'Is that so? I suppose it might be. If you're laying down the law all day, then you'd perhaps not want to continue at home.' 'My experience is the opposite.' 'Oh, Henry. You!'

Laura had smiled, said she must have a quarter of an hour privately with him before she left, as she would be away in the USA for the next month at least.

Jim had been accommodating beyond expectation. He had written again to Molly, had walked beside her at the crematorium, had spent much of his time at his brother's house talking to her. His father, knowing his mind again, had left them a small fortune each from his investments; the sale of the Penarth bungalow and its contents was marginal to the total. Jim could now buy a decent house at inflated London prices and still have money to burn. He took the news with undisguised pleasure.

'The old chap must have known what he was about. I'd never have believed it. This amount. Playing the market? He must have coined it. And never a word.'

'Very typical.'

'I'll say. I wonder what he felt about leaving it to us.' A tasteless expression of delight.

'He'd see it as his duty,' Henry answered, drily, equally pleased. 'That's one thing I do remember about him. He never took his ill temper or miseries out on us.' Henry looked stern. 'He could be very angry.'

'Yes, I know. I once upset my mother; she found some cigarettes I'd bought. I didn't think she'd mind; I didn't really. I was about fifteen. And I cheeked her. She burst into tears for no reason and the old man came in. His face very slowly blew up, all mottled red, but he spoke gently, asking me my side, and I suppose I gave him some lip. He suddenly signalled my mother out. I didn't realize until afterwards, but I saw him with his fingers pointing, ushering her out. She went quick as lightning. And he stood there, fists like great lumps of stone, and a torrent burst out of him. "Don't sit there squinting at me, you ungrateful little bastard. Get yourself up and out of my sight before I lay hands on you." I was as big as he was, but by God he frightened me. "And if ever you speak to your mother like that again, you deceitful, slimy little turd, you'll go straight out of that back fucking door with my foot up your arse." I was shaken to the back teeth. I mean he never swore. But his voice was like ground glass. His army days perhaps. I shifted myself bloody sharp, I'll tell you. He apologized afterwards. I think my mother had been on to him. He's a bit, no, you're a bit like him.'

He told Henry this in the study after the funeral at the handing over of the gold-framed portraits from Penarth.

Henry nodded.

In the post that morning there had been a missive from the BBC.

Dear Henry,
Tom O'Riordan passed your letter over to me. You sounded very cross, and in my view rightly. I don't know exactly what Tom said, but if he gave you the impression that *Two Sisters* had to be rewritten he was very wide of the mark. It is a powerful play, strongly conceived, beautifully scripted and an enormous advance on anything you have done so far for us. I look forward with real enthusiasm to producing it, and am already inquiring round for a top-line cast. The one or two little changes I'd like to see won't occupy you long, I promise.

I'm sorry about. this misunderstanding. You're quite right to take the view you did. Please pass me the word to carry on, and we'll draw up a contract at once. Apologies and best wishes,

Yours sincerely,
Tony (Anthony Friend)

His relief had taken a curious form.

Blinding anger had fired him so that he screwed up the letter and threw it furiously at the wall. His fists were clenched; his eyes stood out of his head; his jaw locked. He growled. Rage trembled in his face.

The hurling of the letter had eventually cooled him. Embarrassed, glad no one observed his actions, he retrieved the paper and straightened it. He had won his own way. And yet that spasm of anger against those who had, however temporarily, the power to wound him had been, he knew, unavoidable, suddenly overriding everything and for the moment irresistible. He hated authority and their decisions, but unreasonably, weirdly, even after they had seen reason. The episode had unnerved him. He rarely lost his temper at work. Perhaps this death had troubled him more than he realized. Or he regarded his plays, know it or not, as his soul, his supreme achievement and, hurt to the quick, had reacted thus. He frightened himself.

'I'm mildness personified,' he told Jim.

'I'll believe that when I see it.'

Jim had paused, then gone on to mention pleasantly that he and Molly had made one or two moves towards reconciliation, both by letter and this morning. They had arranged to meet again next weekend, and though it was all very tentative at present, well, they never knew. He'd acted badly; he realized that now. He couldn't excuse himself.

'She's an attractive woman,' Henry said. 'And I guess outstanding in her field.'

'And I'm a bloody fool.'

'Who says so?'

'You, for one. Don't you?'

Jim clapped him on the shoulder, and began to boast about his work. It tested him, as teaching had not, but he would win. Laura's promotion to glory had left their office stacked with challenging schedules. 'Sometimes I even surprise myself.'

They laughed. Jim's phrase 'promotion to glory' had been lifted from their father's vocabulary. It was a Salvation Army expression for death, and had greatly tickled the old man, the most unmilitary of ex-soldiers, when he'd heard it at the funeral of a Salvationist he'd attended. Jim could now put Laura in her place, at least in her absence, with his father's private words.

The brothers laughed again, clasped arms, friends.

A little later Laura had claimed her quarter of an hour and marched him upstairs to his bedroom. Down below Molly and Jim acted as hosts to the few stragglers.

'It all went off well,' Laura said, from a chair. 'Con would be sorry he couldn't come. He's in the Virgin Islands. Very fond of your father.'

'Had Dad given him a hand? When he was starting?'

'No idea. It's possible, I suppose.'

Laura wasted no more time on that.

'Now, about us,' she began.

Henry sat down on the bed.

'You've still time to think,' she continued, 'because I go away next week for at least a month.' She waited, receiving no answer. 'That's if you need time. I've made *my* mind up.'

'What's your conclusion, then?'

'You know. Or at least you should. I've been through this in my head time and time again.' She smiled grimly at her phraseology. 'I am . . . You want me to say it, don't you?' She hesitated. 'I don't want to bully you, Henry. Or force you. I'm too used to getting my own way. You understand that it makes me chary in a delicate matter like this.' She stared across, quite still, formidable under affability. 'I am quite willing to remarry, Henry.' Her eyes brightened. 'And none of your pedantry about "quite". It means "absolutely".'

'Thank you.'

She waited again.

'But you're not sure, are you?' she asked, easily.

'I'm very flattered,' he began.

'That won't do. Come on. Let's have the truth.'

'What troubles me is this. I don't see what's in it for you.' He held his hand up. 'No. Give me half a tick. We worked ourselves into a bad state and I can't forget it. Nor can I forget that it was you who wanted to end the marriage. I would have hung on. I'm not blaming you at all. Obviously you were right to throw me over, to break out, and give yourself some elbow room. It was what you needed, and you've made the most of it. You're successful now in a way that I never shall be. I'm pleased and proud about that. I'm not jealous. You're a notable now, but you must see that that makes a difference. To me. And to you, if you're honest. What will you get for yourself out of such a marriage? That's intensely worrying to me.'

'Yerss.' She twined her fingers and sat back, apparently enjoying the view through the window, large cotton-wool clouds on bright blue sky, over tiled roofs. 'I was always slightly frightened of you, Henry, when we were married. Perhaps that's why I kicked so hard to get rid of you. This time it will be different. We probably shan't live together. I take it from what you've said that you'll want to stay here and keep your job running. That's fine by me. On the other hand it's worth considering writing as

234

a full-time occupation. I'm prepared to subsidise you, and delighted, but from what Jim tells me even that won't be necessary; your father's will makes you independent. I shall have to travel, at least for a year or two. I might even have to live in America. And I'm afraid there's no question of children. That might alter your position. I'm trying to put this as fairly as I can. I mean, at our age, you can't expect explosions of love, now.'

'Why not?'

'We were married damned near nine years. That's why.'

Her voice carried neither urgency nor ill temper. She sounded thoroughly equable, distanced from all hurt.

'There's one thing,' he said.

'Yes?'

'You haven't yet told me what's in it for you.'

She nodded as if convinced by his argument.

'You'll meet,' he continued, 'all sorts of interesting and successful men who will find you attractive, will want to court or bed or marry you. Now, given all these millionaires or aristocrats or actors or politicians or what-have-you, why should you want to hang your future up with a mediocre provincial manager, and one moreover with whom you tried once and failed?'

'In different, very different circumstances.'

Now she sat quite still, legs together, white hands clasped in the lap of her becoming, expensive black dress. Whether she was marshalling arguments or found herself defeated or had decided to take no more trouble, he did not know.

Henry gripped the duvet on which he sat. He had scared himself. It seemed necessary to succeed, to convince both, to find correct, sufficient, unassailable answers. He did not know if Laura would speak again. Possibly he had said enough to close the question for ever. He did not want it so. He wanted too much. To marry Laura and not marry her. Perhaps that's what she was proposing. Married in name; living together occasionally; half-and-halfers. What did such an arrangement amount to? She'd mentioned commitment before. But to what? To

235

be called Mrs Henry Fairfax and live Ms Laura Le Jeune? He was too broken to answer. There was no sense about. Feeling, half-contained seethings of emotion had made reason ineffectual. He sat on a bed in a smart suit with a white shirt and black tie in a perturbation that was shallow, ephemeral, but capable of dulling his will.

He snatched in a gulp of breath.

'Let me try to tell you,' she said.

The small voice made him suddenly, unexpectedly grateful.

'Please.'

'It's difficult without sounding like a soap opera. I suppose I've done well with my life, made much more than I ever could have expected, and in a shorter time. And I imagine that that makes you think that I don't know how I stand. With myself. Emotionally. And that's true in a way. You can't see why I should want you back in my new inflated status, is that it? I'll tell you. You might laugh, or crow over me, or even suspect I'm up to some dirty trick to do you down but I've been over this time and again, arguing with myself. That means I ought to be able to put it straightforwardly into words. Well, I can. I don't much like the words, and I don't know whether you will, either, but they approximate to the truth.'

She stopped again.

'Go on, Laura. Please.'

'You might see me as super-woman, but I'm in no way different fundamentally, from that uncertain school-teacher you asked to dance eleven, twelve years ago. You were the man I wanted then, when I didn't know what I could do, and you're the man I want now. I ballsed it up. Yes, it was my fault, not yours. I put my future and my need to do my own thing before our relationship. That's not a good sign, or so it perhaps appears to you. But that's exactly what I mean. I chose right the first time, but I wasn't ready for you. Now I know better.'

Henry did not look at her. He too stared out of the window at the slightly sloping corrugated roof of a garden hut. The sun shone after a day and night's rain. Ten or a dozen sparrows, feathers fluffed, light grey breasts proud in the light, drank and bathed in a puddle, fussily, at speed, darting away, returning. Behind them a huge shrub rose, Nevada, swayed in the wind. The twitching of the sparrows, a late butterfly, sun-bursts, the straight darting flight of birds, the wag of cherry branches, the variegations of movement, of wind, luminously conveyed life, its impulsions, and brilliant newnesses. Hillocks of March clouds sailed stately above. September shone richly.

'Thank you, Laura.'

'You needn't give me any answer just now. We'll wait until I come back again. I might learn that I'm talking rubbish, but I don't think so.'

'You're a marvel,' he said, rising. 'I love you.'

They kissed hard, like teenagers at a bus stop. She stepped back.

'Look at the time. I'll go and make up my face and collect Jim and be on our way. Tell him to hurry, will you?'

Downstairs Jim and Molly were talking still, hand in hand. No one else was about except an old, silent aunt and uncle from Huddersfield and the women from the caterer's hard at work clearing and washing up.

'Laura's about ready. You're to get a move on.'

The young people nodded seriously, broke apart, straight-backed.

'I'll collect my things,' Jim said, striding out.

'He's coming on Friday night to stay the weekend.' A whisper from Molly.

'Great.' He joined her in solemnity of face. 'That's great.'

They sat saying nothing. Jim returned first, the energetic man, then Laura. All kissed. Jim lifted his wife from the floor. The Londoners shook hands with, embraced the old Yorkshire pair, before the young people made for front garden, where they kissed again, in an almost clumsy hurry.

The parting was quick. Jim patted the bonnet of Laura's new Mercedes, saying, 'Pick the bones out of this, then.'

Laura took the wheel. Four hands were raised in salute. It was over.

On Molly's face a tear shone. She dashed it away. Promptly.